# LUCY ZEEZOU'S GLAMOUR GAME

## LIZ DEEP-JONES

# LUCY ZEEZOU'S GLAMOUR GAME

## LIZ DEEP-JONES

First published in 2008 by Random House.

Second Edition published in 2023 by Popcorn Press,
the fiction imprint of Fair Play Publishing
PO Box 4101, Balgowlah Heights, NSW 2093, Australia

www.popcornpress.com.au

ISBN: 978-1-925914-82-5
ISBN: 978-1-925914-83-2 (ePub)
© Liz Deep-Jones 2010, 2023



Front cover photograph by Tim Bauer
Model Izabella Deep-Jones
Cover design and typesetting by Ana Secivanovic

All inquiries should be made to the Publisher via sales@fairplaypublishing.com.au

# DEDICATION

*This book is dedicated to my amazing husband Derek,*
*and my gorgeous children, Dylan and Izabella,*
*who gave me the wings to fly and achieve my dreams.*

*I'm grateful for your love and inspiring me to keep sharing*
*my stories and ideas, no matter how crazy and giving me*
*the time in my unshakeable quest for a more inclusive*
*and equitable society. Thank you for joining me on*
*this challenging and exciting journey.*
*Never a dull moment with the Deep-Joneses.*
*Love you, forever!*

'This is a book for kids which features a young girl who is passionate about football. You can't help but love Lucy. She's a character that rings true for anyone aspiring to be a professional footballer just like me. An imaginative and exciting story for everyone with a dream.'

*Paolo Maldini, Former AC Milan and Italy National team*

'This book is a must read for all girls who love their football and fashion, a match made in heaven. This story is so engaging. I feel like I know Lucy. I love it!'

*Heather Garriock, former Matilda*

'It is inspiring to follow Lucy's trials and tribulations as she pursues her footballing dream with such passion and gusto. A must read.'

*Clare Hunt, Matilda*

'Lucy Zeezou's wonderful story is for anyone passionate about football, fashion and the challenges of chasing your dream. A must read!'

*Craig Foster, AM, former Socceroo*

'A must-read from the incredible mind of Liz Deep-Jones as part of her brilliant LucyZeezou series!'

*Phil Moss - Football Analyst*

'This is an inspiring story, encouraging girls to play football and chase their dreams as I did when I was a kid. It's a great mix of football and fashion so it's appealing to everyone and a must read.'

*Christian Vieri, Former ACF Fiorentina and Italy National team*

# CONTENTS

# Chapter 1

# Rumours

A barrage of lights flashed in our faces, blinding us, while relentless clicking and snapping sounds polluted the air.

The reporter at the front of the pack shouted questions at my father. 'Paolo, Italy's leading actress, Loretta Sophirelli, has revealed your secret to the world. AC Milan's new signing is Tommaso Sophirelli – or should that be Tommaso *Zoffi*? What's your response?'

Pins and needles travelled along my body. What were they saying?

'Your son is being touted as Italian football's new hope, "Tommy the Tiger". What do you think his chances are for a spot in the World Cup squad?'

'How have you kept your son a secret for so long?' yelled another reporter.

My mama, usually so composed in front of the cameras after her years of modelling and being paparazzi fodder, released a searing scream. 'Ahhhhhhhh!'

'Mama!' I yelled, but her eyes were wild as she faced Papa and unleashed a tirade.

'How could you? How could you do this to me? To us?' she bellowed, banging her fists on his chest.

*Click, click, click.* The cameras were working overtime. That was all we needed: pictures of the Zoffis fighting being spread all around the world.

Papa tried to console her. 'Frida, please, not now. We'll discuss this later.'

Huh? He wasn't even trying to deny anything. Was this an admission of guilt? Did I really have a brother? I'd always wanted a brother, especially one who loved football too . . . But wait, that was hardly the point! How could Papa have kept this secret from us?

And where did the reporters get this information? Where was the proof? My papa was a very famous footballer back home in Italy, always under the media glare – so why hadn't these rumours come out before now?

My thoughts were brought to an abrupt halt when Mama screamed again, even louder than before. Everyone froze, giving us a short break from the madness.

Papa shook his head at the crazy scene unfolding before him. Then the flashes and obnoxious questions started once more.

'Signora Sophirelli claims that her seventeen-year-old son is your love child. He just scored the winner in his first game with your club. What do you want to say to him?'

'Lucy!' shouted another reporter. 'Do you have anything to say about the news that your runaway team mate, Max Spitzer, has been found? His uncle has come forward to take him in.'

It was such a relief to hear that Max was okay – but I'd never heard him talk about an uncle. He'd told me that his parents had died in a car accident a couple of years ago. Since then he'd been a ward of the state, forced to live in foster care, which he loathed, or running away to live on the streets. It was awful to think he'd had family who could have looked out for him all this time.

Seeing the media pack turn on his daughter must have been the last straw for my papa. This time he exploded, yelling words in Italian that I can't repeat. He pushed the troublesome Italian paparazzo who'd been hounding us since we arrived in Sydney, grabbed his camera and threw it to the ground, smashing it to pieces. It looked as though a fight was about to erupt when the photographer regained his balance and started shouting at Papa.

The other photographers were still snapping away and the reporters continued shouting their invasive questions. Then, screeching sirens overwhelmed their noise as police cars surged onto the footpath and officers piled out. There was a struggle, a jumble of limbs and angry shouts and then my papa was held by the policemen and searched – which he definitely didn't like. He started yelling and tried to break free from their grip. They handcuffed him, apparently for resisting arrest. It was shocking to watch this happening to Papa but the photographers took great pleasure in the drama, unleashing an eruption of flashes. The police officer told Papa his rights and arrested him, saying that he would probably be charged with malicious damage of another person's property. He was forced into a police van and whisked away with the sirens blaring. The troublesome paparazzo was also taken in for questioning, with the smashed pieces of his camera cradled in his hands, but he exited in less dramatic fashion.

My heart was breaking at the thought that my papa had been arrested. It was even worse that he had been lying to us all this time. Beneath that, my blood was boiling at the absurdity of the situation. The famous life just doesn't stop, it doesn't give you a break!

All this was last Saturday. The day had started so well. My family and I had arrived at Nanna and Grandpa's fruit shop after my football team, the Dunbar Lions, had won the Champion of Champions cup. I was elated, and not just by the match: I thought my life was finally on the right track. My precious Nanna Betty had been in hospital, the victim of a car accident, but now she was on the mend, walking with a cane almost as fast as she once had without it. My parents had decided we'd stay in Sydney a while longer, which was perfect – I'd started to make friends here, with Bella from school, and Max, Harry and Dylan from my team. But more surprising than any of those things, Mama and Papa had seen me play football and after much convincing from my beloved grandparents they had agreed to lift the ban and allow me to pursue my dream. We'd been planning to celebrate the Lions' victory with my team mates at a friend's restaurant, but as we'd dropped by my grandparents' home we had been confronted by that media frenzy.

Now it was almost a week later and Papa still hadn't been home. He'd called and told Grandpa that he was going to stay away for a few days to keep the media off our backs and let Mama calm down. She wouldn't take his calls, and wouldn't let me talk to him either, which made me furious. But she'd been crying in her room for most of the week, so although I was upset, I couldn't stay too angry with her. I was cooped up indoors too, trying to keep away from the media, and too upset to go to school. My mother and I had been staying with her parents in their small above-shop apartment for a while now, enjoying Sydney and helping Nanna recover. Papa had stayed in our home in Brera, Milan, at first, but now he was here too, although staying in a hotel while he and Mama made arrangements for our new home in Sydney. Now I wondered whether all that effort had been a waste – would we ever move into that house together?

Nanna and Grandpa were also shocked by the sensational news but they were doing their best not to judge anyone. I was just so confused and afraid that my parents might break up over it. They hadn't even been able to discuss the reporters' crazy claims.

Now it was Friday, and although I was still upset I was *so* bored. As soon as I woke up, I found Nanna and asked her if Papa had called. She hugged me and said, 'Not yet, sweetheart, but don't you worry. He'll be here soon enough. He's hoping his absence will quell the storm. Your parents might have a tough time in the next little while, but they'll work it out. Let's get all the facts first and then we'll see what's best for the family.'

I couldn't imagine dealing with this on my own. Thank goodness I had the most amazing grandparents in the world. They were my rock, my foundation. I knew that they accepted me for who I was and would always support me. I didn't know what I'd do without them.

I nestled into Nanna's arms. Her words were as warm and wise as ever, but I was still worried.

'Lucy, school finishes early on Friday, doesn't it? Why don't you go to Bella's after lunch? You've been stuck here all week and I'm sure she'll take your mind off things. I promise I'll call when I next hear from your papa, okay?'

He was right. And *I* had things to work out too. Like how I felt about my alleged half-brother – if it was true. And what about Max? All I really wanted to do was escape to the football pitch. That was the only place my life ever felt normal.

# Chapter 2

# Milan, Paris, London

'Lucy, are you okay?' Bella opened the bedroom door and launched straight at me with yet another hug.

It was late in the afternoon and there was still no word from Papa. I wished he'd come home so I could see him. The media were still lurking outside the shop anyway. Bella had been trying to keep me entertained and distracted from my family dramas, but I couldn't stop worrying. After a bite to eat I'd mumbled an excuse about having a shower, but instead I'd sunk onto the bed and sat crying.

'I'm not sure,' I said, trying not to sniffle into her hair. 'What if my parents break up? I don't know what to do.'

She pulled back and gave me a sympathetic frown. 'I'm sure Mum can help sort things out. How about we get out of the house? We could escape and catch a movie.'

'Watching some actress flounce around is the last thing I want to do. *That* actress in Italy supposedly had a son with my papa. Poor Mama, imagine what she's going through! The media will be making up all kinds of lies. They must be having a field day at my family's expense.'

'You don't know that,' said Bella. 'And those rumours are probably all just made up. Mum will get to the bottom of this. Politicians always have heaps of connections. I'm sure everything will get back to normal soon.' Bella's mum, Helen, was the state premier – she was definitely very important, but I wasn't too sure that gave her contacts in the Italian acting and football worlds.

'What's normal?' I asked. 'I don't think my life's ever been normal. It's always been crazy and out of control.'

'Well, it may be nuts now but it *will* settle down. Do you want to go for a bike ride, instead? You can use Dylan's bike,' she said.

'I'd rather just hang out here. I really don't want to face anyone out there. Let's watch some football,' I suggested.

Bella hid a small smile. She was definitely not a football fan like me and her brother Dylan. 'Oh, um … okay then.' 'You really are my best friend, Bella. I couldn't get through this without you.'

'Well, watching football *is* a huge sacrifice. I'm glad you appreciate it.' She gave me another gentle smile and reached for the TV remote on the bedside table.

I was staying in one of the guest rooms, which looked as though it was set up for a magazine shoot. The all-white room opened up to a balcony with views of picturesque gardens and a glimpse of the harbour. A large plasma TV was planted on the wall opposite the bed, perfect for a lazy day.

Bella hit the buttons, and gave an excited yelp. The first channel she'd found was playing a fashion show.

'Hey, what about the football?' I shouted.

'We'll get to that, I promise. Just check this out for a minute.'

On the screen, one model after another paraded like prancing ponies, pouting and looking bored with the clothes hanging off their bony bodies. '*Milan, Paris, London …*' the voice-over boasted. '*All the latest fashion shows, the most beautiful models and most exotic locations brought to you from all over the globe. Keep watching for your chance to go into the draw to model in an exclusive photo shoot in a dream location.*'

'Oh please, Bella, are you serious? This is what you love watching?' I cracked up. I knew she liked glamour, but the nonstop fashion TV channel was just so silly. My mama was an ex-model and she constantly pushed me into fashion shows. I didn't even like dressing up and found the whole modelling thing utterly boring.

'What? Are you mad? What girl doesn't like being pampered and looking fabulous? Look at those models, they're so gorgeous. They have the best lives – making lots of money, wearing designer clothes and working in the most beautiful places. There's nothing wrong with that! I want to be just like them. Tall, thin and leading a glamorous life!' she exclaimed.

'Bella, it's not as glamorous as you think. And why on earth would you want to be a stick? They look as though they haven't eaten in months. You're more gorgeous than them. Anyway, it's more important to have brains, like you do, than to be a clothes horse.' I tapped her on the head. 'Pity you're not using them,' I teased.

'It's all right for you. You're gorgeous and wear cool clothes *and* you have brains. I just want to be beautiful too.' Wow. Bella always worried me with this talk. I wished she wasn't so body conscious. 'But Bella, you are beautiful. I'm just tall and thin like my parents.' I thought for a second. 'Maybe I can organise for you to join me in one of those fashion shows Mama makes me parade in and then you'll get to experience what it's really like.

But you'll have to come to Italy.'

'That would be so cool!' she squealed.

'Now, can we please, *please* watch some football?' I begged.

'All right.' Bella flicked channels. She eyed the TV suspiciously. 'I think I'm going to need snacks to make this entertaining. Do you want a green tea? It's good for when you're stressed, you know.'

I raised an eyebrow at her. Bella knew I was dubious about green tea. She could get a scientist to tell me it could cure all the world's diseases, but I just didn't like the taste. 'Juice? Hot chocolate?' I suggested.

Bella winked and headed downstairs with her best modellish flick of her shiny black hair.

I turned back to the TV, wishing I was playing in the match being broadcast instead of sitting here worrying. It'd be sweet relief out there on the pitch, working my way past the defenders to take a crack at goal.

Suddenly I heard a tapping noise at the window.

I raced over to inspect. At first I couldn't see anything in the beautifully manicured garden below. It was as still as a photograph. But then I caught a glimpse of movement in the rosebush.

Was it – could it be Max? It was his style to sneakily try to grab my attention instead of just knocking at the door.

'Bella, I think Max might be outside, there's something moving in the rosebushes. I'm going out there,' I yelled into the hall, trying and failing to play down my excitement.

She was on her way back up the stairs, struggling to carry chips and fruit while holding onto two mugs.

'Girls? Is everything all right?' Helen's voice drifted up the stairs from her study.

Bella shot me a look. 'Yes, Mum, Lucy's just getting excited about a match on TV.' She lowered her voice. 'Why do you always think anything you hear is Max? It could just be a bird in the bushes. Anyway, Max has an uncle now, so he doesn't need us any more.'

I was shocked at her harsh tone. 'I don't believe that. We're still his friends. We always need our friends. I'm going to see if it's him. Are you coming?'

She set the snacks down in the guest room with a sigh and followed me back down the stairs. I raced ahead, anxious to see Max.

When I got to the rosebush there was a scribbled note pressed onto a thorn on one of the stems.

*Meet me @ corner store. M*

# Chapter 3

# The crab

I waved frantically at Bella to join me as I headed for the gate. I knew I shouldn't sneak out when Helen was trying to watch out for me, but I doubted my parents' situation was going to be resolved any time soon. Besides, I couldn't wait to catch up with Max and find out what he'd been up to.

'Where are we going?' Bella asked when she got to my side.

'Just keep up,' I insisted, my stomach churning with excitement.

As we moved closer to the corner store I could see a lone figure waving in our direction. The mop of hair was a dead giveaway. I picked up my pace, my feet in sync with my racing heart, while Bella stumbled behind. Running felt good after being so shocked and still for hours. Pity I wasn't running towards goal, dribbling the ball left and right around defenders.

We followed him past the store and down the street, hitting a set of steep stairs that led us down to a park on the edge of the glittering harbour. He continued walking through the park and out onto the wharf, casually strolling along the boardwalk. He inspected the surroundings and then disappeared beneath the wooden structure like a crab crawling under rocks.

I carefully followed him and was captivated by the sight before me. We were in a little makeshift hide-out with the best views of Sydney. As the sun hit the water it looked like we were surrounded by sparkling diamonds. A broken wooden boat resting on the rocks acted as a lounge, complete with worn blankets and old cushions.

Max finally spoke, 'So, what do you think of my hangout?'

'Oh, it looks nice and cosy. Great views!' I said carefully. I thought his uncle had come forward to look after him. Why would he be camping out by the water? I hoped he wasn't living rough again.

'Yeah, it's a great spot,' added Bella.

'This is one of the places I come to when I need to get away and have some time to myself,' Max admitted.

'What about your uncle's place? Aren't you staying with him?' I asked.

'Well, he's trying to make me feel comfortable and he's an okay bloke but it's kinda hard to get used to living with someone else again. I'm not used to all the rules.'

'I don't get you. He's a family member, your only living relative, and you'd rather be on your own. Why?' Bella asked. I'd been thinking the same thing, but I wished Bella had asked a little more gently.

Max looked annoyed for a second, but he took a breath and explained calmly, 'He disappeared years ago. I still don't know why he took so long to come forward. Where was he when I lost Mum and Dad? Where was he when I needed him most? I've managed without him for this long, so why do I need him now?' He crossed his arms, trying to look as tough as he sounded.

'Have you actually asked him? He must have an explanation. And anyway he's here now – it's a chance to make up for lost time,' I said.

He sat staring out into the harbour for what seemed like ages, then sighed. 'You're probably right. And I am trying to make it work. I suppose it's just going to take time to get used to living with someone.' He cocked an eyebrow at me. 'Anyway, we should talk about the important stuff.'

I sucked in a breath, thinking he was going to ask about my papa and all the rumours. I'd managed to forget about that whole mess for the first time all day.

'Are you playing football with the boys again next season or are you going to join a girlie team?' he asked.

Bella scoffed and tried to cover it with a cough.

*Girlie?* Well, the question was still better than the one I'd been expecting. 'Not sure what the rules are now that I'll be in the under 15s. I can't wait to get back onto the pitch.' Now I raised my eyebrows back at Max. 'But stop changing the subject. I want to know more about your uncle.'

'He's the complete opposite of me. He likes to wear fancy trendy clothes and he can because he's loaded.' Max grinned. 'And he talks a lot, like someone else I know.' His face went glum then. 'He didn't get along with my mum. They fought a lot over spending time with my dad, who had some problems. Mum was very protective of her time with my dad and didn't even like him hanging out with his own brother. It was a bit weird and it caused a lot of trouble.' He became silent, dropping his head for a moment.

'Just before the crash they had a huge argument and Uncle Rick stormed out of the house . . . I remember him yelling, "Have a good life, see ya!" and slamming the door. And that was it. I never saw him again.' Max stared at me with his big brown eyes, then looked back out to the water. 'He used to take me to the park and we'd play football, chasing, all that stuff. He'd test my strength and we'd roll around and have play fights. I loved it.

'But when he left he didn't even bother to say goodbye to me. I was shattered. Couldn't understand how he could do that to me. We were so close . . . well, so I thought.'

Bella and I threw each other a look of concern.

Max tried to put on a brave face. 'Anyway it doesn't matter any more, I've grown up and can survive on my own. I want different things now . . . he's too late.'

Footsteps overhead interrupted Max's rant. We sat silently, gazing through the wooden cracks above and trying to check out who was there.

Max quietly moved further along the rocks to investigate.

'It was just a couple getting cosy,' he coyly reported, flicking me a look.

I caught myself blushing and tried to restore some sort of coolness. 'Come on Max, it's never too late. Did your uncle tell you where he was all this time?'

'Yeah, what's he been up to?' Bella added, glancing at me with a little smirk on her face.

'He reckons he's been travelling around the world and most recently he's been spending time in the outback,' Max said with a shrug.

'Does he have a family or girlfriend?' I pressed.

'Nup, no family left that I know of and he doesn't seem to have a girlfriend. But he has a lot of friends that pop over, and a housemate.' He fished around under a cushion and pulled out a rough wooden figurine of a boat and a small knife. He started whittling away ribbons of wood from the unfinished end.

'Oh, I love that boat,' I said. 'I didn't know you liked to make things.'

'Yep, it's a yacht, actually. One day, I'm going to sail around the world. That's after I make it big in football,' he said dreamily, admiring his work.

'Is your uncle a yachtsman?' Bella asked.

Max's face tensed up again. 'I wish. He's an architect.' 'That's cool . . . designing buildings,' I enthused.

'Not really. Anyway, I don't care,' he declared.

'Oh Max, you've got to try and make it work. I'd love to meet him,' I added.

'Yeah, yeah, soon. Look, I've got to go.' He put away his carving hurriedly and got to his feet.

'Max, what are you up to?' I asked. 'Nothing. I've just gotta go.'

But he was lying, I could feel that something wasn't right.

'Okay, fine,' I said, trying not to freak him out. 'Can you at least tell us where you're living?'

He pointed. 'I'm just up this road in my uncle's artyfarty apartment – number eighty-nine, unit seven – but try here first if you want to find me. I've gotta go. Check you soon,' he mumbled.

He slipped away as he always does, like his neighbours, the crabs; carefully yet quickly negotiating his moves, preferring not to be seen, lying low and coming out only when it suited him. One minute there, the next . . . gone!

# Chapter 4

# Skin

I sat there for a few moments, my thoughts drifting with the sound of the water hitting the rocks. What was it about Max that made me feel funny in the tummy?

'Wow, what's going on with you two?' Bella asked, jolting me back to reality.

'Nothing!'

'Yeah right. You're so into each other. It was like I wasn't even here. His eyes were on you the whole time,' she mocked.

'I think you're getting too much sea air. Max and I are just friends and I'm *so* not interested like that. I'm just into my football, there's no time for boys.'

Bella sniggered. 'You like him. I mean *r-e-all-y* like him!' She paused, looking more serious. 'What would your mum think about you going out with a black guy?'

'*What?*' I couldn't believe that question. 'It's none of her business, and so what if he's dark? She wouldn't care about that.' Although she'd probably rather he was some self-obsessed rich kid whose parents were in fashion or something like that, I thought to myself. 'For the zillionth time, we're not going out together. And you know what? I'd never even thought about Max's skin colour till you brought it up.'

Bella looked a little contrite. 'Jeez, Lucy, I don't mean anything by it. I'm half-Chinese, remember? I get comments about my background all the time. I'm just curious about where he got his gorgeous looks. You've got to admit that he's very cute.'

I tried not to blush again at the thought of Max's smile. This was ridiculous! 'He's my friend and that's it, so will you please drop it? Anyway, we've been out for ages. We should call your mum before she sends a search party!' I said, trying to steer her away from any more questioning.

'I'll call her, but I'm telling you that you guys are into each other. It's so obvious!' she insisted, hoisting herself up onto the pier.

Bella's words kept ringing in my ears. I don't understand why Max can't just be my friend – even though he makes my stomach flutter every time we're together.

'Princess, are you down there?' Came a voice from overhead.

Grandpa! How did he know I was here? I was busted! I sat silently for a moment and thought. But I couldn't hide from him; he'd always been on my side. I'd be lost without him.

'Here I am, Grandpa,' I said, ducking my head out from under the boardwalk.

He threw me a warm smile. 'What are you doing down there?'

'You know I love adventure. How did you know I was here?' I said, climbing up.

He kept smiling, 'I have my sources. And Bella's a little giveaway.' He winked and pointed down the pier, where Bella was chatting to her mother on her mobile.

And then I realised the area was part of the route he takes on his regular walk.

'I'm glad I bumped into you, I was planning to head to Bella's after my walk,' he said.

My stomach dropped. 'What is it? Is Papa home yet?' 'No, not yet, sweetheart. But Coach James popped by.

He wanted to check that you were all right. And he wants to know if you'd be interested in trialling for the Sydney Dolphins under 15s team tomorrow. I can't believe the trials are so soon after your other finals, but he said the rep teams like to get cracking early. He also wanted to know if you've heard back from the David Beckham Academy about that scholarship they were offering you?'

'Oh! You know I'm desperate to keep playing football and I'd love to trial for a rep team – that's the next step up the ladder! But I haven't heard anything from the Beckham Academy. I wonder if they'll send my parents a letter or something?'

The strange thing was that the Beckham scholarship suddenly wasn't exciting me as much as it should have.

I realised that my life was in Sydney now with my friends and Max.

'Well, if so, I'm sure she'll tell you about it when it comes. Now, how about I walk you and Bella back to her place?' he said, squeezing me close as we caught up with her.

'Hey Bella, how did you go with your mum?' I asked. 'Hi, Mr Dib. Lucy, Mum's not very happy with us but

I think we may have got away with it this time. We have to go home now or we'll get into major trouble,' Bella grumbled.

Grandpa threw his arms into the air. 'Girls, you didn't tell Helen where you were going? Even though you, Lucy, were supposed to be staying somewhere safe and avoiding the press? What am I going to do with you? Yes, Bella, we better go speak to your mother, then you, Miss Lucy, are coming with me!'

Oops. But when I looked up at him, I'm sure I saw an amused glint in his eye.

I apologised to Helen in a bit of a daze. All the way to Bella's I'd been hoping there'd be good news about Papa waiting for us by the time we got home. As we turned into Grandpa's street, we were shocked to see a police car pull up in front of the shop, while a small media contingent stalked along the footpath, cameras and microphones at the ready. Why couldn't they just leave us alone?

'Well, Lucy, there's never a dull moment. Let's take the back entrance. We don't want to cause too much of a stir,' he said with a dry smile.

'What is it now? Why won't they all go away?' I asked.

I wished we had some security guys with us here to shield us from the media pack. Papa's football club had hired security men for us a little while back just after I was the victim of an attempted kidnapping. They might have come in handy now – to protect us from the paparazzi.

Grandpa and I snuck in unnoticed through the back door and walked into the shop, where Mama was crying in Nanna's arms.

'I don't know what to believe. I'm not sure if I can face him,' she sobbed.

My heart sank as I heard her – Mama loved Papa with her heart and soul. Now she looked as lost and helpless as a bird with broken wings. It was worse because it was just so unlike her; she'd always been such a strong and confident figure.

Grandpa gave me a gentle nudge and I found myself trying to console her.

'Mama, it's all right. Everything will be fine,' I said as I stroked her hair.

'Lucy, thank goodness you're here.' She grabbed me and squeezed me tight.

Grandpa cleared his throat. 'Well, I think you should all go upstairs and settle down over a good cuppa and a piece of cake. I'll follow you up in a few minutes.'

I went to the shop window to catch a glimpse of the movement outside before I headed upstairs.

I shrieked at what I saw. 'Grandpa, the police are –' 'Princess, you're to go upstairs and that's an order,' he interrupted. He gave Nanna a reassuring look and added, 'I think you need to have a good chat with your mum. Off you go.'

'But Grandpa –'

Again he interjected. 'Lucy, I won't be long, now take your mother upstairs. Nanna has some pasta on the stove and a cake in the oven.'

Mama just nodded and started to climb the stairs. I trailed after Nanna, looking back towards the shop. Grandpa was up to something, and I wanted to see what it was.

At the top of the stairs, Gigi ran up to me. 'Gigi, I've missed you too!' I said as my little dog jumped up at me. I'd had Gigi since I was six years old – she was a gift from my late Nonno Dino and she's been my faithful companion ever since.

I went into the kitchen to give her some dog biscuits and noticed an empty milk bottle on the bench. Perfect!

'Gigi, be a good girl and stay here . . . stay. I'll be back,'

I ordered. She wasted no time in munching into the bickies.

'Nanna, I'm just going downstairs to get some more milk, won't be long,' I yelled as I took off.

I couldn't see Grandpa anywhere in the shop and it didn't sound like he was out the back. Strange. I snuck to the front, peeping through the window from behind the shelves full of fruit.

Outside, two policemen were addressing the media. 'Your vehicles are obstructing traffic and must be moved immediately.'

But they were ignored. Papa made his entrance with his lawyer, and the cameras turned to capture every step. Again the reporters fired their questions.

'Paolo, have you been charged?'

'Do you have anything to say to the photographer you fought with?

'Is Frida leaving you?'

'What's the response from AC Milan?' 'Has your family met Tommy yet?'

Papa's lawyer responded. 'Mr Zoffi will not be answering any questions at this stage. No comment!'

Who did these people think they were? What gave them the right to pry into our personal lives?

Just then Grandpa emerged from the side street and marched into the middle of the scrum, stretching his arms out to stop the media getting any closer. The reporters thrust out their microphones and Grandpa suddenly found himself taking centre stage.

'You should all be ashamed of yourselves, causing our family such distress. Leave us alone,' Grandpa ordered, rushing to Papa's side.

But the media hounds weren't satisfied. They broke into a frenzy trying to get to Papa. While the others continued their charge, one reporter slipped on the ground and Grandpa, always the gentleman, helped her to her feet. The officers tried to quell the madness but weren't having much success.

Amid the chaos, Papa grabbed Grandpa and the lawyer and, together like team mates on the pitch, they wove past the defenders towards their goal. Once inside the shop they broke into laughter.

I popped up from behind the shelving and gave Papa a huge hug. 'Papa!' I bellowed happily. It was such a relief to see him here that all my worries disappeared. He had a knack for making me feel like I was the only person on earth. I loved him so much.

He hugged me tightly and then gently pulled away to clasp my hands. 'Oh, I love my Lucy. Darling, I'm so sorry that you've had to put up with this.'

I gulped back the lump in my throat. 'Papa, I'm so glad you're back. Those idiots should leave us alone. I'm glad you smashed that photographer's camera!'

His face scrunched up in disappointment. He stared into my eyes and said, 'No, Lucy. I was wrong. I should never have allowed it to get that far. In hindsight, walking away was the answer. I was wrong and now I have to face the consequences. We were born into this famous life and we have to know how to deal with it while maintaining our respect and dignity.'

I knew he was right, really, but it still didn't seem fair. He'd dealt with it growing up, when his own papa, my Nonno Dino, was a star with AC Milan. The spotlight had only grown stronger as Papa developed his own football career, and especially now that he and Mama had the family fashion business. They were one of the most sought-after celebrity couples in Italy and made headlines around the world. It made it extremely difficult to lead a normal life . . . whatever that was!

Papa interrupted my train of thought. 'Stefano, thank you for your help. I need some time with my family. Let's talk tomorrow.'

'It's been my pleasure. And don't worry – you haven't been formally charged. I'll resolve this matter as soon as possible.'

Grandpa escorted the lawyer out the back entrance, while Papa's mind seemed to shift back to matters of the heart.

'I must speak with your mama. Where is she?' Papa asked anxiously.

I was dreading their encounter. It was bound to be dramatic and highly emotional. I leaned in for another hug, trying to delay the fireworks. 'She's upstairs with Nanna.'

Papa gave me a kiss on the cheek. 'I love you, princess,' he said, and ran up the stairs.

Grandpa promptly returned, 'Ha, I heard that. More like a cheeky monkey. I thought I told you to stay upstairs.'

'Sorry Grandpa, you know I can't help myself.'

He looked at me with his warm sparkly eyes. 'You're just as mischievous as I once was. I'm getting too old for all this drama. It's not easy keeping up with the Zoffis, especially you! Now, let's go upstairs.'

I was very apprehensive about what could be happening up there. I stopped on the bottom step.

'Oh god, Grandpa. What's going to happen to our family? I'm so worried that Mama and Papa are going to break up. I don't understand how I could suddenly have a half-brother. How could Papa keep him from us?'

'Princess, I'm sure your parents will work it out. They love each other very much. Your mother may need some time to herself to sort things out but I don't think she'd ever leave Paolo. And as for your half-brother, well, only your papa can tell us if it's true or not. You're a tough cookie, so you'll be fine – and don't forget we're always here for you.' He pointed to himself with a grin. 'Your old grandpa here would move the earth for his little princess, so stop worrying.'

'Well,' I said, wiping my eyes and trying to smile, 'can you move it a little to the left so we can have longer days for me to fit in more football training?'

He laughed and put his arm around me. 'Come on, football nut, let's go and join the rest of the family.'

# Chapter 5

# Buddy

Grandpa and I walked into chaos. I could hear Mama and Papa arguing behind the closed door of the spare bedroom. Gigi was barking at the door, despite Nanna's attempts to calm her, and the phone was ringing. I hoped it wasn't for me. I didn't want to talk to anyone right now.

The best place for me when I felt this awful was the football pitch. I could see myself running with the ball, heading towards the target, skipping around one defender then another. I found more space and an opportunity to shoot. I kicked the ball with all my might, aiming for the top right-hand corner. It was sailing high . . . 'Lucy? Lucy, dear, Bella's on the phone,' called Nanna, snapping me back to reality.

'Oh . . .' I hesitated, glancing towards Mama's room. Nanna shook her head and thrust the phone at me. 'Thanks, Nanna.' It was rotten timing for a phone call. But maybe talking to Bella would calm me down. She was my best buddy, after all. She was ringing me on the house phone because I'd lost my mobile a while ago, otherwise, she probably would have sent me a text. I had to get a new phone.

I took the call in the kitchen, patting Gigi and trying to get her to settle. 'Hey, Bella, what's happening?'

'I just wanted to make sure you're okay. Your dad is all over the news. You'd think that nothing else was happening in the world. How are you doing?' she asked.

'I'm not sure. I think I'm just about to find out what's going on with my parents. You can probably hear them arguing in the background. Mama's furious, and for once I don't blame her. I just want to get out of here,' I blurted.

'Lucy, we've all had tough times, and I'll be here for you. My parents split up a few years ago and I thought that I'd never get over it, but I did. You might get lucky and they'll stay together.' Bella paused, a little hitch in her voice. 'Just try to be strong, especially for your mum, okay? She needs you right now, more than you realise – especially if you *do* have a half-brother. You never know, this could turn out to be the best thing that's ever happened to you. You've always said you wanted a brother.'

'Yeah, I'd love a big brother but this might cost my parents their relationship. Uh-oh, I've got to go. It's really kicking off. Talk soon. Oh! And thanks, Bella. Ciao,' I said quickly as Mama and Papa's argument intensified.

'I don't want to talk to you right now. I don't even want to look at you! Just leave, will you!' Mama cried, opening the bedroom door and pointing to the stairs. Her eyes were swollen and the tears flowed freely down her face.

Papa moved into the doorway, pleading. 'Frida, it's not what you think. Please, let's discuss this. It happened before we met. Please!'

But there was no answer and the room filled with a bitter silence. I had to look away from their pained faces. Out the window, the sky had filled with low clouds, threatening heavy rain. Papa reached towards Mama, but she strode away from him.

They'd argued before – Mama had a dramatic temper, after all, and Papa could match her when he wanted to – but it'd never been as bad as this. They weren't just angry – they both looked so hurt. It was heartbreaking to watch.

Grandpa deliberately disturbed the mood, 'Ah, Frida, Paolo, I think we'd better leave you both to talk about this in private. You just need a little time to work things out.' 'No,' Mama said quietly. 'I want him out of here . . . now!'

I shuddered at the thought and erupted into tears. I hid behind Grandpa, hoping no one would notice, while Gigi nuzzled me.

Nanna tried her best. 'Frida, I think you're overreacting. It's only fair to listen to Paolo's side of the story. Give him a chance to explain himself. Of all people, you should know how the media twists things around. Don't let them destroy what you have because of some rumour!'

But to my horror, Papa said, 'I think it's best I leave until Frida's ready to discuss this further. I'm sorry to have caused so much trouble. Please forgive me.'

I couldn't hold back any longer. I put Gigi down and pleaded, 'Papa, I want you to stay. I don't want you to leave us. Please.' I ran over and squeezed him close to me.

He stroked my hair. 'Lucy, I've caused enough trouble for now. Don't worry, everything will be okay. Mama just needs a bit of time. I'll be back to see you soon. You know I love you, princess.'

He gently wiped my tears and kissed me on both cheeks. His eyes were shining, but he wouldn't let the tears flow. 'Ciao, my Lucia, Tony, Betty. Please forgive me for this mess. Ciao, Frida, I love you.'

And my papa left. He was gone . . . just like that! I ran to the window and watched him disappear up the street. His head down, his stride slow and uncertain, he didn't look back. He didn't even try to capture a glimpse of the daughter who was wishing he'd return.

I was so upset and angry. Angry that she didn't stop him. Angry that she didn't let him explain. Why? We are . . . we *were* such a close family. Mama adored Papa. They adored each other. But now it looked like my family was shattered.

# Chapter 6

# All about me

Mama was staring blankly out the window. I moved towards her, but Nanna reached out to stop me.

'Lucy, it's been a long day. I think it would be a good idea for you to have a quick wash and then we'll have tea,' she said softly.

Grandpa took the hint too and excused himself to make a fresh pot of coffee. I tried to put my anger aside and gave Mama a kiss on the cheek. She needed our support, even if I was cross with the way she hadn't let Papa give his explanation.

'Lucy, I'm so sorry you had to see all this. I just need to think about things for a while,' Mama said gently.

'Please talk to Papa, please let him come back!' I begged.

I was already starting to imagine how things might be if she didn't. Dividing my time between his and her places, like most of my friends whose parents were divorced. Trying not to talk about one to the other. Watching them avoid talking when they dropped me off at the other one's house. No way, that can't happen. I won't let it.

And as if she could read my mind, she said, 'I don't want you to worry about this. I do love your father, but at the moment I'm very hurt and confused. We'll work it out, okay?'

I hugged her again, tighter this time. I could see in her face that her world had been flipped upside down. I loved her so deeply, but for some reason Papa had always had my whole heart. Maybe it was because we had more in common, that mad passion for football, or because I never got to spend as much time with him.

I slipped into the bathroom and locked the door. I didn't jump into the shower right away; I ran the tap and placed my ear to the door. I felt a bit guilty being so sneaky, but I was sick of being in the dark. What had Papa said to Mama when Grandpa and I were downstairs?

Through the door I heard Nanna start speaking. 'Frida, sweetheart, I know this must be hard, but don't you think you were harsh on Paolo? You really should give him a chance to explain himself.'

Nanna never had been one to mince her words.

'No, Mum, I don't. You don't understand. This is a big blow, and I can't even deal with it in private. How would you like your dirty laundry revealed to the world? How would you like to find out through some hack that your husband has a child with *another* woman? And that woman just happens to be a very famous and much-loved actress? What am I supposed to do?' she asked, getting more agitated with each word.

'Oh, Frida, you know my heart aches for you. But you also know that Paolo loves you very deeply. He deserves a chance. You know this could all have been made up,' Nanna said sensibly.

That's it Nanna, keep reminding her that this could all be a big fat lie.

'I'm doing my best to understand, but you don't realise what's really going on. I know the woman the media are talking about. I met her once at a party and I sensed that she knew Paolo rather too well, so I asked him about her. He said they'd dated just before I'd met him but it was nothing serious. He seemed aloof around her but she had eyes only for him – she wouldn't leave him alone! We argued about her later. I suspected something was going on but I couldn't work it out . . . and now I know!' she started sobbing again.

'Oh dear, there must be an explanation. And you must consider that even if he does have a son, the boy was born before you met. If so, well, that's something we'll have to deal with – but we will embrace the child. We must if he's a Zoffi.'

Suddenly I heard Grandpa grumble and there came a knock on the door. 'Lucy!' he chided. 'I can see your feet in the gap under the door. Are you eavesdropping, young lady?'

Oh no, how stupid . . . As I stepped back I tripped over my shoes and knocked over a bottle of perfume. Smash! 'Lucy, what was that? Open this door,' Grandpa demanded.

I'd be better off living on the football pitch. Why was I so clumsy off it?

I opened the door slowly. 'Um, I'm sorry, I –'

'Lucy, let's clean up this mess and give Frida some privacy,' Grandpa said. 'I think you need some time out too. The media have probably had their fun for the day and gone home – why don't you go down to the Reg with Gigi and run off some steam.'

Grandpa gets me. He knows that football's the best medicine for me.

'Thank you, Grandpa.' I was so excited at the prospect I burst into a pirouette, just at the moment when Mama looked over. Oh no, I thought with horror, this wasn't exactly the time to be dancing about the room.

She lifted her mouth in a half-smile and nodded towards the door. 'Oh, off you go. It's nice to see someone happy.'

I ran into the bedroom to change, eager to get down to the Reg Bartley Oval. It was a perfect distraction from all this madness.

I threw on my favourite Love Lucy tracksuit. The family label, 23 (named after Papa's famous number on his jersey, of course), produced a lot of stuff that was too glitzy for my taste, but I had to admit our teen line had a cool sporty look.

As I was stuffing my boots and ball into a bag, Mama called out, 'Lucy, how would you like to go shopping tomorrow? I think some retail therapy might just be what the doctor ordered.' She paused. 'And I could do with some company.'

Shopping was the last thing I wanted to do. But, I couldn't say no to her right now.

Grandpa came to the rescue. 'Frida, Lucy has her football trials tomorrow. They're first thing in the morning, so you'll have plenty of time together in the afternoon. Although I *was* planning on taking you out tomorrow. It'll give you some time to clear your head, and Lucy some time to prepare for the trials. What do you think? We'd love to take you out, and a friend of mine can look after the shop. We could do with more of a break.'

Grandpa really was my saviour. I was so glad he was being encouraging about the trials. Mama might not have actually been saying 'no' right now, but she was never going to encourage my football career. I started to wonder whether she had got my scholarship letter from the David Beckham Academy but now *really* was not the time to ask.

'Maybe, you're right. I'm not sure what I want at the moment. Anyway, Lucy probably isn't the best person to take shopping,' she muttered.

'A good night's rest is what you need,' insisted Nanna. I took that as my cue to leave with Gigi.

I wanted to pretend that everything was back to normal for a while and that Papa would soon return. Some football drills were exactly what I needed to distract myself. I wanted to get back onto the pitch and forget everything for a while.

I ran down to the Reg, chasing after Gigi and hoping to see the one person I knew could take my mind off things.

# Chapter 7

# Street life

The sun was about to meet the horizon and the breeze off the harbour gently brushed my face. The seagulls swooped and dogs barked, chasing the wind.

This was the place I first met Max Spitzer, the football pitch in the park that lay nestled by the harbour and played host to sports clubs including my Dunbar Lions football team. It was such a beautiful part of the world. It was also where Max would sometimes find shelter, making its grandstand a substitute home.

My favourite noise in the world suddenly grabbed my attention: the ball pounding the back of the net. That sweet sound gave me such a warm feeling.

A few seconds later we were at the pitch, and Gigi sprinted out, chasing the ball and running back to jump on Max. But her playful greeting was being shunned. He was urging her away and as I moved closer he stepped back into an unlit part of the pitch – but it was too late for him to run.

'Hey Max, what's up? Gigi's just happy to see you.' His cool manner was making me uneasy. He wouldn't look at me. He kept his head down, his long fringe covering one eye. I couldn't make out his expression in the dissipating light.

'Nothing's up. I'm just kicking the ball for a bit of a laugh.' His head was still angled at the ground and he tucked his hands into the pockets of his torn jeans. He wasn't dressed for a football session – although Max wasn't really one to have a dress code.

He must have wanted to see me. Surely that's why he was here, otherwise he'd be hanging out at the Double Bay park further along the harbour near his uncle's place. Something was up.

'Well, you're not exactly laughing, Max,' I said, as I instinctively went to tap him on the shoulder.

He swiftly knocked my hand out of the way. Gigi started barking ferociously. I was shocked and didn't know what to do.

'Gigi, it's all right. That's enough,' I ordered, trying to calm her down although I was also annoyed at Max's behaviour.

'You shouldn't have done that,' he said, and before I could argue, he lifted his face and peered at me. He was holding back tears, clenching his teeth.

'Oh my god, Max, what happened?'

We sat down and my hand reached out for his. To my surprise he actually let me grasp it. An uncomfortable moment slipped by, but then it started to feel right. It was the first time I'd held a boy's hand. I gently stroked the side of his face. A strange sensation came over me. I edged closer, but he suddenly pulled away. So we just sat there in silence. I was trying to figure out what had happened, and hoping he'd confide in me. Why was he so upset?

I was too scared to delve further. I knew he wouldn't want to answer any questions and I didn't want him to suffer any more, even though I was suffering seeing him like this. We were both in a mess. I was going through the most difficult time in my life but Max needed me, especially now.

Gigi broke the silence, barking and nudging the football, trying to get our attention.

I kicked the ball down the pitch and she was happy, tearing off to fetch.

Max seemed to enjoy the distraction. He got up and took off after the ball, claiming possession and kicking it to me. We practised goals, taking aim at the top corners while Gigi ran back and forth. She'd stop, panting, then race back into the action, trying to get the ball.

It only felt like minutes later when the lights in the park thumped off and I realised the sky was dark. It never got truly black this close to the city, but even the reflected light was too dim to show the ball clearly. The activity I'd barely noticed on my way in had disappeared: no more tennis players or joggers or kids running around while their parents had a last cup of coffee.

The surrounding bay was perfectly still and could have been eerie, but I felt safe with Max.

We headed to the grandstand, where the streetlights lit the path.

'Max, what's up? Did you have an argument with your uncle?'

'Lucy, it's hard to explain, but I –'

He suddenly stopped, dropping his head and turning away from me.

'Please, Max, I just want to help,' I pressed.

'I don't want to talk about it. It's nothing.' He kept his head low, concentrating on the ball at his feet.

And before I could press him any further, I heard a shout and saw a figure approaching.

'Max, thank god I found you. I've been looking everywhere for you. Come on, let's go home,' he said.

He was dressed immaculately, just as I should have expected from Max's description. His wavy black hair was neatly cut, his suit smartly tailored and I caught a hint of the same Armani aftershave my papa wore.

Max stood tall. 'I'm not going anywhere with you.

Leave me alone.'

The man stared, upset. 'Max, please come home.' 'No, all right? I don't need anyone to look out for me,

I've taken care of myself for years,' Max argued.

'Well, I think you can do better. I'm here for you now and I'm responsible for you so please let me help,' his uncle urged.

'Where were you when I lost my parents? Where were you when I *really* needed you?' Max asked. He was doing his best to sound forceful, but I could hear the sadness beneath it.

'Max, this is something we need to discuss at home – your home – so please let's go.'

'We're outta here. Come on, Lucy,' Max spluttered and turned his back on his uncle.

Max grabbed my hand, collected his bag from the stand and we marched up the hill towards my grandparents' store.

'Max, please let me help you. I love you. I don't want to lose you a second time. Please come back,' pleaded his uncle, but Max barely paused before continuing to stride up the hill.

# Chapter 8

# Shelter

I think that was the first time Max had heard the words 'I love you' since he lost his parents. I caught a little tear sliding down his face but I knew him well enough to pretend not to notice.

'Max, your uncle obviously loves you. He seems like a really cool guy and he's trying to make it work. What's up? Why are you pushing him away?' I asked.

'Look, Lucy, it's like I've told you. I do like my uncle, but I've been on my own for a long time and it's weird having to answer to someone, having to trust them. And I'm still angry with him for disappearing from my life. I'll probably go back to his place tomorrow,' he said.

'As long as it's just for one night. But where are we going to stay? I'm not sure we can go to my grandparents' place. My parents have had a huge fight and Mama's a mess. Where else can we go?' I asked as we headed up the street.

'I was going to stay at the Reg in my old spot in the corner of the grandstand, but someone else has taken it, so I thought about trying the refuge up the road. Hopefully they'll have room for me to spend the night. But Lucy, you're going home,' he insisted.

I didn't want to leave him like this. 'No, I'm staying with you.' I quickly changed tack. 'Well, I mean . . . um, this could be a new experience for me. It's exciting.' Oh, that sounded so stupid.

'Lucy, you really have no idea. There's nothing exciting about having nowhere to stay.' He gave me an appraising look. 'Fine. You can get a taste of my old life, so you can see it's not some big romantic adventure. But what about Gigi? She won't be able to stay at the refuge,' he said, patting her.

That's the thing about Max. He puts up a tough exterior but deep down he's a softie.

'Let me sneak her back into my grandparents' place. I'll just put her into her bed and at least then I'll know that she'll be safe,' I replied.

We rushed back to the shop. I eased the back door open and heard the sounds of TV and quiet conversation filtering down the stairs. Luckily Gigi had fallen asleep in my arms, so she wouldn't bark and alert everyone that I was home. I laid her on some old towels in the shop's back room. She'd be comfy there until I returned.

'Phew. No one heard me,' I told him as we headed back up the street.

We arrived at a rundown building on a back street. It looked shabby and distinctly uninviting.

'Max, is *this* the refuge?' I asked, a little shocked.

He stopped and looked deep into my eyes. 'What was I thinking? You're the daughter of the legendary footballer Paolo Zoffi. You've never been without a roof over your head. This is crazy. Lucy, you really should go home. This isn't a place for you and I'm sorry I let you come.'

'Please, I want to hang out with you. It'll be fine,' I stumbled, trying to avoid his gaze. 'And I'm coming with you whether you like it or not. If it's not a place for me, it's not a place for you either.' He had a sheepish look on his face, as if to say that he knew he wasn't going to get rid of me that easily. I knew that deep down he wanted me to stay.

That thought stuck with me for a moment. I'd never had such a close friendship with a boy before. They'd always been my team mates and friends off the pitch, but only to hang out with, playing and talking about football. This was different and I liked it.

'Okay, you can check it out but then you've gotta go home,' he said. 'Besides, I'll be lucky if they have a bed available, and they don't have mixed rooms. You'd be in with a bunch of strange girls. It's no palace and it's not a social club. If we get inside, stay close to me and don't talk to anyone,' he instructed.

'Don't you worry, Max, I can look after myself,' I insisted, with my hands on my hips.

He raised his eyebrows and mumbled, 'Yeah, right, Lucy. You're one *really* tough girl.'

I hadn't realised that this place existed so close to my grandparents' store. I looked around and spotted kids about my age – some even younger – peering suspiciously at us, some chatting and others just sitting on a broken lounge staring at a tiny old TV.

We walked through a small hallway, the paint peeling off the walls, and climbed a set of squeaky stairs that led to an office. A sign above the desk read 'CRISIS HELP NETWORK DROP-IN CENTRE', and posters around the room gave instructions to 'SAY NO TO DOMESTIC VIOLENCE', 'THINK BEFORE YOU DRINK' and a whole load of other warnings. The place was giving me chills.

'Max, you're back!' said the tired-looking woman at the desk. 'To be honest I was hoping you wouldn't need to come here again. Who's your friend?' she asked, while continuing to tap at her computer.

'This is Lucy, she's not going to stay but I need to hang out here just for the night. Is that cool?' he asked.

I didn't think I could have stayed here anyway. The whole building reeked of damp and dirt and some other unpleasant smells. It was desolate, despite the woman's attempt to be friendly. All grouped together, those posters suggested more problems and dangers than I'd ever even thought about. I didn't want Max to stay either.

'Max, it's your lucky night. We have one spare bed, so you can stay on one condition,' she said with a serious look on her face.

How could I get him out of here? This was no place for Max – it wasn't for anyone.

'What's that?' he asked.

'You tell me why you're here. Take your time and explain it to me. Does your uncle know where you are? You know I have to notify him,' she said gently, while typing more notes into her computer.

Max fidgeted.

'What's it matter? I just need somewhere to sleep for a night. Please, just this once, no questions asked,' he pleaded.

'I'd like to, Max, but I have a duty of care and I must follow our procedures. I just want to help you. So, what's it going to be?' she asked.

Without warning Max ran out the door. I took a deep breath and chased after him.

The lady called out, 'Max, come back or I'm going to have to call the police. You should be with your uncle.' But he kept running, and soon we were sprinting around to the church and down the back alley.

'Max, wait. No one's chasing us. Max . . . stop!' I squealed, trying not to lose him.

He knew every nook and cranny in this area so he could easily have slipped away, but I managed to stay right on his tail. He suddenly turned a corner and disappeared into a dark alley. I kept running, even though I couldn't see a thing. All I could hear was my breathing. My heart raced and beads of sweat trickled down my face.

I could just make out something in the distance but I wasn't sure what it was. I kept running. Suddenly someone grabbed me and pulled me back into a doorway. I screamed, but I was held so tightly that my pleas were muffled. I started kicking to loosen the grip. I'd been kidnapped only a matter of months ago and panic flooded me, making me think 'It's happening again!' over and over. I kept kicking until I heard 'Ow!' and then, a voice whispered, 'Lucy, Lucy it's me. It's Max . . . keep quiet.'

I was relieved but angry. 'Did you have to do that?

You scared the hell out of me.'

He still had his arms around me and we looked at each other intently. He let me go suddenly, glancing away.

'Max, please let's go to your uncle's. He wants to do the right thing and so do I,' I said carefully, putting my hand on his shoulder.

He shrugged it off. 'I don't want sympathy, Lucy. Everyone reckons they want to help, but I want to be independent. I need a friend, not someone feeling sorry for me.'

'Max, you know I'm your friend,' I said, giving his foot a gentle kick.

But he didn't look up.

'Maybe I don't want anyone's help! This afternoon my uncle was going on about my future. School, uni, jobs. It felt like my whole life was being planned for me. Like I was trapped. I like being free.' He shook his head. 'Some of the street kids around here are okay. We try and help each other out. But a few of them are facing jail or are messed up from drugs and alcohol. I don't want to get sucked into that vicious cycle. I had to deal with that stuff when my parents were alive. I've seen how it can turn good people into monsters.' He stopped and looked at me, panicked. 'Being back at the refuge reminded me of all the stuff I've gotta avoid. But I don't want to plan my whole life away either. I want to make my *own* decisions, as they come, you know? I reckon the best thing is if I get out of Sydney and make a new go of it. Find a school, a good football club, then I'll be right.'

My jaw dropped. I couldn't stand the thought of Max living elsewhere, but if that's what would help him then I had to support the idea. It was so hard to comprehend how anyone could have such a troubled life. I'd never been exposed to this sort of thing before. I wasn't sure how to respond, but I figured I should be positive.

'Max, that's what's great about you. You have dreams, even when things are tough. I know that you'll make it, because you want it so badly. And I know the perfect person to help you,' I finished with a smile. An idea hit me – why hadn't I thought of this earlier?

'Let's get out of here. You can stay at my new house. I think they're still renovating, so it must be empty. The only problem is that we'll have to break in.'

'That's not a problem –' he started, then looked around quickly and put a finger to his lips.

A small beam of light was highlighting the walls around us, and soon I heard voices headed in our direction. Max motioned me towards another lane and we ran through a narrow gate hidden behind a large block of flats. We scurried down the path beside the flats and emerged back onto Grandpa's street.

The sound of voices was soon followed by footsteps, getting louder with each step. We carefully moved along the walls, past Grandpa's shop and around the corner. Then we spotted trouble. Parked halfway up the footpath was an empty police car with its lights flickering silently.

# Chapter 9

# Uptown girl

It'd been a long evening and I just wanted to curl up in my comfy bed and drift into a nice long dream. But that wasn't going to happen. Max took one look at the police car and quickly ran away.

I caught up to him and tugged on his sleeve.

'This way . . . the house,' I said breathlessly, and he nodded that he'd follow me.

As we ran I thought about Max's life on the streets. It must have been this exhausting all the time; constantly on the lookout, not knowing where it might be safe to stay, let alone where his next meal would come from.

We passed an open window and a pungent waft of coffee sent me back to the Italy I loved. My beautiful quaint neighbourhood of Brera in the city of Milan, where I grew up. I could see the florist's shop window overflowing with brightly coloured flowers, and hear the familiar sound of the baristas greeting their customers. I missed my football friend, Pino, who'd join me for a football session before school – as long as he didn't sleep in.

But Max didn't have a place that he called home. For the past few years, the Reg Bartley Oval had been the closest thing he'd had to one. Max would huddle in a makeshift bed in one corner of the stand, with just a few blankets strewn on the wooden seating. Evenings must have been the worst – cold and alone, he'd be left with just his thoughts. No television to let his mind wander from reality. Just the screeching of bats, dogs barking and cars careering down the street.

I could understand why Max wanted to leave and make a fresh start, but Sydney was his home – it must have some good memories as well as the scary and tough ones. And right now it was my home. I didn't want him to go. I hated the thought of not being near him.

Max seemed to tune into my thoughts. 'Lucy, the new house your parents have done up down near the harbour – it means you're staying here, right?'

'I suppose so. I think Mama plans to spend part of the year here and the rest in Milan while Papa is still playing football. But I'd be staying here with my grandparents when she goes, so I could stay at one school. I'd just fly back to Italy for visits.' I snuck a look at Max while I caught my breath. 'But at the moment we may not be going anywhere. You know that my papa was arrested after he smashed that paparazzo's camera? I've seen him mad before, but that was a bit frightening.'

'That photographer deserved it. He should stick his nose out of other people's business. I wish I'd been there to see it,' he said, smiling grimly.

The thought of the scuffle seemed to excite Max, but it was a scene I'd rather forget. I was sure that Papa would rather it was erased completely. But as much as I worried that the incident could affect my family in the future, I didn't want to share my problems with Max. They seemed so small compared to his.

'Max, what are you going to do about your uncle? Couldn't you make your fresh start here in Sydney, with him?' I asked.

He looked a little sheepish. 'Maybe. If running off hasn't ruined everything. I wish I could just do it on my own.' He looked back up the way we'd come. 'But if that's my only option for going it alone, maybe I should just suck it up and go back to his place. But not tonight. Where's this place of yours anyway?'

Typical Max. He seemed to be coming around for just a minute, but then he went back to his own plans. Still, I was sure that I could help bring Max and his uncle back together somehow.

'It's just up here, at the end of the street,' I said. 'The white house, the last one before the park.'

This part of Darling Point was considered exclusive. When I'd mentioned the new house to Bella, she'd grinned and started telling me about all the famous actors and other celebrities who owned homes in the street. Some had modern facades and others were built in another era, but they were all massive properties, their hedges and fencing doing little to hide their grandeur and spectacular views of the harbour. This was the kind of neighbourhood my family was used to, as we had holiday houses in Europe overlooking the Mediterranean, and even one overlooking Lake Como in Italy. Nonno Dino used to tell me I was a very lucky girl. Now, having stayed in my grandparents' sweet but crowded flat and having seen how Max lived, I knew how right my nonno was.

'Wow, these houses are more like mansions. Lucy, you're so lucky. You're such an uptown daddy's girl – ha, uptown girl!' he said with a cheeky expression.

I didn't like that tag and I was pretty sure Max knew it. What a stirrer. I decided not to bite.

'Mmm, I suppose so. Let's see if the little rich girl can break into her own place,' I said as we came to the fence around my house. We both chuckled at the prospect.

My blood was bubbling wildly again. This time it wasn't fear – it was excitement. There was something invigorating about breaking the rules – although it was probably no big deal for Max.

I'd only been past here once before, so I didn't know it that well. The house nestled on the end of the street facing the harbour, with a park on one side. It was a great spot; private, with lush trees enveloping the property.

We walked into the park, trying to act natural. The darkness and the trees made it difficult to see and the screeching bats were spooky.

Of course! I pointed to a tree a few steps ahead. It was close to the wall separating my house from the park and had low branches. I hoisted myself onto a branch and – after a tricky moment with a face full of leaves – found my footing on top of the wall.

Max followed, swearing and then laughing as he copped a load of twigs to the head. In the yard below us was a heap of soft soil, ready to even out the yard again once the renovating was done. Perfect.

'Oof!' I landed a little heavily, winding myself. Light from the house on the other side spilled into the yard, dazzling me. I turned around, and as my eyes adjusted again, I found myself staring at something completely unexpected.

A jetty projected into the harbour from the backyard. And there, bobbing gently among the silvery ripples of the moonlit water, was a beautiful surprise. 'Oh my god, Lucy, check it out! Is that really yours?' Max asked, starryeyed.

I raised my shoulders in disbelief.

It was majestic. A long black yacht with 'LOVE LUCY' painted in big red letters through an outline of a large red heart.

'Now, that's very cool, Lucy,' he whispered.

'Yep, it looks amazing. I had no idea we owned a boat here,' I said.

'You mean you have more? Why didn't you tell me you like sailing?' he demanded.

'Well, I didn't think it was important. We have a bigger one moored in Portofino but I didn't know about this one. Papa and I love escaping to the sea . . . no one to bother us!' I whispered back.

It was something special I shared with him. The captain would take us to a secluded beach and Papa and I would dive in and swim in the crystal-clear water while Mama would just watch us from the deck, sipping champagne. She didn't like to swim because she didn't want to wet her hair. Even when she did come in she'd never put her head under – can't ruin the hairdo! But I didn't mind, since it meant I could splash about with Papa.

'Lucy, you don't have to be embarrassed about being rich. Just enjoy it. I know I would. I mean, what a dream, having a yacht named after you. It must be a surprise for Christmas or your birthday. It's coming up soon, isn't it?' he said, glancing at me briefly before continuing to admire the yacht.

I didn't want to sound like a brat, but it really wasn't that big a deal to me. Papa's private plane is also named 'Love Lucy'. It was sweet, but I was also kind of used to it. Besides, it was also the name of one of our clothing lines, so there was business mixed in there too.

'My birthday's still a few months away. How did you know?' I warily said.

'I don't reveal my sources,' he said, in a silly voice. 'But this is fantastic. Maybe we could just hang out on the yacht. And we wouldn't be breaking in, because it has your name on it,' he said, winking. I had to laugh at his dodgy reasoning. 'By the way, when's your birthday?' I asked.

Max's shoulders hunched up and he glanced away. I wished I hadn't asked him – but it was such a simple question!

'Um . . . I turned fifteen a little while ago. But I don't really do birthdays. Not my thing,' he said quietly.

'Well, from now on we're celebrating them,' I insisted. 'Anyway, I'm cold and hungry and there probably won't be any food onboard. We're much better off trying the house.'

'Oh, come on, Lucy. Where's your sense of adventure?' I hesitated. I didn't like sleeping on boats – the cramped spaces made me a little uneasy. And I also felt a bit nervous about staying out all night with a boy, even if it was just Max.

'Come on. Don't you trust me?' he teased, looking back at the boat excitedly.

That did it, I couldn't back out now. I wanted Max to know that I was his true friend. Besides, it was so cute to see him so enthusiastic and it was uncanny that he picked up on my fear.

'Okay then, let's make it your belated birthday present – but you go first.'

Just as Max attempted to board, a flash of light flooded us. 'Hey, don't move!' came a voice from behind us.

# Chapter 10

# The two of us

The light flashed in our faces as the stranger with the torch moved closer.

Max dropped into a boxing stance. He looked ready to play the knight, but he had no armour, just his wits to get us through the danger we faced.

'Don't worry, Lucy, I'll sort this out. When I have him pinned to the ground, you run,' he whispered.

The light moved closer towards us. 'What are you doing here? This is private property. And what –'

But before he could say anything else, Max pounced. I screamed, 'No, Max. No!' I knew the voice but it was too late.

A fight broke out and they rolled further away from me towards the end of the jetty. Somehow Max managed to yell, 'Zeezou, run, run!'

'Lucia, stay where you are,' he bellowed as he wrapped his legs around Max, pinning him to the ground.

That voice warmed my heart. Of course it was him. I ran closer to them and nervously laughed at the sight before me.

'Max, it's my papa!' I yelled.

Max lay there stunned while Papa stood above him and rubbed his chin. I ran straight into my papa's arms.

'Lucy, what are you doing here at this time of night? Who is this boy?' he asked. He released me to help Max up.

Max took his hand. 'I'm Max. I'm Lucy's friend. I'm sorry about your chin. I didn't realise who you were. I thought we were in some sort of danger and I didn't want Lucy hurt.'

'Oh Max, you're so sweet, but I keep telling you that I can take care of myself,' I grinned.

'Mmmm.' Papa rolled his eyes. 'Well, Max, I must say you do have a good right hook. Since you were trying to protect my daughter, no harm done. And you can call me Paolo.' He reached forward to shake hands.

'Thank you, Paolo,' Max replied in a strange squeaky voice.

'Are you all right?' I asked.

'Um, yeah. It's so cool to finally meet your dad. Pity it's like this. I'm so sorry Paolo,' he mumbled in awe.

'Let's go into the house. I'd still like to know what you two were doing here, especially at this time of night. Lucy, does Mama know that you're here?' he asked.

'Um, no Papa. I was meaning to call her but lost track of time,' I said sheepishly.

'She'll be worried sick! We must call her.'

'Could you please call her for me? I couldn't face her yelling at me right now. Please, Papa.'

'Lucy, this isn't right,' he insisted. 'Please, Papa, just this once,' I begged.

'Fine. I'll do it this once,' he said, reaching into his pocket for his phone and walking back towards the house. That was a relief. I was hoping I could make them speak to each other. But as Max and I walked up the yard, all I could hear was yelling coming from inside the house.

'Wow, Lucy this place is so cool,' said Max.

'Yeah … I'm amazed myself!' I knew they'd bought the place and started renovating a little while ago, but I hadn't realised Mama had progressed so far with decorating the house.

Papa came towards us with a glum look. 'Well, she isn't happy. She thinks that I had something to do with you disappearing like that. She's madder than before. I have to take you to your grandparents first thing in the morning. Lucy, you must start thinking about other people and being more responsible.'

Max was silent the whole time, staring at Papa like he'd never seen a man before.

'I'm sorry, Papa. The last thing I wanted was to cause more trouble,' I said carefully. If I admitted I'd been out so late because I wanted to help Max, my parents would view him as a troublemaker. I wanted them to like him.

'Well, it's done now, so don't you worry. Your mama and I will sort it out,' he said gently, then turned his attention to Max. 'So, young Max, what's your story? And why did you call Lucy "Zeezou"?'

This was fantastic! Max was proving to be a great distraction – hopefully I'd be let off the hook.

Max bounced to attention, but seemed to have lost his ability to speak. I think Papa was used to this from young football fans.

I jumped in to the rescue. 'Papa, my team mates in the Lions call me Zeezou – it's my nickname! I thought you knew. You know my favourite footballer is Zinedine Zidane, well, after you. I'm called after his nickname, Zizou. Anyway, Max is a really good footballer and a crazy AC Milan fan. He's also a left-back and –'

'Um, yes, it's my favourite position. I want to be like you, one day,' Max said shyly.

'Well, I'd like to check out your football skills. Right now, though, it's time we all got to bed. Max, I'll drive you home. Or you're welcome to stay in one of the guest rooms if you're allowed and I can drop you off in the morning,' Papa offered.

'Oh, thank you, but I've taken up enough of your time.

I'd better head off,' he said.

'No Max, please stay here. Where are you going to go?' I asked.

Papa sensed that something was wrong. 'Max, a friend of Lucy's is a friend of mine. I'd really like you to stay with us tonight and in the morning you can join Lucy and me in a football session. Would you like that?'

'Oh . . . ah, wow. Yes, brilliant. Um, this is a dream come true. Oh my god, I mean, this is so cool. I'm staying right here!'

We all had a chuckle.

'So Max, I gather you're staying.' Papa grinned.

'I'd be honoured to stay in your home, Mr Zo . . . um, I mean, Paolo!' Max replied. I guess I could understand why he was being so goofy. He had just met his idol, one of the greatest footballers on the planet.

'Great, who should I call? Your mother?' asked Papa. To my surprise Max tentatively offered, 'Oh, um . . .

my Uncle Rick, but he's probably asleep.'

'That's okay. If he doesn't answer I'll leave a message to let him know that you're safe with us so he doesn't worry about you,' Papa said coolly.

Max gave Papa his uncle's phone number. While he made the call, Max and I chatted.

'Sounds like you've made your decision, Max,' I said, relieved.

'Yeah, meeting your dad is a bit freaky. I was so thrilled at the thought of a kick-around with my idol – it reminded me just how much I want to make football my life, my career. I'm so lucky to have this chance,' he said, his eyes full of excitement.

'Yep, and I think from now on the ball is going to roll your way.'

Max had the biggest smile planted across his face, 'Yeah, Lucy, you're right. Finally, I'm going to be mixing it with the best on and off the pitch! It's my destiny.'

I thought about the trials tomorrow and the missing letter from the Beckham Academy. I wished that I was as sure about mine. What was my destiny?

# Chapter 11

# Idol

After Papa left a message for Rick, we all settled down in the lounge room. Papa had come back here after his fight with Mama, and planned to stay on while the finishing touches to the house were being made. He'd even arranged for Rosa, our lovely housekeeper in Milan, to come to Sydney for the next few months. She'd be arriving later in the month. I took all this as a sign that he was confident he and Mama would be getting back together sooner rather than later.

Soon we were engrossed in a conversation about our favourite subject – football, specifically AC Milan's season and the Champions League, which Papa had missed because of my attempted abduction. This had happened a few months back. The kidnappers grabbed me and demanded a ransom, but luckily I'd managed to escape from them.

Papa and Max were getting along very well and Max seemed more comfortable as the conversation continued. But eventually I couldn't keep my eyes open any longer. I wished them both good night, and as I walked away, I heard their conversation continuing.

'Paolo, I love the way you guard the backline. You play with so much . . . what's the word? Finesse,' Max blurted.

I smiled to myself. Max had been staring at Papa, as though he was trying to work out whether he was real or not. Maybe I'd be the same way if I met someone I admired, someone like my favourite singer, Pink? I kind of hoped not.

'Thank you, Max. That's a great compliment. So, tell me, why do you play football?' Papa asked.

'It makes me feel free. There's nothing like it in the world,' he said. I could hear in his voice that he was talking about his greatest love.

And that was exactly how I felt when I played. Free as a bird gliding in the sky. I had to get back on track and really focus on the game – live and breathe it like never before.

Uh-oh! The football trials were tomorrow. I really had to get some sleep.

'Max, let me know if there's any way that I can help you,' I overheard Papa offer as I walked into my room.

I was so happy that they were getting along. I'd never heard Max open up so freely. Maybe it was because he felt like he already knew Papa, having followed his career all his life. I also got the feeling Papa had sensed that Max needed his help.

Mama should be here with us, I thought, sharing this time with Papa. He was so good with Max. He'd probably be a good father to Tommaso, if it was true that he was the father – and if he ever got the chance. Before too long, I drifted off into a deep slumber.

I was awakened the next morning by bright sunlight slicing through the small gap in my curtains. I was still tired; my body was heavy and my tummy was screaming for food. I opened the curtains to a wide view of the twinkling harbour and sailors tending to their yachts on the neighbouring jetties.

I couldn't wait to have breakfast with Papa and Max. The house was very quiet, so I guessed they must still be in bed. I threw on my tracksuit. Mama really had been planning for a long stay here. The wall-to-wall wardrobe was already full of clothes I'd left behind in Milan and some new outfits that she'd obviously hand-picked; they were a bit too girly for my liking. Her desperate and relentless efforts to make me more fashion-conscious gave me a giggle sometimes – she just wouldn't give up.

I ran downstairs, looking forward to telling Papa and Max about my trial.

To my disbelief I found the breakfast room a mess. A platter of pastries and fruit had already been munched on. Two plates of half-eaten food lay on the table, but the culprits were nowhere to be seen. I started devouring a brioche as I went on the hunt.

They weren't hard to find. From the backyard I could hear that beautiful smack of a boot connecting perfectly to the ball. The sound was coming from the park next door. It was like listening to your favourite song. It's a godgiven talent to deliver such perfection and it's something both my papa and Max possess in copious amounts.

I decided to watch them for a bit before joining in. I scrambled up onto the fence and found myself a nice spot in the fork of a tree. Max had the eye of a tiger, totally focused and in his element. He was playing so well and showing Papa all his tricks and moves with great ease and precision. Papa seemed to be enjoying himself too, and I decided I'd waited long enough. I hopped down silently and worked my way in to win the ball from an unsuspecting Max.

'Excellent, Lucia. Good move,' Papa yelled. But that just spurred Max on and before I knew it he had the ball at his feet, running back towards Papa and scoring a goal between the two marked tree trunks. Max celebrated with his shirt over his head.

'Max, no ... look *out*!' I yelled but it was too late. We watched, cringing, as he ran straight into one of the trunks. He fell on his back and lay still.

I didn't know whether to laugh or cry. It was the funniest sight, but of course I hoped that he wasn't hurt, especially after what he'd been through last night. Papa and I ran to his side.

'Max, are you okay?' I asked, growing worried when I realised his eyes were closed.

After what seemed like eternity he screamed 'Ha!' and burst out laughing.

'You scared the hell out of me! But I'll give it to you – that was funny,' I laughed.

'How's your head feeling?' Papa asked.

'It's a bit sore but what the hell. I've had the most amazing morning!' he gushed.

'That's good news, Max. Let's get you up on your feet. You're a very gifted footballer and my club could use your skills. If this is something you really want, well, I think I can help you, but try to take it easy with your celebrations for a while,' Papa said thoughtfully.

Aspiring footballers asked Papa for help all the time. I'd seen him struggling to encourage less talented players to keep playing, without giving them false hope that they'd reach professional level. He was obviously very impressed with Max's talent to make an offer like that.

'It's my dream to be a professional footballer. I'd give anything to get a crack at the big time,' Max said, rubbing his head.

'Oh, Papa you're the best! I knew you'd be able to help Max,' I said, thrilled.

'Of course I would, and not just because he's your friend. He truly has great potential,' Papa replied.

I couldn't help but feel a little twinge of jealousy when I heard that remark. It was exactly what *I* wanted to hear from him about my football – but I'd show him at my trial.

'Papa, I have to hurry. I have a football trial at the Reg for a representative team. Will you please come and watch me?' I asked.

'Of course, I'd love to watch my girl play football. And then we'll visit Frida,' he answered, running his fingers through his hair.

I realised then just how selfish I'd been. 'Oh Papa, I'm so sorry. I'm carrying on about my problems without even thinking about what you must be going through. I want you to know that if I do have a half-brother, I'd be really happy about it. You know I've always wanted a big brother, especially one who plays football.' I thought I saw a hint of a tear come to his eyes.

'Lucy, you don't know how much that means to me.' He paused and then whispered, 'It's true, and his name is Tommaso! He can't wait to meet you.' He grabbed me for a big hug. Over his shoulder I saw Max throw me a wink.

'Oh Papa, that's great news. I can't wait to meet him, either.' And I meant it, although I was a little shocked by the news. I had so many questions, but they would have to wait. I couldn't let Papa see my surprise – I had to let him know that he had my support.

'All right then,' said Papa, wiping his eyes roughly with the back of his hand. 'We'd better get moving. I promised Max's uncle I'd drop him off too.'

'Cool, I think it's time for me to go home,' Max admitted, as I contemplated life with my new big brother.

# Chapter 12

# Game on

We dropped Max at his uncle's, then headed to the Reg. My preparation for this trial hadn't been the best but I couldn't wait to get back to playing the game I love. I tried to keep the news of my big brother well and truly in the back of my mind. I had to be fully focused if I was going to make it onto this team. It was almost a good thing that I'd been so distracted; I hadn't had any time to get nervous.

As we approached the Reg, I heard the balls being pounded into the back of the net and my heart lifted.

'Papa, please don't take this the wrong way, but can you keep your distance? I don't want the players or coach to know you're here. I want to get in on my own terms. Is that okay?' I asked.

'Don't worry, I understand. It was the same when my papa came to watch me play. I respect you more for trying to do it on your own. I'll keep a very low profile. Will this do?' He hunched his shoulders and pulled down the brim of his cap.

He knew how to make me smile, but my thoughts were elsewhere. 'I miss Nonno Dino. I wish he was here,' I said.

'Me too, but just remember, every time you kick the ball he's with you.' Papa gave me a last hug and headed off to a quiet spot away from the other parents.

It was good to think he considered my love of football the same as his and his father's. It made me feel even closer to him.

As I headed to the registration area, I was surprised by the number of girls here to trial. There wasn't a boy in sight. It was silly – I should have known a rep team would be single sex, but I suddenly felt strange and nervous. I wasn't used to playing with or against other girls. I was facing the unknown and wasn't sure if I would fit in.

I looked about, hoping to spot a familiar face. A very fit footballer caught my eye. She was manoeuvring the ball as though she was practising some kind of mind control over it. It was magical to watch the way she effortlessly flicked the ball up into the air and cracked it into the back of the net. She was awesome.

She collected the ball and suddenly started walking in my direction.

'Glad you could make it, Ms Zoffi,' she said, while I stood speechless.

'You *are* Lucia Zoffi, aren't you? Or do you prefer Lucy Zeezou?' she continued.

'Oh, um, yes, they are all me, but I prefer Lucy. Everyone calls me Lucy, although my team mates call me Zeezou on the pitch.' I smiled cautiously, wondering how she knew me.

'It's good to finally meet you. I'm the coach of the Sydney Dolphins under 15s team. Coach Tilly is what they call me here. Coach James has told me so much about you. I actually caught a glimpse of you playing in last season's final and I must say that I was very impressed with your performance.'

This was amazing. I was off to a good start before I'd even hit the pitch, although she was clearly expecting a lot and I wasn't exactly prepared.

Before I could respond, she said, 'Well, Lucy, we're not here to get acquainted. Go and change into your kit and join the rest of the girls.'

By now the Reg was overflowing with girls handing in their registrations, chatting and mingling. I'd never seen so many girls interested in football. It was obviously very popular in Australia. Maybe it had something to do with the new national women's league that had just kicked off. There must have been about a hundred players here fighting for just fifteen or sixteen spots.

'Oh, um, I don't have my kit. Can I trial in my tracksuit?' I mumbled, embarrassed.

'Well, I don't usually accept that. You're lucky that I'm in a good mood and it's your first day,' she said, suddenly all-business. She sighed. 'Just this once I'll allow you to play as you are. But if you make the team, don't ever let me see you turn up to any of my sessions dressed like this again. We're not here for fashion; football's the name of the game and I expect you and any player under my tutelage to be dressed in full kit and behaving appropriately,' she ordered, motioning me onto the pitch. I noticed the rest of the players stealing a glance, some checking me out and giggling at my bad start.

She had me all wrong – I wasn't here for fashion either. How could things turn around so quickly? Now I really had to prove myself.

The only thing lifting my spirits was having Papa on my side, finally getting his approval to play. It was a little strange not having to quietly slip away to play in secret. Here at last was my chance to show him what I could do. I wished Grandpa was here too. I was sorry for staying out so late and worrying him, and Nanna and Mama. My mind drifted to the good old days, training with my dear Nonno Dino, who inspired me to play from the moment I took my first steps. His wise words came to me, as they so often did. 'Lucia, keep it simple. Enjoy your football, believe in yourself and, most importantly, never give up!' 'Lucy Zoffi, group 3,' yelled Coach Tilly.

I ran over and stood in my group as my stomach started to churn. All the girls were checking each other out, whispering to friends and old team mates.

'Did you hear that last season's star striker has signed with another club?' one girl said to her friends.

'Yeah, it's not surprising. Apparently she didn't get along with the assistant coach,' another answered. 'It was getting nasty, so her parents pulled her out.'

'Okay, girls, enough chatter. To compete at representative level I expect my players to train hard, have good touch on the ball and be consistent at every game. This is nothing like park football and I expect 110 per cent dedication and commitment or you may as well leave now,' ordered Coach Tilly as she looked around at her hopeful players.

No one uttered a sound. She had their full attention and obviously their respect. She must have a good reputation – or maybe everyone else also found her a little scary. I knew then that this was going to be extremely tough. All the girls here were serious about their football. That was a pretty exciting thought – I couldn't wait to check out their skills.

Coach Tilly continued. 'It's great to have such a good turn-up but I can only choose fifteen players for my squad. Please remember that if you don't make it this time around, it just means you need to work harder and try again next time. And for those selected, congratulations. Right, I want you to start heading out onto the pitch and give me two laps to warm up and then straight into drills. I expect you all to be focused and showing me your best … Good luck!'

It was the first time I'd been on a pitch full of female footballers. The atmosphere was very different from being around the boys. I wasn't even sure why. There was a hint more chatter, but the girls moved with the same intensity and work ethic.

'That's it … lay the ball off … good movement … stay focused,' yelled the coach from the sidelines.

Everyone was switched on, desperate to impress for a spot in the squad. Oh, it felt so good to be doing what I love best, but I was so nervous. I was trying so hard – maybe too hard. When the teams were chosen to play a proper game I decided to try a more relaxed approach. I was told to start as a left-back, which certainly wasn't my preferred position.

'Lucy, what are you doing?' yelled the coach as the ball rolled past me and a rival player claimed possession, beating the keeper for the opening goal.

'Oh, I'm sorry, Tilly. I wasn't expecting it,' I nervously replied.

'It's *Coach* Tilly and it's time to wake up. Goal-scorer, well done. As for the rest of you, I want to see more effort. Don't waste your time or mine,' she said sternly.

Everyone moved back into position with an extra bounce in their step. I was used to playing as an attacking midfielder or a striker. She said she saw me play in the final, so surely she knew I'm best up front. Luckily, Nonno Dino had taught me how to play in all areas of the park, although tackling was still the weakest part of my game.

The rival team was celebrating their first goal thanks to my mistake. I'd failed in my position as the last line of defence in the opening minutes.

The screeching of car tyres and yelling suddenly filled the air. A shrill scream followed, and the players looked up, startled. It was an awful sound, but I assumed it was just another Sydney traffic incident.

Coach Tilly blew her whistle. 'Minds on the game, girls!'

As we resumed play I tried to steal a look at Papa. I immediately wished I hadn't. His face was sombre with disappointment, although he motioned for me to press on. My heart sank. This was not how I wanted him to see me play.

I had to pull myself together. It was just one mistake and now I had time to set it right. Nonno Dino taught me to be better than this, to keep fighting, to give it my best.

Soon the opposition was on the attack and fast closing in. I went in hard, winning the ball. The striker went down in the process and the coach blew her whistle as my rival struggled to get up, moaning and gripping her ankle. I offered my hand but she wouldn't take it.

'Get lost, prancer,' she moaned. 'Don't think you can get away with it just cause you're a Zoffi.'

'I don't know who you are but you've got the wrong girl. Get up and stop acting. I won that ball fair and square,' I demanded, sweating and hoping that she'd apologise.

'Ha, that's a joke. I know who you are. We're at the same school! But of course you've never even noticed me. Well, we all know the famous Zoffi family thanks to our principal. She made such a big deal about you, rolling out the red carpet for the princess's arrival from Italy. La di da!' she mocked with a sour laugh.

And that's when I realised who she was. Angie, the school bully. I'd only been at the school a couple of months and had managed to stay clear of her, although I'd seen her taunting other girls. I'd had no idea that she was a footballer – let alone a good one. Great. Life at school was going to get even worse, and she clearly wanted to make things tough for me on the pitch.

'Okay, girls, that's enough. Good tackle, Lucy. I want more of that,' yelled Coach Tilly.

I tried to mask a satisfied smile. I'd won the coach's approval – for now – although it was still going to be an uphill battle to get a player like Angie on side.

But I knew that Papa would be impressed, as tackling was his specialty. I just hoped that he'd caught me in action. I looked over. Thankfully he was alone, keeping a low profile, but to my disappointment he was on his phone. He probably missed the tackle!

Suddenly he looked up, his gaze met mine and he gave me the thumbs up.

That was just what I needed. Now I could really kick butt. But then he gestured that he was leaving. I couldn't believe it. Where was he going?

All I could do was wave back with a forced smile, as though it wasn't a big deal. I'd played without his support for years. I was tough. I'd just have to play that way again.

I was thrown back into the game when a player called out and the ball came spiralling over to me. I pushed up from the back and fed the midfielder, who switched back to me thanks to a tight defence. I decided to take them on myself and started running with the ball, weaving past one defender and then another until I reached the 6-yard box and came up against Angie. The bully was in my way.

She was a solid girl covered in freckles and she had lots of brilliant red hair. She looked tough, very tough. But I wasn't afraid. She was in my domain and this time I was the one to be feared. I threw a dummy but she didn't fall for it. She tried to grab my shirt but I moved to her right and managed to get around her, smacking the ball into the top right-hand corner, far from the goalkeeper's outstretched hand. But before I could celebrate, my feet were taken from under me and I found myself flat on my back.

I knew who was responsible and she was not going to get away with it. I slowly rose to my feet, and even though my left leg was throbbing with pain,

I launched towards her.

'What do you think you're doing? You could have broken my leg. You should be off the pitch, you silly cow!' I yelled with fury.

Angie's face suddenly matched the colour of her hair. 'Really? I was just doing my job, putting you in your place – on the ground where you belong.'

'You should be put out to pasture, because you certainly can't play football,' I sneered, moving closer. We were standing face to face as the girls looked on, amused, and the parents started to murmur among themselves.

'Girls! That's enough bickering. I love the passion you both have for the game but you must calm down. You were *both* playing out of position, but Angie your tackle from behind was unnecessary and warranted a red card. In fact, I think you should sit out for the rest of the game,' ordered Coach Tilly.

'But Coach, it wasn't just me. What about Lucy?' Angie exploded.

'That's for me to decide,' Coach Tilly snapped as she gestured for Angie to get off the pitch. She turned to me. 'Lucy, you played out of position but you demonstrated great movement on the ball, and that was a superb finish. That's the kind of play I like to encourage. But you need a cooler head. Go and have a drink and I'll let you back on in a few minutes.'

'Yes, Coach,' I said meekly.

I didn't think it was fair but I didn't want to cause any more drama. Besides, I was happy with her positive comments about my game.

Unfortunately my bag was right behind Angie and a few other players on the sideline. I had no choice but to walk straight over and grab it.

'Oh, look, it's Little Miss Catwalk looking for the red carpet,' said Angie, while the others sniggered.

'Oh, very funny! Don't be such a sore loser,' I bit back as I took my water out of my bag.

'Listen here, Zoffi or Zithead, or whatever your name is. I'm not a loser and I'd watch my mouth if I were you,' she barked, walking towards me.

'You can't threaten me. Go back to eating grass, you cow. You certainly can't play on it,' I snapped. I regretted it right away.

In an instant, she threw herself on top of me. I couldn't believe it. I'd never been in a fight before. I struggled to get her solid frame off me. She had me pinned to the ground, and to make matters worse, she started pulling my hair. I did my best to fight her off, kicking my legs and hitting out with my arms, but to no avail. She was too strong and obviously used to this sort of thing.

Thankfully, Coach Tilly put a stop to it. 'What on earth is going on? Angie get off her … now! This is totally unacceptable!' she screamed.

I scrambled to my feet, my face burning with fury. Oh, I just wanted to crawl into a hole and disappear. This was too awful. I straightened myself up, trying to prepare myself for the blasting.

'I'm extremely disappointed in both of you. I do not tolerate any type of aggressive behaviour from my players, especially players of your calibre.'

'But Coach Tilly, she just lunged at –' I tried to explain.

'Not now, Lucy. I'll speak to you both privately after I address all the players. Can everyone please gather round and sit down.'

'Well, girls, today was your chance to be selected for the under 15s team representing the Sydney Dolphins in the New South Wales Super League. Those who make it will be up against the best teams in the state, so my staff and I are choosing players who we think are dedicated, talented, committed and passionate. And *respectful* to others.' She faced Angie and me for those last words.

She continued with the full attention of the prospective squad members. 'When they wear the sky blue, I expect my players to devote themselves to the game and always perform at their best both on and off the pitch. A letter will be sent to all players over the next few weeks informing them of their selection or otherwise. This club is well known for nurturing the best football talent in the country and it's where I spent most of my youth. Now, I'm playing for Australia. Maybe one day you too will become a Matilda …'

Oh, of course! *Tilly* was Tatiana Katrovic. I'd heard of her before. Since arriving in Sydney I'd heard more and more about the Matildas – playing for Australia was now on my radar even more than representing Italy. There seemed to be so many more opportunities for female footballers and the Matildas were awesome. Papa wouldn't be pleased, but you've got to stay true to yourself and follow your own dream!

Now I had to hope twice as hard that today's incident wasn't going to hamper my chances of making the squad. If I made it, I decided then, I was going to put all my energies back into the game I loved more than anything. I'd make it to the top just like Coach Tilly.

I tuned back into her speech: 'I'd like to thank you all for participating in these trials and for those who miss out, I wish you all the best. And don't be too disheartened, keep training and try again next year. Okay, off you go. You'll hear from us.' The girls started to disperse.

Suddenly, Papa was running towards us, calling out, 'Lucy, you have to get home now!'

Oh, god, what now? I buried my head, hoping he'd stop. I didn't want them all to know about my background. What could be so bad that I had to be embarrassed in front of the girls and the coach? They all stood dumbstruck at his dramatic entrance. But as Papa moved closer, Coach Tilly's expression softened and she appeared to be more welcoming.

'*The* Paolo Zoffi?' she said. She was practically purring. 'Yes, hello, I'm Paolo, lovely to meet you,' Papa replied. 'I'm Killy Tatrovic, um, I mean, sorry, I'm Tilly Katrovic. I'm the girls' coach. It's such a great honour to meet you,' she gushed, flicking her ponytail and holding out her hand.

I tried hard to contain my laughter and so did the rest of the players. She was behaving like a silly schoolgirl, but unfortunately Papa seemed to have that effect on people. Of course she'd know who Papa was – and now everyone did!

Papa pretended not to notice anything. 'Apologies for the interruption, but I need to take Lucy home right now. Please excuse us.' He quickly shook her hand, then went to put his arm around me.

'Of course. Lucy may go, but I do need to have a chat with her about an earlier incident. If you don't mind I'll call you to discuss it further.' Her voice was soft and inviting now, and she fluttered her eyelashes. She looked utterly ridiculous.

'That's fine. You can reach Lucy on my wife Frida's number, which is on the registration form,' Papa blurted. The girls' attention was fixed on Papa's conversation with Coach Tilly. It was so funny to watch the hard, tough coach transform into a flirtatious awkward teenager.

They couldn't contain themselves any further and burst into laughter.

But Coach Tilly wasn't about to be ridiculed. 'That's enough, girls. Mind your manners. This is Paolo Zoffi, one of the best defenders in world football and one of the most recognised players on the planet.'

If I hadn't been so embarrassed it would have been funny: the girls turned their heads towards Papa as one, murmuring 'Ooooh'. Ugh. I just wanted to leave as quickly as possible, but apparently Papa thought he should share some words of wisdom. Sometimes I wondered whether he didn't *like* all the attention just a tiny bit.

'Girls, it's great to see so many aspiring footballers. I'm sure Tatiana has also told you that even if you weren't selected it doesn't mean that you're not good enough, so never ever give up on your dream. Now, please excuse us, we must go. Ciao!' Papa told the players. I was stuck standing alongside him with everyone's eyes locked on us. I just wanted to melt into the ground.

'Oh, thank you, Paolo. That was very kind of you,' Coach Tilly said.

'Sorry I have to go, Coach Tilly,' I said, shrugging my shoulders. I knew that my chances of making it were dwindling.

'Oh Lucy, I understand. Family comes first. Don't worry, we'll talk soon,' she replied with a massive smile. Well, that lifted my spirits, even though my true identity had now been revealed.

So much for the low profile. We just couldn't blend in anywhere. It was silly of me to think that Papa would go unnoticed. How could he? There was always someone who recognised him. There was no escaping his celebrity.

Now I had some mysterious, pressing issue to face and I wasn't looking forward to it. I didn't know what could have been so urgent that Papa would make such a scene. That was more Mama's style.

He took my hand and we raced up the hill to Grandpa's shop.

'Papa, please tell me what's going on. What's the rush?

'Lucy, we'll discuss this at your grandparents'. What's the incident she mentioned?' he asked, looking worried.

'Oh, it's really no big deal. I'll explain later,' I shrugged, hoping he wouldn't press me further.

'On a good note, I thought you played very well. I was very impressed by your tackle on the red-haired girl. And you always told me you were just a striker!' he joked. 'Maybe you're following in your papa's footsteps, after all,' he added, rubbing my head.

I threw him a smile. There weren't many things that topped hearing his praise.

My smile soon disappeared, though, when we walked into the snap of a camera lens. A paparazzo desperate for a picture caught us off guard. I don't know how he knew Papa was there, but we made the best of it – we kept walking, ignoring him as well as we could. The famous life was definitely not for me!

# Chapter 13

# Gigi

Papa and I walked back to the shop without being hounded by other paparazzi. What a relief! He seemed distracted, though, and I worried about what I was going to hear when we got there. I hoped he'd been called away from the Reg so he and Mama could talk properly at last – but I had my doubts. Either way, I was looking forward to cuddling my little Gigi. She'd probably be cranky with me for dumping her back home last night, but it'd be comforting to have her with me while I heard whatever my parents had to say.

She is such a gorgeous little chihuahua, with beautiful white fluffy hair and huge brown eyes. I've always told her all my secrets – especially about sneaking off to play football. That was one advantage of having a friend who couldn't talk!

Once we reached the shop, I raced up the stairs, waiting for her to jump up at me, eager to be cradled in my arms.

But there was no barking, just an uncomfortable silence. Something was very wrong. I stood in the lounge room, calling, 'Gigi? Come on girl . . . Gigi, where are you?'

But the room was completely silent. This wasn't what I was expecting. Oh, please, take me back to the football pitch! I didn't think I could handle any more drama.

'Ciao, Mama, Nanna, Grandpa,' I said, running over to kiss them all hello, and wondering who the man with them was. He looked sort of familiar.

'Lucy, this is Rick Spitzer,' said Mama.

'Oh, hello, Rick, nice to meet you. Is Max okay?' I was surprised that Max's uncle was here.

'Hi Lucy. Nice to meet you properly. We didn't get a chance to talk last night. And I'm sure that Max is fine,' he said, although he didn't look completely convinced.

I was about to ask why he looked so uncertain about Max when Grandpa got up and put his arms around me. 'Now, princess, there's no need to be alarmed, but Gigi's been in an accident.'

A little shriek escaped me. 'When? Is she all right? Where is she?' I cried. My breath had already grown ragged and my heart seemed to stop beating.

Papa came over and gently sat me down. 'Gigi's going to be all right. She's been injured, but she's at the vet now being cared for. That's why I brought you home so quickly.'

'But she was fine last night. I put her to bed while she was sleeping. How was she hurt?'

Nanna spoke softly. 'Lucy, darling, we woke in the morning to Gigi barking. She was running in and out of your bedroom, howling because you weren't here.'

Nanna tried to compose herself, but I could see the glimmer of tears in her eyes. She continued as Grandpa stroked her hand. 'We decided to take Gigi down to watch you at the trials. But my hip started playing up so we had to head back and on the way we ran into Rick. When Paolo left that message for Rick last night, Rick realised that Max's friend "Lucy" was you, our granddaughter, and decided to visit the shop.' She paused to sip her coffee.

I was getting frustrated, wishing that she'd get to the point.

'We've known Rick for years – he used to be one of our regular customers – but we lost contact, so we had a lot of catching up to do. We never realised he and Max were related. Well, we got caught up discussing Max's future. Paolo had told Rick how gifted Max is at football, and that he wanted to help him. All of a sudden Gigi bolted across the road. She must have been chasing something. I yelled for her to stop but it was too late.'

'Oh no! How badly was she hurt?' I asked, shocked to the core.

'Well, it could have been a tragedy, but she's going to be fine. A cyclist came flying down the hill just as Gigi ran out. He tried to swerve but clipped her back legs. He stopped to pick her up just as a car came down the hill and had to brake hard to avoid hitting them both. There was a terrible screech from the brakes – the car only just missed them! All I could do was scream!' She paused and looked at Grandpa, then back at me. 'Well, finally we crossed over. I tried to soothe Gigi while your grandpa rang your papa.'

Now I could put the pieces together; the screeching of the car and the scream I'd heard at the trials, Papa abruptly leaving the oval. It all added up.

I gave Nanna a huge hug. 'Thank you, Nanna. I'm just so relieved that she's going to be all right. I don't know what I would have done if she was . . . well you know . . .' The adults settled themselves back into their seats, and I plopped down on the lounge and poured myself a glass of lemonade. I was desperate to visit Gigi at the vet's, but was told that we had to leave her to rest for a few days.

My focus shifted to my parents.

Mama appeared a little more like her usual self. She wore a fitted, plunging red dress and kept throwing inviting looks across the room at Papa. Something had definitely changed.

Rick coughed politely and started to speak. 'Tony and Betty, it was no accident that I ran into you. I wanted to visit to thank you for keeping an eye on Max over the past few years. I wish I'd been here and known what was going on.'

'It's been our pleasure. We would have liked to do more for Max, but well, I'm sure you're learning just what an independent boy he is,' Grandpa replied as Nanna nodded in agreement.

'You did all you can and I really appreciate it. And I want to thank Paolo for looking out for Max last night. I was so worried that he'd end up back on the streets. He's a good kid and I'm trying to work out how to help him feel comfortable living in a safe, home environment. But I know it's going to take time to earn his trust and respect.' Rick stopped and gave a half-smile. 'To be honest, I'm trying to get used to the city again after having spent a fair bit of time in the country with my people.'

'Your people?' Mama asked. I'm glad she asked, because I wasn't too sure what he meant.

'I'm from the Wiradjuri tribe. It's the biggest Indigenous group in New South Wales,' he explained. 'It's a shame that Max doesn't seem to know a lot about his background, but I'm going to teach him about our mob. He's at the age now where he can make his own choices and I want to make sure he doesn't fall back into that street scene. I think he could have a bright future. I owe it to my late brother and I owe it to Max.'

'I think you're right, Rick,' said Papa. 'Max seems like a good kid and he's a very gifted footballer. I meant it when I said that I think we could help him on that career path.' Mama stepped in. 'Paolo, excuse me for interrupting, but football isn't the answer to everything. What happens if he doesn't make it and there's no backup plan?'

'But he *will* make it –' I started.

'It's not just his talent, Lucy. What if he's injured and has to retire young? Or decides he doesn't like the travelling a footballer must do?' she said gently.

'Of course, there's no guarantee, but he's hungry to succeed. He can get a good education at the same time. And Lucy will set an example with her own football pursuits. Support is half the battle, isn't it, princess?' he said, winking at me.

'Yep. I'm going to train really hard to become a Matilda, just like Coach Tilly,' I announced.

'A Matilda?' Mama said with a blank stare.

Papa also gave me a funny look. 'The Matildas are the national women's team here, aren't they, Lucy?'

I nodded, a little worried by his expression.

'But football is the most popular sport in Italy. Why don't you want to play, for the *Azzurre*?' Papa queried.

'Sorry, Papa, but the football here for girls seems to be much more popular and it also seems better funded. Just the fact that they have a national women's league here like the men must mean that there are so many more opportunities for girls here than in Italy,' I explained.

Mama seized the moment. 'There's nothing wrong with wanting to represent Australia.' Nanna and Grandpa nodded in agreement. But Mama wasn't stopping there. 'Although, while we're on this track, I still think you'd be much better off on the catwalks of Europe where you belong. And there's a perfect opportunity coming up . . .'

Oh no, why did she have to keep making plans for me?

'Our friends Dolce & Gabbana are throwing their support behind a young and funky new Italian label, Molto and Favolosa. They're launching the label with a fashion charity show. They've invited us to model in the event, thanks to D&G's recommendation. Don't look at me like that, *Lucia*, you'll be interested in this one. It's to raise money for animal shelters. They want to include Gigi in the show – all the models will be parading their pets. As long as they're not too big and wild. Honestly, that Jelena and her ostrich, it's just *too* silly.'

Jelena wasn't exactly the only silly model, I thought, looking at Mama. 'Um, well, that is a very worthy cause. Gigi will love all the attention. Okay, Mama, you've got me. But I thought we were discussing Max's future. He deserves a break and I know for a fact that he doesn't want to end up back on the streets. He's even more crazy about being a footballer than me,' I claimed, turning my gaze back to Papa and Rick.

'Max is very lucky to have a friend like you, Lucy,' Rick said seriously.

'No, I'm lucky to have a friend like Max! He's made me realise how fortunate I am to have such a supportive family. Max is one of the only people who really gets me!' I blurted.

Whoops. I had no idea I was going to say anything like that. Everyone looked as surprised as I felt.

Eventually Papa said, 'Well, thankfully Gigi is going to be all right in time for the show. Rick, it's been very good to meet you, and I look forward to sitting down with you and Max to discuss how we can help his football career.' He leaned forward to shake Rick's hand, then turned to me. 'Lucy, your Mama and I have a lot to discuss, so we're going to step out for a while.'

I moved forward to give him a huge hug, to show him that he had my support. He winked.

'Of course, Papa. Please go! Enjoy dinner, Mama,' I said with a big grin. Would a nice meal be enough for them to resolve what was going on? Papa had told me yesterday that the rumours about him having a son were true – did Mama know that? She seemed very calm as they left together, just like the good old days, so perhaps she didn't. I kept my fingers crossed, hoping they'd reconcile.

Rick set down his coffee cup and got to his feet. 'Betty, Tony, thank you for your hospitality. Lucy, it was lovely to finally meet you. Max has told me so much about you. I'm sure he's fine and I don't want to alarm you, but I thought he would have come back here with you. He told me that he was going to watch your trial. Did you see him?'

'Um, to be honest, no. I was so focused on my game I didn't really notice anyone. Maybe he watched for a while and then met up with friends?' I suggested, trying to cover up for him. Oh Max. I wished he could have told Rick what he was doing just this once. What about all his talk last night of trying to get along with his uncle? If only he knew how much Rick really cared. I had to find him.

'You're probably right,' Rick replied. 'I need to learn to give him some space.'

Grandpa walked Rick down to the front door, as I tried not to look concerned.

# Chapter 14

# Ventitré

I was having trouble sleeping. I lay there missing my Gigi and wondering about my parents and about Max. I thought about us chasing our dream together. I couldn't wait to tell him about the conversation we'd had with his uncle. I must have dozed off eventually, because I was jolted awake to an argument brewing on the other side of my door.

'Frida, please. I told you everything at dinner. There was nothing going on between Loretta and I,' Papa pleaded.

'Don't *mention* that woman's name again. I don't want to hear it!' Mama hissed.

'Fine. But you must believe that you're the only woman in my life. I love you and only you. It happened a long time ago, before we met. Tommaso is seventeen – do the maths. I've never betrayed you.'

'You think keeping him secret from me – and from Lucy – wasn't a betrayal? How could you keep something so important from us? How can I trust you again?'

I could hear the trembling in her usually confident voice. She stopped speaking and sobbed.

Papa murmured to her softly. I couldn't make out the words through the door, but at least she wasn't screaming for him to get away. My eyelids drooped.

The phone's ring woke me late the next morning.

'Lucy!' Nanna bellowed from the hall. Then, 'Oh, morning, Paolo. How's that couch treating you?'

I rocketed out of the room. Papa was stirring on the couch. He was whiskery and crumpled, with one cheek striped red by the cushion's fabric. Well, I suppose staying on the couch all night was better than being sent back to Darling Point in disgrace.

Nanna waved the phone at me, her hand over the mouthpiece. 'Lucy?'

Please be good news about Max, I thought.

'Max? Max is that you?' I asked groggily, then dropped the phone from my face as I saw Mama poke her head out of the spare room. She spotted Papa on the couch and slammed the door shut again.

'Lucy? Lucy? No, It's *NOT* Max,' buzzed an angry voice from the phone. Oops. Bella.

'Bella, Bella!' I said at last, trying to hide my disappointment.

'Yeah, hello to you too. Honestly, if you call me Max once more . . . Anyway, I've been worried about you. What on earth is going on?' she grumbled.

'Well, I –'She kept going. 'Have you found your mobile yet, or got a new one? I haven't heard from you for days and I'm never sure when you're going to be home. I thought we were best friends. What are you doing? Are you hanging out with Max because I'm not cool enough?'

Oh no, poor Bella was flipping out. I excused myself so that I could explain everything to Bella in privacy. I escaped into the bathroom. Ew. I really needed a shower anyway.

'Well, I've been trying to help Max, but actually we've had a bigger drama, well a few. Gigi's at the vet, Mama and Papa are probably starting another argument as we speak and I just want to get a good night's sleep,' I said.

'Oh no, Lucy, I'm so sorry. Is Gigi all right?' she asked. 'She's going to be fine, thank goodness. But I can't stay on for long – I really need to talk to my parents before they go off and get a divorce.' I wondered whether it was worth mentioning Max going missing again.

'Yeah, I'm not surprised. Your dad's still making the headlines this morning. His camera smashing episode is a big hit on YouTube,' she informed me, in true Bella fashion. She should be a spy or a journalist. She was always one step ahead of me and everyone at school on the latest news and gossip. Why on earth she dreamt of being a model was beyond me. Oh well, there was no point trying to keep anything from her.

'Bella, I know you probably don't want to hear this, but I think Max may have run off again. We have to look for him. I'm not sure what's going on, but I've met his uncle and he really wants to help him. So do I!' I really didn't mean to blurt that last bit out.

'Well, I thought as much. You're obsessed with him! But we'll find him. Well, he'll find you. Between the two of you I'm going to end up in the loony bin.'

'Oh yeah, that'll be *our* fault!' I giggled. 'But don't worry about my so-called obsession. I want to help Max, but that's it. From now on I'm focusing on my football. I trialled for a new team yesterday. All girls. Ooh, and guess who else was trying to make it into the team?'

'Do I want to know?' Bella said.

'Yup, you do. Angie. I didn't even know she played. I hate to say it, but she's quite good. But *such* a cow. She actually started a fight with me. Can you believe it? Anyway, I still want to make the team. The coach plays for the Matildas.' I thought for a second. 'Well, she must be retired now if she's coaching. But that's what I want to be!'

'Retired?' Bella asked.

I groaned. 'Ugh, that was a terrible joke. I want to be a Matilda.' There was a knock at the door.

'Lucy, can you get off the phone, please? Mama and I have something very important to discuss with you,' Papa called.

'Sorry Bella, I've got to go. I've been ordered to get off the phone, pronto. Sorry!'

'Okay, but can you call later? Maybe you should come over here so we can work out a plan to find Max before he gets himself into more trouble. Hang on . . .' I heard muffled words and a bang, as if the phone had been dropped. 'Dylan's here, asking after you. He wants you to know that if you don't marry Max, he'll step in – ow!'

Bella rang off with a clunk. Somehow I suspected that *wasn't* what her brother Dylan wanted to say. He was my team mate with the Dunbar Lions. Well, he used to be.

'Lucy, come on. Off you get,' Papa called again.

I stamped out into the lounge room, unsure what to expect. Thankfully Nanna was still there with Mama and Papa. Grandpa was probably downstairs in the shop already.

'What's so important that it couldn't wait?' I tried to sound casual.

'Princess, sit down. I stayed here last night because your mama and I wanted to speak to you as soon as possible,' Papa said with a serious frown. 'I know you've had a rough few days, especially with Gigi being hurt, but we will visit her soon. I promise. I'm sorry, sweetheart, but your mama and I have decided to take a little break.' 'But you went to dinner together and I thought everything was fine again. I want you to stay together. Please don't do this,' I said sadly.

I *thought* I'd been expecting this news, but I still couldn't believe how terrible it was to hear him say it.

'Lucy dear,' said Nanna, coming towards me, 'sometimes adults need time apart to realise what they're missing. It'll be fine, sweetheart.'

'No, it won't! I know so many kids whose parents have split up. They never get back together.' And that was it – I started crying in big hiccupping gasps.

Papa gently stroked my hair. 'Lucy, Lucy,' he said, his own voice croaky. 'Shh, it'll be okay. Your mama's going back to Milan to check on our latest range before it goes out to the buyers. *Ventitré*, or should I say in English, 23, needs the boss, while I must stay here until this silly court thing is over. My football is on hold, as you must have guessed by now. Maybe we can spend more time together and play football? Just you and me, now that will be fun!'

I loved the sound of that!

Mama broke in. 'Well, that's fine up to a point, Paolo. I still don't think

Lucy should be playing football and especially no more games with boys! It's too rough. You're coming to Milan with me for the charity fashion show and we don't want any bruises or scratches showing when you hit the catwalk. Honestly, Lucy, you should focus on modelling and school, and that's it,' she finished with a sigh.

'She'll be playing in an all-girls team this year, won't you, princess? Unless Coach Tilly has bad news?' Papa said with a teasing smile.

Oh no. I still hadn't told Papa what Coach Tilly was annoyed about. Best not to mention that now.

'Yes, of course. Please, Mama, I'll stay out of trouble. I promise,' I told her quickly. She was twisting her bracelet around her wrist and biting her lip, trying to keep her face calm.

'Well, see that you do! Anyway, I think we should film the Love Lucy commercial while we're over there. We might as well take advantage of your school holidays and the new ad campaign must be out in time for the upcoming fashion season. That will keep our little star busy and out of trouble,' she declared.

'But what about Papa?' I stressed.

'He's going to stay here, in the house in Darling Point, until his court appearance. All we can do is take it one step at a time,' said Mama.

The only step I wanted to take was back onto the football field.

# Chapter 15

# Peas in a pod

After Papa left, Nanna busied herself cleaning the flat and Mama took herself back to bed. I called Bella back and promised to go over there as soon as I could. As I put the phone down, I noticed Mama's handbag sitting on the side table. It was hard to miss, as it was a sparkly Gucci number. Peeking out of the top was a corner of white paper decorated with a red football motif. The temptation was too great. I had to take a look. And there it was, folded in half and shoved into her bag: the letter from the David Beckham Academy, addressed to me.

*Dear Lucy,*

*We'd like to inform you that you have been selected to take up a full-time scholarship with the David Beckham Football Academy. If you are interested in taking up the offer please reply no later than . . .*

How could she do this to her own daughter? I'd missed the deadline. They'd think I wasn't interested in their scholarship. Unbelievable! How could she keep this from me? Now was not the time to confront her. I had to lay low until I'd worked out what I was going to do about it.

I got dressed quietly and crept into the room. She was asleep, her face tense and anxious. I squeezed her shoulder gently until she stirred.

'Mama, do you mind if I get the driver to take me to Bella's for a little while?' I asked, desperate to get away and clear my head.

'Mmm, what? As long as the driver takes you,' she murmured.

I told Nanna where I was headed, called our driver to pick me up, grabbed a few things, and scooted downstairs into the shop.

Grandpa was just finishing up serving a customer. A box neatly packed with fresh fruit and veggies sat on the counter.

'How are the kids?' he asked the customer. 'All fine, growing up too quickly,' she said.

'I'll take that to the car for you,' he said, picking up the box before she could answer.

'Oh, that's so sweet of you. Thanks, Tony.'

'It's my pleasure. Lucy, can you please hold the fort for a few minutes?' he asked as they walked out of the shop. 'Of course, Grandpa.' I was left alone with my thoughts and the horse races being called in the background on his precious ancient radio. It was an old unit in a brown leather cover, and took pride of place on the counter next to his old-fashioned register and scales.

He loved all of his old stuff and refused to update to the latest equipment. He was attached to anything from 'the good old days' and he *loved* the horses. They were an escape from all the hard work he put in at the shop. He even had a few customers who were jockeys and loved nattering to them about the track. He'd try to head off to the Randwick races as often as possible, but Nanna tried to keep a tight rein on him – ha ha.

When the races weren't on, he'd listen to his favourite singers. There was a record-player upstairs, but down here the single cassette slot in his old radio played Johnny O'Keefe (whom I'd never heard of until a few months ago) and Elvis Presley, plus some Lebanese music later in the evening.

But right now, the races were on. It must have been an exciting race, because the commentator was getting so carried away with the call that his voice was starting to break. Through the door, I spotted our driver, pulling up in front of the shop.

I stepped out to the car and tapped on the passengerside window. The driver lowered the glass and smiled hello. 'Hi, I won't be long. I'm just waiting for Grandpa to come back,' I explained.

'No problem, Lucy,' he said.

I walked back into the shop and started polishing the apples while I waited.

Soon I could hear Grandpa approaching the shop, singing one of his favourite Elvis songs. He danced his way into the store and kept singing. I grinned. Even when everything was going badly, he was a ray of sunshine. He grabbed me to join him in for a dance. We laughed and twisted together until he stopped to take a breath.

'Now, that's better, princess . . . I haven't seen that beautiful smile for a while. Let's keep it planted on your lovely face. Remember, be happy, just be happy – that's what life's about. You're too young to be wandering around looking gloomy. Have no fear, Grandpa is here.'

'Thanks, Grandpa. You always know how to make me feel better.'

'Good! Where are you off to?' he said.

'I'm meeting Bella at her place. Oh, and Grandpa – do you know where Max is?' I asked hopefully.

'No, I don't, but I'm sure he'll be okay. Max will come and find you when he's ready. Go and have fun,' he ordered, urging me out the door.

I couldn't push Grandpa for any more information. I gave him a kiss on the cheek and popped into the car.

I slid across the back seat and as I went to settle my feet on the car floor I felt something bumpy. I looked down and couldn't believe my eyes. Of course it was bumpy. There was a person there. He signalled for me to close the window that separated the driver and me.

I did as I was told and he squirmed up onto the seat opposite me, his face and hair obscured by his hooded jacket. He leant forward, looked at me intently and then kissed me on the cheek. It made me melt and sent my heart racing. I couldn't move. I didn't know what to do.

Then he smiled and said, 'Surprise!'

'Oh my god, Max, you really scared me for a second.' I pulled back and just stared at him.

'I wanted to surprise you. I thought you liked spontaneity! I saw the car pull up and hoped you'd be getting in it.'

He was still looking at me closely and I remembered the kiss. I had to look away.

'Why can't I stay cross with you? Yes, you know that I do love surprises, but please, not so scary next time. I've had enough surprises to last a lifetime.'

He dropped his head. 'You haven't answered my question. Are we friends? I'm serious.'

'I thought we were already, but friends don't run off when they've said they wouldn't,' I said firmly. I'd tried so hard to be patient and understanding. Maybe it was time to be really direct.

'I was freaked out about talking to your dad. It was so weird chatting to my idol and being in his house … amazing and a dream come true but weird. I just needed some time to work things out. I don't want to get my hopes up and then be disappointed.' He looked up at me from under his messy hair. 'But I had to see you. I reckon we're like peas in a pod – except I'm the bad, dried-up one and you're the perfectly good one, opposites but from the same pod. Y' know? You get me and I get you … it's as simple as that.'

Wow. I didn't want anything to ruin this moment. I just wanted to bottle it up and keep it forever. But of course we were interrupted: the driver started knocking on the window.

'Lucy, we're here,' he called.

'Hey, tell him to turn around. I have a surprise for you,' Max said, smiling.

'But we're at Bella's house. She's expecting me and I can't run out on her.'

I wanted to savour this time with him for as long as possible, but I couldn't let Bella down, not again!

I looked at Max and then at Bella's house, and lowered the window to the driver.

'Um, could we please turn around? We've … um, I mean, I've changed my mind. We're going to –' I turned to Max and hissed, 'Where are we going?'

'Centennial Park.'

'We're off to Centennial Park,' I instructed, a little disappointed. I was secretly hoping we'd be off to the Reg to play some football.

The driver must have been suspicious then – I caught him peering in the rear-view mirror, but Max had slumped down again.

Eventually the driver said, 'Centennial Park it is, Lucy.' I raised the window between him and me again.

'What am I going to say to Bella? She'll never forgive me,' I said to Max.

'She'll get over it, just send her a text,' said Max. 'I can't. I lost my phone, remember?'

'No probs, use mine.' He handed me his phone.

'Oh, very snazzy, when did you get this?' I asked cautiously.

'Uncle Rick gave it to me, so just text her so you can enjoy the rest of the day,' he said, shuffling up and back into the plush seat. 'Now, this is a great way to travel. You really don't know how lucky you are, Lucy.'

I nodded, distracted by texting Bella. I was nervous about cancelling our catch-up at the last minute. This really was bad form. But at least it was better to text her than not show up at all.

*Hey Bella, sorry cant make it 2 yrs. Will explain later. Ciao Lucy xxx*

I was starting to doubt my decision until he leant across and placed his hand on my shoulder and said, 'Lucy, I've never let anyone into my world, but you're different.'

Wow. His big chocolate eyes fixed on mine and nothing else mattered – but I wasn't sure where it was going to lead us.

# Chapter 16

# Cinque

I thought about the time Max and I first met on the pitch, playfully sussing each other out, our competitive streaks in full flight as we fiercely chased the ball, each one of us fighting to create the chance to crack one into the back of the net. It was so much fun. Something changed in me that night; a warmth came over me. It was a feeling I've never experienced before. It was like a sudden flash of excitement in my tummy and everything was different. I just clicked with Max and I have the same feeling every time I'm with him; it won't go away. That first night, we played on that pitch until the sky turned black and thousands of stars twinkled as though they were winking at me. It was an unforgettable night, but since then, so many things have happened to me. In many ways, my life has changed. One thing hasn't, though – I still feel the same about Max.

All of a sudden, the quiet moment we were sharing in the car was broken by an earth-shattering noise. It was his phone ringing. What a racket! It was some sort of noisy rock band. I screwed up my face and raised my shoulders.

'You don't like Guns N' Roses?' Max yelped.

'Uh, no. Is that who it is? They're not really my thing.

I think maybe my papa likes them.'

'They were only one of the biggest bands in the world, ever. I love them and so did my dad,' he boasted.

Thankfully the music stopped as Max answered the call, 'Yep, yep … fine … I'll put her on.'

'It's Bella, for you,' he said, handing me the phone. 'Oh no, what am I going to say?' I whispered, putting my hand over the phone's speaker.

'Simple … tell her the truth,' he said, shrugging his shoulders. 'You've got nothing to be ashamed of. You can catch up at school tomorrow,' he added.

I knew she would be furious that I'd dumped her – especially for Max.

'Hey Bella, I'm so so sorry I couldn't make it but let's catch up tomorrow. I've got so much to tell you.' I squirmed in my seat, hoping that she'd forgive me.

'I saw you pull up in front of the house. What the hell's going on? And why are you using Max's phone?' she bellowed.

'Good question and we'll discuss that when I see you. But um … I'm just helping him out with something that suddenly came up. Sorry!' I squealed.

Max was rolling his eyes; all I could do was shrug. 'Sorry isn't good enough. I thought we were best friends. I'm not your dumping ground … someone you see only when you've got a problem. It's not all about you, Lucy. I'm sorry that Gigi was in an accident and about all your other dramas but really, this is ridiculous. Have you even asked about my life and what's been going on with me? Do you care about anything other than yourself and your precious Max? See ya!' And with that, she hung up on me.

'Well, I messed that up. I've just upset my best and only school friend. Now what?' I moaned.

'Don't worry, she'll come around. And what happened to Gigi?' he asked.

'A cyclist hit her and now she's in the vet hospital. She's going to be okay but she won't be home for a few days. I really miss her. And my parents are still fighting with each other. And now Bella's angry with me. Oooh, nothing seems to be going right!' I cried and threw myself into his arms.

'Oh, that's awful, but things will work out with your parents. And I'm glad Gigi's going to be fine. I'll come with you to pick her up. Look, we're here. This will cheer you up.' He gently propped me up.

The driver called out, 'Lucy, are you happy to be dropped off here?'

'Mmmm … Yes, this is good, thank you,' I replied, pulling myself together.

'Are you okay?' he inquired.

'Yes, I'm fine, thanks,' I answered.

'Don't worry, Lucy, your secret's safe with me.' He pointed to the front gates of the park where, surprisingly, Max was standing tall in full view, bowing forward to welcome me into the park.

The driver and I both laughed and he said, 'He seems like a good kid, Lucy. Don't you worry, just call me when you want to be picked up.'

Now my head was doing backflips. It seems that whenever I feel like I'm getting to know Max, he does something to surprise me. He's really a bit of a mystery.

I walked up and stood by his side at the majestic entrance to the park. I wondered what he wanted to show me.

'Welcome to Centennial Park, Lucy Zeezou. Surprised? You look as if you're away with the pixies,' Max grinned. 'What do you think of this place?'

'You're full of surprises!' I said.

'Yup! Come on, let's have some fun and escape to one of my favourite haunts.' He winked at me, then grabbed my hand.

And we started running into the green sprawling parkland ... birds were furiously chatting, kids in the playground were laughing, crying and shouting with joy as they climbed the equipment and played on the swings. All around us were beautiful gardens filled with stunning flowers, bursting with colour and releasing their gorgeous, powerful aromas. This was so lovely and so invigorating, it really helped me to forget my troubles.

It reminded me of one of my main hangouts in Milan, Parco Sempione. It's one of the most popular parks in Milan, a leafy oasis where Pino and I used to meet up with the rest of the boys for a game of football.

I had to give Pino a call ... it'd been too long. My past and present hit me and I realised that I was now in the process of setting up a new life in Sydney and that Max was going to play a big part in it.

We walked through the grounds, the leaves and twigs crunching beneath our feet as we wove a passage through spectacularly tall gum trees, their trunks bare. The lush bush and long iridescent grass reminded me of the landscape of a fairytale. I was almost waiting for some gumnut babies and fairies to magically appear from behind the trees.

We emerged in a landscape that looked like something painted by the famous artist Sidney Nolan, then ran down the hill, where an old cannon with an engraving dating back to 1888 took pride of place. Then civilisation and the natural environment came together as we crossed the road below and saw a swanky modern restaurant. Amazingly, a creeping vine covered much of the restaurant's exterior, and it gave the impression that it was being cradled by nature. The water feature in its beautifully kept garden made it even more picturesque and serene.

Even in the short time since we'd been back in Australia, I had learned a bit about Australian art. Mama sometimes dragged me to art exhibitions, and although I complained about it, I actually enjoyed going to the various galleries. I loved the colours and the landscapes. The park was making me think of brushes and paint and capturing this beautiful place on a canvas. I imagined that the brush strokes marked out our every move as we went from adventure to adventure.

As we climbed into new territory, I wondered if there was a purpose to this visit, 'Max, I'm really enjoying our walk, but where are you taking me?' I asked, curious to see which canvas we'd next step into, as a horse and its rider cantered by along the track.

'It's a surprise. I think it's something you'll really enjoy,' he teased as we walked on.

And then my ears pricked up at my favourite sound. I felt a surge of excitement run through my veins, and as we climbed to the top of a small hill, I looked across a field. I wasn't disappointed.

A group of players, dressed in the famous Brazilian yellow jersey nicknamed *canarinho* – little canary – were battling it out for the ball on a pitch that was lined on one side by tall palm trees.

'Max, this is fantastic. Who are these guys?' I asked. I increased my pace, itching to get close to the action.

'It's a local football club made up of Brazilians who live in Sydney. They get together every week to play football and to hang out with friends. It keeps their culture alive too.

They play here every Sunday and I thought you'd like to be part of the whole Brazilian football thing. They give me a game whenever I turn up, they're a great bunch of people. Maybe they'll let you play too.' He laughed and gave me a nudge. 'Come and meet Gelcimar, he's expecting us.'

My adrenaline was soaring and I had a huge smile on my face. 'This is one surprise that I love.'

'This is just a part of it,' he teased.

Now he really had me . . . what could be better than this?

We walked behind the goal posts towards the barbecue area, where a large group of people were packing away the leftovers of delicious-smelling meats and luscious green salads. The group was made up of players, their friends and families. It was a great atmosphere.

Max walked up to a small athletic guy wearing the Brazilian kit. He had a neat black ponytail and wrapped around his wrists were a bunch of woven bracelets.

'Hey Gelcimar, I told you I'd make it today. This is my friend, Lucy,' Max said with a grin.

'I'm glad you're here, Max,' Gelcimar said, giving him a friendly, yet kind of unusual handshake, which looked a whole lot cooler than the conventional type. 'And lovely to meet you, Lucy. I've heard that you're a very good footballer. Are you up for a game?' he asked.

'Oh, sure, that'd be great, I'd love to play,' I answered enthusiastically, 'but I don't have my kit with me.'

'There's no need to worry about that. We've got some spare boots,' Gelcimar responded, smiling. He reached into a bag and handed me a pair of boots and some shin pads. 'We were hoping you'd come down here some time soon with Max.' He winked at Max, then sauntered off to speak to a friend.

'Thank you so much,' I gasped. 'Max, this is the best surprise.' I hugged him and sat down to put on the boots, while Max followed Gelcimar.

There was a stone or something in the toe of the right boot, and I took it off again. When I shook out the boot, I found something that totally blew me away.

Instead of a stone, I pulled out a silver charm bracelet. It had my name dangling from it, a red heart, a football and my number, *cinque*!

Wow, what a special gift. Max had obviously put a lot of thought into this, so I was really touched.

Max came back, a nervous smile on his face. 'Lucy, what are you doing? They're waiting for you. Come on.'

'Oh, sorry, I'm coming, I'm coming. Max, thanks so much for the present. It's so beautiful, I love it,' I gushed. 'Ah, yep. No probs. Glad you like it,' he replied bashfully, his eyes focused on the ground.

'Come on, Lucy and Max. Get moving, we're eager to kick off,' Gelcimar called.

I wanted to ask Max more about the bracelet, but that would have to wait. We jogged onto the pitch, where we were greeted by the other players, most of them Brazilian. Wow! This was great. Brazilian players have a great reputation and they all seemed quite a few years older than Max and me, so it would probably be a very tough clash. But I love a challenge! The only other girl on the pitch was the opposition's goalie, but the shortage of girls was no problem as I was used to competing with boys – or should I say in this case, men!

'Lucy, we're playing 4 4 2. You're up front alongside Danillo. Max, you're on the other team with the bibs and you're in your usual left-back position, alongside Baltazar, Vasco, Luiz and Zeca . . .' I listened intently to Gelcimar's instructions. I was ready for action.

We ran into our positions and the next thing I knew the whistle blew and we were on the attack. I was running with the ball, weaving in and out of a couple of defenders. It was so uplifting to be in control, although it didn't last for too long – a determined defender swiftly claimed possession.

The game was challenging – these guys weren't messing around and they were pretty skilful. They weren't treating Max and me with kid gloves either. They treated us as equals, so I had to be at my best. Unfortunately, down the other end of the pitch our defenders couldn't hold off our opponents' star striker. He weaved in and out of the players with relative ease, and once in space he unleashed one from outside the 18-yard box. Our keeper dived, his arms outstretched, willing the ball to come to him, but he had no chance of stopping the powerful strike. Everyone watched in awe as the ball was spectacularly planted into the top left-hand corner.

The goal-scorer celebrated in stunning fashion – he did a couple of effortless backflips and finished with a bow. His team mates, including Max, ran over to him to join in his jubilation. They were jumping and cheering as though he'd scored a World Cup winner. Well, it certainly was impressive, and we knew we had a big job ahead.

We restarted and tried to keep possession as we pushed up the pitch, but their defenders were giving us some trouble – mainly Max. He won the ball and sent it flying towards the star striker, a man blessed with speed. And before we knew it, he had banged in another breathtaking shot, this time from a tight angle with very little space to spare. He somehow managed to drive it in, beating the keeper and the defender guarding the near post for goal number two. Needless to say their celebrations were again dazzling and Max was certainly enjoying their success.

Our side was deflated and we had to come up with a better strategy to try to keep the star out of the game. So we decided to get one of our defenders to heavily mark the rival star striker.

We made our way back to the centre of the pitch and when the whistle blew, I had a renewed determination.

From the kick-off, the ball was passed back to me and at that moment, I decided to take the players on and fight my way up the pitch. I managed to weave past two players, then three but I suddenly came up against Max and he was relentless. I had to lose him, so I quickly managed to switch the play to the left. The ball met the winger at his feet. He flew down the line and threw in a few fancy moves as I ran into the box. He sent in a swirling cross and suddenly, as though I was the only player on the pitch, like a pouncing panther I leapt into the air and volleyed the ball past the hapless keeper. My team mates went berserk while I was in a daze.

'You really are Zeezou!'

'That was magnificent.'

'You must play for Brazil. We will adopt you.'

I was completely dumbstruck. I didn't really know how it had happened. It was just one of those instinctive things. It felt as though it was someone else who had scored that goal. Not me. I did it without a second thought.

Our opponents were also impressed, running over to give me a pat on the back.

'Hey Lucy, that was one hell of a goal. How did you do it?' Max asked.

'I don't know. I just did it,' I replied, still in something of a daze.

'You were in the zone. The ideal head space for any athlete. Just do . . . don't think!' Max commented.

'Now you're getting too philosophical, Max. I'm just having fun and doing what I love. This is it, this is where I feel I belong more than anywhere,' I said.

'Yeah, I know what you mean. I'm with you.' We gave each other a look that meant more than I can describe. It was an awkward moment, but an honest one. We had a real connection – we understood each other.

'Hey, you two . . . we're taking a break,' said Gelcimar.

We walked back to our bags and grabbed our bottles of water, but as I was having a sip, my eyes fixed onto a police car which had suddenly pulled up onto the kerb.

I sensed that trouble was brewing so I alerted Max with a nudge from my elbow. He looked up and we snatched up our bags, ready to make a move. Two tall bulky policemen moved in our direction as we started stepping backwards, while our new friends looked on in astonishment.

Gelcimar looked puzzled. 'Max is everything all right?'

They were close enough now that we could see their determined faces and they knew they had Max. One yelled, 'Max! Max Spitzer, we just want to ask you a few questions.'

Max grabbed my hand and within an instant we were running . . .

# Chapter 17

# Il Diavolo's den

Oh great, police trouble, just when we were getting stuck into a fantastic game and given a chance to test our skills against extremely talented players. Brazilians absolutely love their football and the players I met today were no exception. I knew that lots of Brazilian kids dreamt of making a better life for themselves through football, just like Max. But at this particular moment, that dream, for Max at least, seemed a long way off.

We flew through a stand of pine trees at the other side of the pitch.

As we ran I gasped, 'Max, why don't we stop and talk to them? They probably just want to take you back to your uncle. We can't run forever.'

I looked back and they were weaving in and out of the trees, hot on our trail as if we were ruthless criminals. One officer was yelling, 'Max, stop, stop . . . we just want to talk to you. We're concerned about your welfare.'

But Max ignored their calls and continued with his fast pace, making sure that we were always a step ahead as we moved deeper into the park.

He finally answered me. 'I'm not ready to go back. I need more time. I'll go back on my own terms,' he insisted.

Max seemed to know where he was going. I tried to keep pace with him as we passed a small pond covered in tall green reeds. We negotiated our way through more bush, jumping over small mounds and large broken branches. It was a frantic run and I lost my footing, falling flat on my face in a muddy patch.

I called, 'Max, wait!'

He turned and quickly ran back to me. 'Gee, Lucy, sorry,' he puffed, 'I thought you were just behind me. Are you okay?'

'I think so. I was trying to keep up with you but you're too fast. I'm not used to climbing over all these things,' I growled, wiping my face.

My anger didn't last long. Even though it wasn't funny, we found ourselves laughing at the craziness of the situation.

'I'm sorry to get you caught up in this. It's my problem, not yours. Let's just wait for them to catch up. I suppose it's for the best,' he relented.

I suddenly snapped, 'Oh no no no, we've gone this far, let's keep going. You're not stopping on my account. Anyway, I don't think they're going to catch us. I can't even see them. They've probably given up by now.'

'I can't argue with that. I like your attitude, Zeezou,' he smiled.

'Well, anyway, I'm having a ball. And this mud pack is a great beauty treatment. Don't you think?' I oinked and we broke into an even bigger chuckle. Max stretched out his hand to help me up and unwittingly pulled me straight into his arms. I caught myself giving him a muddy peck on the cheek.

That brought our laughter to an abrupt halt and we awkwardly stared at each other for what seemed an eternity. Max broke the uncomfortable silence. 'Come on piglet, we'd better hurry or the police will catch up to us.' His face was a distinct beetroot red.

'Yep, let's go . . . *Andiamo*! That's Italian for "hurry"!

Oink, oink,' I laughed.

'Lucy, come on, no more messing around. Let's get moving! *Andiamo*!' Max ordered. 'Pretend we're on the pitch and we're on the attack. You have the ball at your feet and you're fighting past the defenders on your way to the goal. Stay focused and you'll make it. There's only a few seconds left on the clock so this will be our only chance to win. You must score for victory.' His voice was urgent.

I looked behind me and could see them quite a way from us, but we weren't out of danger yet. It didn't look like they were going to give up the chase. I desperately wanted to score that goal. I didn't want to let Max down and I certainly didn't want to get caught. Oh my god, I'll be in major trouble with my parents. They're going to go ballistic.

We powered ahead easily, but were suddenly faced with another obstacle – a big flock of squeaking geese. And they didn't seem to be very happy about our presence. They chased us, pecking at our bottoms, trying to scare us out of their territory. They were pretty aggressive and I wanted to tell them that we were just passing through, but they weren't up for a discussion. Max couldn't stop laughing as I screamed and giggled at the same time. I didn't know that geese were such intimidating creatures, although their wobbly attempts at running were so cute you couldn't help but like them.

We managed to make it through with our bottoms intact and found ourselves near a community of brown and sea-green ducks. Thankfully, they were far gentler than the geese. They waddled along the edges of the pond, in sharp contrast with the swans, whose elegant posture and deep red lipstick beaks reminded me of catwalk queens.

We ran around the pond and found ourselves on a dirt path surrounded by even taller trees and thick bushes. Max came to a sudden halt near a lovely old building covered in vines, overlooking a sports oval.

Max looked around to make sure no one was in sight and then with a proud voice said, 'Okay, Lucy, here we are. Please, after you.' He beckoned me forward.

'But where are we going?' I said, confused.

He opened a door that had been hidden under the vines and he extended his arm with a royal gesture.

I took one step in and screamed. I was covered in spider webs, frantically trying to wipe them off.

'What are you laughing at?' I cried. 'I can't stand spiders, they give me the creeps.'

'You are being such a girlie,' he mocked. 'You try to act tough like a guy, but your feminine side comes flying out when tested.'

'It does not. And anyway, I am a girl, in case you hadn't noticed. Well, a girl who is a tomboy. And what are you staring at?' I retorted.

His eyes flicked up to my face and he stuttered, 'Um, nothing.' He smiled, then slapped his hands against the wall in a drum roll. 'Anyway, SURPRISE! I'd like to welcome you to Il Diavolo's Den . . . my other hangout.'

'Mmmm, clever! It sounds sinister, but of course I know what it means,' I boasted with a cheeky smile. '*Il Diavolo* is the devil in Italian and it's AC Milan's nickname and of course I love it!'

He nodded, 'I thought you would. Signorina, after you.'

'Oh thanks, but I'm not going to meet any more spiders am I?' I nervously asked.

'No, trust me. You'll love it in there.' He was proud of his hangout.

He stepped in past me and held out his hand. I took it and carefully climbed down behind him, peering into a neat, compact furnished room, covered in the famous AC Milan colours.

'Well, Max you could have called it AC Milan's other famous nickname, the *Rossoneri*. This is like a shrine to the club. Papa would be very impressed,' I said. I was trying to be positive. Unfortunately, I'd spotted more spider webs but they were well out of reach on the corners of the ceiling. A comfy-looking black lounge leaned against one wall and an AC Milan poster was proudly displayed above it. A made-up small bed with a quilt cover also in the red and black AC Milan colours rested on the opposite side. A black beanbag nestled on a patterned black and red rug which resembled a chessboard. There was a small wooden coffee table in the middle of the room with a couple of chairs, and there was also a big esky near the table.

Max obviously spent a lot of time in this den. It was pretty comfortable, although it wasn't the kind of space I'd like to live in. Still, I tried to be enthusiastic.

'Max, this is impressive. It's so, um, so cosy and well it has just about everything,' I said.

'Yeah, it's cool. I found it by accident one day. Over the past few months I've been trying to fix it up, collecting stuff from the streets to furnish and decorate it, and of course, bringing my AC Milan stuff here. This is where I hang most of the time because it gets too wet and noisy at my other hangout. I really like it here. It's quiet and no one can bother me.'

Even though it was dark in the den, and a bit hot and stuffy, I wanted

Max to think I liked it. He was so proud of his haunt.

'Are you sure no one knows about this place? Surely someone was here before you,' I asked.

'No. It was just an empty shell when I found it. I think it may have been a forgotten hideaway or maybe a shelter from hundreds of years ago. Who knows and who cares . . . it's mine!'

'Okay, cool, but do you think we should get going soon?' I suggested. I was starting to feel a little claustrophobic.

But before Max could answer, our attention turned to a noise outside, footsteps moving closer and closer.

I nervously whispered, 'Max, it must be them. It's the police. They've found us.'

# Chapter 18

# Waratah

He signalled for me to follow him up the steps to the door and I thought he was going to give himself up. I threw him a confused look. But he stopped at the top of the stairs where we could listen more closely to what was happening outside.

'They couldn't just disappear into thin air. I'm sure I saw them move around here somewhere,' said one strong male voice.

The other officer remarked, 'It's been a long day. Let's call it quits. He's a street kid, I'm sure he'll eventually come to his senses and return to his uncle's place for a good feed and a warm bed.'

I whispered to Max, 'I told you, it's the police. Is there another way out?'

He nodded but kept listening.

The policeman with the strong voice protested, 'No, we've got to find them. I'm sure they're here somewhere. The Zoffi girl could be in danger.'

'She seemed to leave with him willingly when we started pursuing them. I've had enough. You can keep searching for them, and I'll stand watch here in case they turn up.'

Max motioned for me to walk back down the stairs. 'Great, I'm dead meat. My parents are going to be so furious. I'm in major trouble,' I groaned.

Max whispered, 'Now I know why they were so determined to find us – they're also after you. Your parents must have alerted them. Let's get a move on. I've got to get you home. Stay close and follow me, this way.' He ran to the opposite wall and heaved open a small high window. The vines outside were even denser and with a shudder I imagined even more spiders hiding in the leaves. I clambered up and through. It was horrible, but we soon emerged into the bright light and the welcoming afternoon sun saturating our faces. It was great to breathe the fresh air.

We found ourselves at another pond, with long, dark-green reeds around the edges. There was a small island in the middle of the water, dominated by weeping willows, their long arms brushing the surface and providing a shady retreat for the ducks, who seemed content with their little haven.

I caught our reflection as we gazed at the water's smooth surface, which broke into small ripples as the ducks coasted by.

My hair was hanging loosely – or as Mama would say, messy and windswept and I was still wearing football boots with my black Love Lucy T-shirt and faded skinny jeans. I hoped Gelcimar had grabbed my trainers for me. Mama would be mortified if she saw me in this state. She was always fussing about my outfits. 'You need to be more lady-like. Why don't you wear a nice dress?' blah blah. When was she ever going to get it?

Max was lucky in that sense, because he could wear what he wanted all the time. There was no one to order him around, although maybe his uncle might have started doing that. It wouldn't matter what Max was wearing, though, he was always so comfortable in his own skin.

I was thinking we made a good pair – young, covered in dirt, but full of dreams . . . the same dream but different circumstances. I couldn't help wondering if maybe we'd end up together one day. Who knew? Still, one thing's for sure, and that was that my football dream came first. And I also knew that I was so so busted.

'Lucy, what are you dreaming about now?' he asked inspecting my face.

I pulled myself together and answered, 'Oh, nothing much. I'm just really loving this park. It's so beautiful.'

Well, I couldn't tell him what I was really thinking.

Sometimes a girl's gotta keep things to herself.

He said, 'Yeah, I love it too. My parents used to bring me here when I was little. Every Sunday we'd have a picnic by the large pond at the other side of the park and feed the ducks, and play ball games and chasing around the trees. I especially loved it when my dad would pick me up and swing me round, like an aeroplane. Mum would freak out but I'd yell for more. I loved my dad when he was sober,' he added, a sad quality to his voice.

I didn't know what to say, so I gazed at the pond. Just beyond it in a small bush garden, I saw an unusual, beautiful large red flower on a very tall thick stem.

'Max, you wouldn't know what that big red flower is over there?' I pointed, just to change the subject. As usual my tongue was far ahead of my brain. I wished I could retract my silly question. As if he'd know anything about flowers.

'Oh yeah, that's a red waratah. It's the floral symbol for New South Wales and this state's rugby union team.'

'Wow, that's impressive. Max, you never cease to amaze me. How on earth did you know that?' I asked, gobsmacked.

It was the first time I'd ever heard a guy talk about anything floral; in fact it's not even something I'm particularly into.

'My mum was an amazing florist. She ran her own successful business for years. She was so talented and was really making a name for herself and then suddenly she died alongside my dad in that horrific car crash. I really miss her. I especially miss her hugs and kisses and even her constant badgering to study. She used to say, "Max, knowledge is power. You can be anything you want to be as long as you put in the hard work. Don't take short cuts" … and … she …' He couldn't continue.

His head fell as he struggled to stop the tears. I tried to comfort him but he brushed my arm away. He was alone in his grieving, alone in his thoughts, alone in the world. He didn't know how to take comfort in someone else's company.

'Max, I'm so sorry, I didn't mean to –'

But before I could finish, he abruptly stood up and announced, 'I think it's time to take you home, Lucy.' He wiped his tears with his sleeve.

My heart broke for him as I tried to hold back my own tears. 'Fine! But how about you? Are you going to go back to your uncle's?' I said, fearing I might not see him again.

'Not yet. I need more time. Anyway, I'll be fine. I know how to look after myself,' he claimed. Regaining his composure, he added, 'Come on, let's get going.'

We marched up a steep tree-lined hill which led us towards Bondi Junction and I thought about his answer. At least there was a glimmer of hope that he was thinking of going back to stay with his uncle. I didn't want to press him any further in his vulnerable state so I tried to stay cool.

'We'll jump on the train and that will take us to Kings Cross station. It's not far from your grandparents' store,' he said.

That didn't appeal to me much! It must have shown on my face. 'You've never been on a train before … have you?' he mocked.

'Ah well, yeah … of course I have,' I lied, cringing. 'But why don't I call my driver instead? He can pick us up if he's free.'

'No, this is going to be more fun than I thought. It's about time that our little uptown signorina learnt about how the other half lives,' he said cheekily.

'Really, I didn't realise that I was such a snob. Well, I'm assuming that's what you mean by uptown. I'm up for the challenge,' I retorted.

He nodded. 'Yep, uptown's Indigenous slang for rich.'

We arrived at the train station, which was buzzing with a huge mix of people, some very casual, some dressed up. The commuters were coming or going, rushing, running or striding, and sometimes you could see that others were more leisurely about getting to their destination.

My mind was filled with the thought of germs and disgusting smells and I was imagining that inside the train we'd be all squashed together like sardines. Yuck!

Max bought a couple of tickets from a machine and we walked to a turnstile. He gave me a ticket as I stepped back to copy his movements. But just as he was about to go through the turnstile a young police officer who seemed to have appeared out of nowhere threw an order at him: 'Stop. I know what you're about to do.'

'What are you talking about? I'm not doing anything wrong,' Max countered as I slowly moved back. Why was the policeman picking on Max? Did he know that he was a runaway?

'You were just about to jump the turnstile. I know what you blokes are like. You think we owe you,' he thundered.

Max stood tall and fearless as if he'd faced this sort of attack before. I stood there full of nerves.

The officer stepped closer to Max and chided, 'You blackfellas are all the same. Troublemakers!'

My eyes popped out of my head. I thought the officer would be trained to be tolerant, and even though I'd never heard the term 'blackfella' before, it was obviously racist.

But Max didn't flinch and hit back, 'Nothing wrong with blackfellas. We're the true Australians and have rights just like the rest of you. Haven't you worked that out yet?'

I'd never thought of Max as black, even though Bella had made a remark about it the other day. He was my friend and his skin colour wasn't an issue.

'Yeah, I thought as much,' the officer said. 'I won't put up with this sort of insolence from your type. I'm serving you with a $200 fine.'

'For what? I've got a ticket. Stuff it. You can stick your train!' And like a flash, Max turned and grabbed me, accelerating into a desperate stride. We had to fight and weave our way past hundreds of commuters rushing all over the place. It was as though we were on the football pitch, manoeuvring past defenders in a determined effort to score a goal, but this wasn't fun. It was serious. We were in serious trouble again. I just wish we were on the pitch being chased by rivals rather than a policeman in pursuit.

We dodged mothers with prams, businessmen and women, elderly people and a group of young kids. But the man in blue stayed on our tail, yelling out orders, 'Stop! Stop!' We kept running . . . running like the fox trying to outwit the hound.

Our heartbeats accelerated as we pounded the streets. We were determined to get away. We made a good team. No one could stop us!

# Chapter 19

# Indigenous

I loved the freedom I experienced when I was with Max, with no rules, no obligations and being answerable to no one. It was something all teens longed for every day. But . . . I was beginning to realise that this wasn't the kind of freedom I really wanted. I didn't want to keep running and hiding and dodging the authorities, especially when I hadn't actually done anything wrong – that was hardly 'freedom'. It was no way to live. Max seemed to be able to survive it, but I hoped he could find more structure to his life. It was lonely and destructive living the way he did.

We came to a car park and plopped down behind a large 4WD which was parked on the edge of a concrete embankment. By now, the sun was setting. Even in my agitated state, I was able to admire the spectacular baby blue and pink sky, with splashes of deep orange filtering through the skyline. It wasn't long before the curtain closed and the sky was black.

The darkness worked to our favour, making it more difficult for the unrelenting policeman to find us in this serious game of hide and seek. A game I was no longer enjoying.

'Lucy, let's slip into that charity bin over there.' He pointed at a large square metal bin, the type people threw their rejected clothing into.

'I can't go in there. It's full of dirty clothes and it will stink!' I announced, turning my nose up.

'But we have no choice and no time to waste discussing this. He's in the car park and we'll be easy pickings out here. Quick, Lucy,' he said urgently.

I scoured the area for a better place to hide. And then as if the angels came down and plucked us away, I saw it. 'Max, look there's an opened door at that church hall over there. Let's go,' I said.

But before we could move, we heard the crunch of footsteps near the front of the car that was shielding us. We peered from behind the large front wheels and spotted a big black pair of boots. The policeman was just a few metres away, and beams of light from his torch were searching the ground.

I thought my heart was going to leap out of my mouth. Luckily, Max placed his hand across my lips, anticipating my scream, which was nanoseconds from disturbing the peace.

Oh, god I just wanted to go home. I felt as though I couldn't breathe. My body froze as the policeman came to a halt. He was so close to capturing us.

He was kneeling on the ground and thrusting the torch light in our direction. We were lying perfectly still, but I feared that the pounding of my heart would give us away. The light moved closer and closer towards us and within a whisker of my shoulder being exposed, Max unexpectedly propelled a rock in the opposite direction. The policeman lunged towards the rock at the other side of the car park while we quickly slid down the embankment into a back lane that led us to the church hall.

The door was ajar. We stepped inside and stumbled into a room full of children dressed in white uniforms practising karate while their parents admired them from the outskirts. All eyes suddenly fixed on us; we stepped straight back out the door, Max checking that the coast was clear and then ran down the street, and squeezed through a hole in the fence of a nearby school.

Luck was on our side, because we came across an unlocked door which opened to a small storeroom. We slumped to the cold floor, exhausted. I crunched up into a ball rubbing my arms.

'Here, Lucy, put this on.' Max tenderly placed his jacket around me.

'Oh, thanks, Max.' The spring evening wasn't *that* cold but I appreciated the gesture.

We sat silently, trying to catch our breath. 'We did it, we lost him,' I proudly cheered.

'Yes, we did,' Max responded, 'but we can't stay here for too long just in case he's still on our tail. We've got to keep moving.'

'Oh no, I've had enough. I'm too tired and hungry. I just want to go home,' I moaned, my hands hiding my face.

'You're right Lucy,' he relented. 'It's time to go home. Call your driver and tell him to pick us up at the school but to wait in the side street. He'll know it.' He handed me his phone.

I made the call and the driver said he'd be there in no time.

'Max, before we go, I need to ask you something. What's a blackfella?' I queried, inspecting his smudged and dirty face.

'It's me and my people. It's who I am – an indigenous Australian, an Aboriginal,' he proudly announced.

'I've heard about Aborigines, in fact your uncle told us that he was from the Wadgery, the biggest Aboriginal group in New South Wales. But I've never heard the name blackfellas.' I was curious to know more.

Max giggled, 'Well, good try Lucy, but our mob is called Wiradjuri and you are right – it's the biggest in this state. I'm still learning about my people. But you're not supposed to call us blackfellas. It's actually a derogatory term, although our own people sometimes use it within our community, but in a nice way. I was just being sarcastic when I said it. That policeman was obviously racist, but I'm used to it.' His big dark eyes dropped down.

'I was appalled by his behaviour, targeting you like that. He was just an ignorant idiot. I can't understand why anyone would judge someone by the colour of their skin. And your skin is so beautiful. You're so lucky,' I exclaimed, a bit red-faced when I realised what I'd just said.

Max was also coy about the compliment and we fell into an uncomfortable silence.

The noise of Guns N' Roses thankfully broke the mood. Max answered his phone, 'Yep ... great. We're coming now, ta.'

'Your driver's here. Let's go,' he ordered, jumping up and leading me out the door.

He carefully scanned the area. 'Quick, the coast is clear. Don't run, just walk quickly. I don't know many street kids, especially blackfellas, who'd have a driver picking them up in a flash car like this! The policeman certainly won't suspect it's us,' he laughed.

'Hi, thanks so much for picking us up,' I said to the driver as I jumped in. I sank into the comfy seat, relieved to be heading home finally.

I closed my eyes, the door slammed shut, and we pulled away from the kerb. Ah, safe at last.

'Oh what a relief! We really appreciate this,' I breathlessly said with my eyes still shut.

'It's a pleasure, Lucy, but what do you mean by "we"?' the driver asked.

My eyes snapped open. I had been so relieved and so tired that I hadn't even noticed that Max didn't get into the car. I looked out the back window to try and get a glimpse of him, but it was no use. He had disappeared into the night without a trace, without even a goodbye!

# Chapter 20

# The cup

I snuggled into Max's jacket and sank deeper into the back seat while he wandered the streets on this cloudy evening. Rain started trickling down the window, followed by a downpour. Thunder and lightning momentarily flashed across the blackened sky.

As the rain hit the windscreen and the wipers rocked back and forth, the driver revealed, 'Lucy, your parents are waiting for you at home. Everyone's been so worried. When you didn't come home for dinner your Grandpa rang Bella's house and she said she didn't know where you were. I'm sorry but I had no choice – I had to tell them that you were with Max. Your Mama was so worried that she called the police. I'm sorry.'

Wow, the good news outweighed the bad. 'I understand you had no choice, and I probably should have called them, but did you say that both my parents are home?' I asked in hope.

'Yes, they're together at the Darling Point residence.' And that's what I was hoping to hear – they are TOGETHER. Oh, god I hope so. I hoped they'd made up.

For the rest of the journey home I distracted myself from the trouble I was bound to be in by thinking about the highlight of my football life, our Cup win. I was running down the pitch, weaving past defenders and managed to kick a perfect cross which found Jared on the right. He spectacularly smacked the ball past the keeper to score the winning goal and claim victory in the final. The boys picked Jared and me up to celebrate our win. I'll never forget it! I finally gained my team mates' acceptance and in one fell swoop, my family supported my dream to be a professional footballer. No more secrets, no more sneaking around, or so I thought. I remembered the time I was kidnapped, how terrified I'd been and how I'd come out of that frightening experience stronger in myself, a survivor, a girl ready to face the world.

'Lucy, you're home,' the driver said.

I opened my eyes to find that we were at my new home. The black waters of the harbour were rippling in rhythm with the rain drops pelting down, while the boats swayed along to the same beat.

I knew that I was in big trouble, but right now all I could think about was crawling into bed. I thanked the driver and walked up to the door but I didn't have a key. I pressed the doorbell and Mama flung it open.

She pulled me tightly into her chest, crying. 'Oh Lucy, we were so worried about you. We thought you may have been kidnapped again. I'm so glad you're home.' She stroked my matted filthy hair.

I was surprised by Mama's greeting. I'm so lucky that I have a loving family to come home to.

We walked into the lounge room, the raging storm spectacularly visible through the large windows. I found myself wondering how Max was doing on such a miserable night. I hoped he went back to his uncle's place.

Papa was sitting on the lounge running his fingers through his hair. As we approached, he stood up and glared at me. There was an uncomfortable silence.

'Lucy, you know how to make my heart race. Your mama and I have been worried sick.' He stared at me as if I was from outer space. 'Come to your papa and give him a hug.' I didn't hesitate and ran into the safety of his arms.

He squeezed me tight and said, 'You're a smelly princess tonight, but I'm so glad you're home. Now sit down, we need to talk. We know that you were with Max. Why did you go against our instructions? We're not happy about this.'

I decided to tell the truth. I didn't like keeping secrets from my parents. I had done it for too long in order to play football. But honesty is definitely the best policy, even if it gets me into trouble. My parents had enough of their own problems to deal with at the moment. At least they were back under the same roof.

I responded from my heart. 'I'm so sorry. I honestly can't explain it but I didn't mean to cause any trouble. Max is my friend and he understands me like no one else. It's hard to stay away from him. When I'm with him he makes me feel like I am capable of anything. It's liberating and I love it. But I'm so sorry I acted against your wishes. I should have at least called you to let you know I was okay. I truly am sorry, Papa.'

Papa gently stroked my hair and replied, 'Yes, it was very thoughtless of you, Lucy. You really should have known better, especially after what happened at the San Siro stadium. You can't imagine what your mama and I have been through. You need to learn to be more responsibile. And we've decided that it's best you to go back to Milano with Mama a little earlier than expected. While you're there, as Mama mentioned, you'll be modelling in Molto and Favolosa's charity show. Mario and Franca have made you their star model, along with little Gigi. It's a great idea and such a worthy cause. You'll be a huge hit!' He tried to make it sound appealing, but I couldn't help smiling. I wouldn't be such a hit if they could see me now!

Papa continued, 'I'm hoping to come too but it depends on whether I have to appear in court. But I'm sure it will be all over soon. My lawyers are quite positive that no charge will be laid. Anyway, my princess, in the meantime it's back to Italy for you.' He stood and went into the next room.

I had been so caught up with my own so-called problems that I selfishly forgot about Papa's court case so I decided to toe the line and agree with whatever my parents had to say. I'd caused enough trouble. I didn't want to go back to Milan just yet but I had no choice. I was struggling to stay awake. I sighed, 'Yep, that all sounds fine. I'm so tired. Can I please go to bed?'

'Oh, okay Lucy, but I just wanted to let you know that I've spoken to Bella's mum and she's given permission for Bella to come to Milan with us.' Mama had a wide smile on her face, but I couldn't get too excited. I was in the bad books with Bella and she probably wouldn't want to come. 'Oh, thanks Mama. That's great,' I glumly responded, much to their dismay.

'Lucy, are you feeling all right?' Mama gently asked. 'Sorry Mama, I'm just exhausted. I can't wait to jump into bed,' I mumbled.

Papa appeared in the doorway with his hands behind his back and said, 'Well, I think you need to have a quick shower before you go to bed. And, Lucy,' he paused, 'maybe this will cheer you up.'

The barking was a dead giveaway. My face lit up as he gently placed Gigi into my arms. I was so happy to have her back.

'Gigi, my little Gigi.' I had to be extra careful with her little bandaged-up legs. She couldn't stop licking me. I kissed and cuddled her.

'You're the best, Papa, Mama.' I kissed them on both cheeks and climbed the stairs towards my bedroom with my beloved Gigi held close to my chest, but as usual my curiosity got the better of me. I rested my head against the banister, intently listening to what my parents were saying.

'Sshhhh, Gigi,' I whispered in her ear, while patting her to keep her quiet. I had to know whether they were back together or not.

'She really likes this boy and to be honest he's not such a bad kid. He was living in very bad circumstances, but there's hope for him now that his uncle is taking care of him. Are we really doing the right thing?' Papa's voice was filled with anxiety.

'Of course we are, Paolo. He still has the mind of a street kid and that's trouble. Look at what happened today. For heaven sakes, we've had the police looking for them. I'm not encouraging my daughter to spend her precious time with someone who has no boundaries. Who knows what kind of bad people he hangs around with and what he gets up to? He's a bad influence. I'm not sure about anything right now except that I want her to forget about him.' Mama was insistent.

'You know that I don't much like her hanging around with boys but I do feel sorry for this kid. I know that I can help him. He's very talented and football could be his way out,' Papa professed.

'You and your football. You know, it's not the answer to everything.

Football is the reason Lucy's in this mess in the first place. I don't even want her playing; it's a waste of time, it's rough, and it's not something girls should really be doing. She should be on the catwalk, where she belongs. Anyway, what does Lucy know about football?' Mama fired.

I knew she didn't want me playing. She'd been against the whole idea from the start. It wasn't fair! What gave her the right to stop me from pursuing my passion?

'Frida, I don't think you understand, but Lucy is a very gifted player and she does in fact belong on the pitch.' My heart skipped with excitement.

Papa was on a roll and there was no stopping him. 'She has a quality you can't teach and she's hungry to play, determined to perform at her best. She has everything you look for in a player. I'm very proud of her. Football is her passion and you can't take that away from her. I think that we should encourage her dream, not thwart her ambitions in life.'

Mama let out a big sigh. 'Come on Paolo, she doesn't really know what she wants and that Max is bad news.'

'I've spent time with him and I know he's basically a good kid. He just needs some guidance and some opportunities. His parents are dead, he's been on his own until Rick came along, so he could do with some good luck right now. I think I'm the one to help him. You know my own papa came from a poor background and football was his ticket out. I never forgot his stories. He ran around with no shoes, there was no hot water in the house where he grew up. And yet look at what he achieved. And don't forget that he was the one who instilled Lucy's passion for football. He had dreams for her to be a footballer, I know that now, and I want to honour his memory.' Papa's voice had a new determination.

'Paolo, your father was a great man. I loved him, but right now I'm worried that Lucy is mixing with the wrong crowd. I want to protect her and give her every opportunity to reach her potential in life, so that she blossoms into a beautiful and successful woman in her own right. She has what it takes to be a star on the catwalk. She has beauty and poise. Why can't she see that? Why can't you see that?' 'Because it's your dream not hers,' Papa responded. 'Let her follow her own path. We all have dreams and they can change and shift as we grow, but we must allow her to be who she wants to be – not what we want her to be. I know that I've also made that mistake. I love the idea of her running around in pretty dresses and looking glamorous like her mama with the world at her feet, but that's not what she wants. She's a footballer, a footballer with enormous potential, not a ballerina or a model.'

'We can't even agree about our own daughter. How are we going to agree about us? How about your son? I actually feel sorry for him having to keep his own papa a secret. I still don't understand why you would do that. I thought I knew you, but I don't! You're not the man I married,' she cried.

He pulled her in close to him. 'Frida, you're the last person I wanted to hurt. I love you more than anything in the world. I didn't want to complicate things at the time and now I know I was wrong. Please let me make it up to you, let me make it up to him. We can all be one happy family, I know we can. I'll do anything to make it right. Please Frida, please say you'll forgive me.'

Tears filled my eyes as I hoped and prayed that she would forgive him.

I waited and waited to hear her response but I heard nothing. I couldn't take it any longer. I carefully climbed down a few stairs and nearly screamed with excitement. They were in a tight embrace, their lips locked in a passionate kiss.

I quietly headed back and slipped into my bedroom thinking about my new big brother, Tommaso. What was he like? Did he want a sister? Would we get along?

I fell into bed, tucking my new bracelet under the pillow and placing Gigi by my side. I'd have an extra long shower in the morning. I was content, warm and safe with my family. I couldn't be happier, but as the rain lashed across the windows my heart was also heavy as my thoughts turned to Max. Where was he?

# Chapter 21

# The Scream

The ball was in full flight, floating towards the goal mouth; defenders were everywhere, all of them trying to thwart the strikers jockeying for the perfect position. I prowled into the box like a hungry cheetah and threw myself into the football's path, propelling my right foot forward, and connected to make a spectacular scissor kick. The cheetah catches its prey.

Goooooooooaaaaaaaal!

Well, so I thought, but at the final moment, just centimetres before the ball crossed the line, the goalkeeper miraculously managed to block it. It must have been just by the tip of his gloves, as everyone thought I'd beaten him but it was parried back. Luckily, my team mate and hero, Zinedine Zidane (nicknamed Zizou) was there to clean up, ensuring the ball went into the back of the net for the winner.

We gave each other a high five and a pat on the back. The rest of the team ran over to celebrate; Papa emerged in the same strip. We were on the same team, rejoicing in our win together. It was magical! I looked over to the side line as the sun shone down on my grandparents clapping with pride and Mama glaring at me with a forced smile.

And a few metres away, there was Max – alone, unkempt, dirty and dressed in black. The sky suddenly turned a deep orange red, rippled through with waves of blue. Max seemed to blend into the swirling, distorted background. He put his hands over his ears and looked as if he was about to belt out a scream. It looked just like that famous painting 'The Scream' by Edvard Munch. It was as though all the pain and hurt in his life was pouring out of him, but you couldn't hear anything. There was an eerie silence in this surreal landscape. I could sense his pain, his loneliness and his deep sadness.

I woke up in a cold sweat, yelling, 'Max! Max!'

Mama and Papa came running into my bedroom, 'Lucy, Lucy, what's wrong?' They cuddled me and stroked my head trying to calm me down.

'I just had a bad dream, but I'm better now that we're together. Are we together again? I mean as a family?' I asked, trying to put Max in the back of my mind.

'Well . . . it seems that way,' Mama sleepily revealed with a shy smile.

'Don't worry, Lucy. We're here for you as a family. You have nothing to worry about,' Papa added reassuringly, his gentle eyes focused on me. His glance shifted in Mama's direction.

She looked like she was going to melt, batting her eyelids and flicking her hair. It was obvious that they still loved each other very much.

'Lucy, everything is okay, so go back to sleep. It's still quite early – you can have a little more shut-eye before you have to get ready for school,' Mama said.

The thought of staying in bed was much more appealing than having to get up for school. I wasn't looking forward to it, as I had to face Bella and I knew that I'd be hearing some snarly remarks from the other girls who would have seen the news about Papa's arrest.

'Okay, I'll stay under the doona for a bit longer.' But I was very restless, thinking about Max. I hoped he'd found shelter and food at a local refuge or had gone back to his uncle's place. I wondered whether I'd see him at the Reg after school with the rest of the boys.

I opened the curtains and was greeted by a bright orange sun rising to reveal a clear blue sky. What an enormous contrast to last night's stormy weather.

After a nice warm shower, where I gave myself an extra good scrubbing, I threw on my uniform and packed my football gear in my bag, hoping for a kick-around with the boys after school.

I ran down to the breakfast table and joined Mama and Papa, who were already tucking into a delicious feast.

'*Buongiorno* Mama, Papa.' I kissed them both on the cheeks and sat down to get stuck into a yummy breakfast. 'Mama, you're all dressed up. You look lovely. Where are you off to this morning?' I asked. She always dresses up in her designer gear wherever she goes but I suspected she had a particular mission today.

'I'm coming to school with you. I have a meeting with your principal, Mrs Zambocelli,' she announced coolly.

'Oh, what's it about?' I was suspicious.

'We're just going to discuss our trip to Milan next week. It's nothing for you to be concerned about.' She patted around her lips with the napkin, ensuring that her make-up was perfect.

'But I'll miss the start of the football season. Why do we have to leave so soon? And how about my school work?' I blurted, knowing that after yesterday I had no choice but to obey. I could no longer get away with doing my own thing. It was much easier at my grandparents' place.

Papa stepped in. 'That's one thing your mama will sort out with your principal. Now, princess, while you're in Milano for the fashion parade we've organised to film the Love Lucy commercial. I know you had your heart set on filming it in Sydney but it makes more sense financially, creatively and logistically for us to film it back home. It's perfect timing and then we'll be ahead of schedule to release it for the upcoming new fashion season.'

Mama nodded in agreement. Well, I guess I should be happy that they were a team again.

He added, 'The other great news is that we've been given special permission to film at the Piazza del Duomo. We thought that it was important to stay true to our label's Italian heritage and use our hometown as the backdrop. We'll have access to the cathedral, fashion stores and cafés. It's ideal and I know it will be a magical shoot. Anyway, you'll get a chance to catch up with your friends. I just hope I'll be with you once this legal mess is cleared up.'

Mama rallied behind Papa. 'So do I. Don't forget Lucy, you'll have your best friend with you to share the experience. You'll have so much fun together.'

There was nothing I could say except, 'Oh, yes, I'm sure Bella will be in her element. Ironically, she wants to be a model so she'll love both events.'

'Oh, no wonder I adore that girl,' Mama enthused. 'I didn't know she loved fashion. Well, that's all the more reason for her to go.'

'But what happens if I make it into the Sydney Dolphins Rep team? I don't want to lose my place.'

'If we don't hear from them over the next few days, I'll give them a call. We'll find a solution,' Papa promptly answered.

Mama looked irritated for a moment, but covered it with a smile and stood up. 'I think we'd better get going. I don't want to keep your principal waiting.'

That was odd, running late had never bothered her before. She loved to make an entrance. She was up to something fishy.

# Chapter 22

# Moreton Bay fig tree

I don't really like going to school, mainly because I find it hard to blend in. The girls aren't sure what box to put me in – pretty or nerd – either way I'm either teased or completely ignored. I love learning, though, and enjoy my subjects, especially ancient history and visual arts, although English is my best subject. It's the making friends bit that I find difficult. And Bella, my best and only friend at the school, probably isn't even speaking to me – and I don't blame her, considering I brushed her off yesterday to hang out with Max.

So, I wasn't looking forward to walking through the big front gates – especially with Mama. She knew how to make an entrance and arriving at school in an over-thetop white Bentley is just going to add to my problems. I can just imagine the sarcastic remarks:

'Everyone stop, the Zoffis are here.' 'She's such a show-off.'

'Who does she think she is?'

'We may as well roll out the red carpet.'

Mama and I didn't speak for the whole trip, which was only about five minutes up the road. I was in my own world, trying on the one hand to figure out how to cope with the girls at school and on the other trying to work out a way to find out about my football trial. I hoped Mama's cross expression at breakfast didn't mean she was going to stop me playing with the Dolphins, like she had with the Beckham Academy scholarship letter.

She was busy retouching her hair, oblivious to my nerves and suspicions.

She checked that she had all her things in her bag, and then proceeded to rearrange her fringe until the car pulled up at the school.

The driver opened Mama's door and when she was ready we headed out, confronted by the stares of the other students. My stomach started churning, anticipating their nasty words and the awkward day ahead.

As usual, Mama oozed confidence and looked as if she'd just stepped off the catwalk into the glare of a sea of photographers instead of just a bunch of nosey students gawking. But Mama didn't care. She even paused, looking over the group, her trademark pout on her face. She was used to the paparazzi. As if on cue, there was a distinct camera flash from the school gates. It was a lone photographer stealing snaps, no doubt in the hope of selling them to one of the gossip mags.

I pulled my school boater hat down as far as I could to avoid the camera's glare and the ogling students, and quickly marched into the school grounds as Mama tiptoed behind in her high heels.

'Ciao, Lucy. Have a good day. And make sure you come straight home,' she ordered sternly, as she headed towards the principal's office.

'But Mama, I was planning to spend some time with Bella after school. I want to talk to her about our trip to Milano. How about I make it home by five, please?' I asked with a hopeful expression on my face.

'Well, okay, but don't be late. Oh, I almost forgot. Here, this is for you. I bought you a new mobile. Don't lose this one. It's charged, so there's no excuse for you not to be in touch,' she said.

'Oh, it's so cool, Mama. I'll keep it close in case you call. Thanks, Mama. You're the best. Ciao.' I gave her a kiss and strode away, happy with my new phone.

Now I had to face Bella. To my surprise, she was sitting in our usual meeting spot on one of the benches under the sprawling Moreton Bay fig tree. We've had so many great chats under this tree. It's where we've revealed our deepest secrets and shared many laughs. I took it as a good sign. She must have been waiting for me.

I hesitantly approached the bench, 'Hey Bella. How are you?'

'Fine, and you?' she coldly replied.

'Yeah, I'm okay. Bella, I'm so sorry about the way I've been acting lately. There's been so much going on. I just hope that we can talk about it and move on.'

'Yeah sure! But there's a lot going on in my life, too. You're not the only one who faces challenges, Lucy. It might help you to think about others for a change. The world doesn't revolve around you, although you drop everything for Max when he comes calling. Oh, and have you heard that Dylan's off to the David Beckham Academy? What happened to your scholarship?' she said in a cutting tone.

'Oh, I decided to stay and play my football in Sydney,' I lied. Now was not the time to explain about Mama's sneakiness. 'But that's so great for Dylan. I'm thrilled for him. Maybe we could –'

But she didn't let me finish, 'Look I've got to go. See you round,' she hissed and walked away.

She may as well have slapped me. That really hurt. I honestly didn't expect her to be that upset. I thought we'd have a chat, I'd tell her what's been happening, and we'd work things out and everything would be fine, but obviously not. Have I really been that selfish? Is it all about me? Why should I have to choose between Bella and Max? They are both my friends. Aren't they? I know I did the wrong thing by her yesterday, but I apologised. Why couldn't things be back to normal?

As Bella walked away, I saw, to my horror, that she was joined by . . . oh I don't even want to mention her name. How could she do this and why? Why would she team up with her? Not Angie 'Baddie' Baggly, the bully I faced at the football trials. I just didn't get it. Of all people! Why would Bella hang out with her?

# Chapter 23

# Bella Bella

I've always had male friends through football and we talk about the latest results, player transfers and club dramas. I'm just like one of the boys, and I love that. It's always been like that, once they accept me on the pitch. We have an affinity, a bond through football. But with Bella it's different.

I mean, she isn't even sporty, but she understands my circumstances, and the best thing is she couldn't care less about the Zoffi name. I can really trust her and so we talk about all sorts of things, including, of course, stuff that boys won't talk about and I wouldn't want to discuss with them.

I can't stand the thought of losing her friendship, especially at a time like this. I desperately want to work things out with Bella but I'm not sure how I'm going to make up for my selfish behaviour. I must admit that I'm at fault in this situation. I was too caught up with my own dramas and with what's been happening with Max, and I don't even know what's going on in Bella's life. And now she won't even talk to me.

How are we going to travel to Milan together? She didn't even mention it, but the conversation was pretty short. Maybe she hasn't been told about it yet. I've got to somehow break the ice and tell her our great news. I can't imagine her turning down a chance to hang out backstage at a fashion parade as well as on the set of a commercial in the centre of Milan.

'Lucy, Lucy, are you paying attention?' I'd been in my own world during the first class after lunch, Geography, although I'd noticed when I arrived that Miss Hopkins was in a foul mood.

I jumped. 'Oh, yes, miss.'

'Well, can you answer the question?' asked the teacher.

Naturally I had no idea what the question was, and it occurred to me that I was going to get into trouble yet again, this time for daydreaming, and was sure that Bella wasn't going to throw me a lifeline. Anyway, she wasn't even sitting next to me as usual. Everyone's eyes darted in my direction at the back of the class room where I was seated alone. I desperately tried to come up with something that would get me out of this situation, or wait for a hint from another student, but I had nothing.

Then a sudden bang caught everyone's attention.

The teacher strode to the cause of the commotion. A large pencil case had fallen to the floor. She growled, 'Who does this belong to?'

The girls looked around, waiting for someone to claim responsibility. I knew who owned that pencil case.

'Well, if no one's going to own up I'll be forced to punish the whole class with a lunchtime detention.'

'Miss Hopkins, I'm so sorry, but it was an accident. I must have knocked it when I went to get something out of my drawer,' a voice piped up.

But Miss Hopkins was in no mood for fun and games. 'Bella, I'm really surprised by your behaviour. I want you to wait outside the classroom.'

We were all a bit shocked, as Bella was rarely in trouble. She was the goodie-goodie and was often teased for being a teacher's pet, but not today. Today she had been sent out of the classroom for the first time. And it was all my fault. I was sure she was trying to distract the class to help me.

I had to do something, 'But Miss, it was an accident. Bella didn't mean it. Anyway it was just a pencil case that fell. It was nothing serious,' I said.

'I will not put up with your cheek, young lady. You can also join Bella outside,' she ordered, pointing to the door.

'But Miss, I didn't . . .'

'Now, Lucy! Out you go!' she directed, much to the class's delight.

I also wasn't used to being shown the red card but at least in a football match, you're sent off only if you've done something really bad like a dangerous tackle or fighting with the opponent. Other than that you normally get two chances if you've committed an offence and they come in the form of two yellow cards. Once you've been shown the second yellow, an automatic red card appears out of the referee's pocket, and you can no longer participate in the game. It's a dreaded walk of shame to the change room. Your head is hanging because you feel as though you've let your team down, since they are left with only ten players for the rest of the match.

But in this case, it wasn't a team environment and my rivals were more than happy that I was in trouble, sneering and laughing as I left the classroom. 'Okay, that's enough or you'll all enjoy extra time with me in detention,' Miss Hopkins threatened.

As my Nonno Dino used to say, you can always turn a negative into a positive and now was the time to do it. I had a chance to mend my friendship with Bella.

We stood at either side of the door staring into space. I made the first move, 'Bella, thanks for making the distraction. I really appreciate it.'

'That was an accident. Don't get ahead of yourself, Lucy,' she sniped as she wiped her glasses.

I had to try harder. 'Oh come on Bella. You're not the clumsy one, that's something I'd do. Please Bella. I'm so sorry for being such a bad friend. How can I make it up to you?' I asked, my fingers crossed behind my back for luck. She was silent for a little while as I desperately waited for an answer. It was agonising, and although I knew I deserved it, my impatience got the better of me.

I walked over to Bella and stood right next to her. I had to break the ice with something out of the ordinary. So I let my feet do the talking, and I fell into an impromptu performance piece, incorporating my dance moves with football routines, but without the ball, so it probably looked quite ridiculous. She started rollicking around in laughter.

Before we knew it we were both in hysterics and for a moment it was like old times – best friends having a laugh. The sun shone through the windows in the corridor and for a moment we forgot that we were in trouble. We were brought back to earth when the door opened. 'What on earth is going on out here?' yelled a very cross Miss Hopkins, catching me being silly.

I stopped on the spot and spluttered, 'Oh, nothing, Miss. We were just –'

'You were just messing around making even more of a racket and disrupting the class. This is the reason you were sent out in the first place. Right, I want both of you marching to the principal's office where you can explain your unacceptable behaviour.' She pointed in the direction of Mrs Zambocelli's office.

'But Miss, Bella didn't do anything. It was my fault,' I admitted.

'I shouldn't have to repeat myself. You are both in trouble. Off you go!' she shouted.

We headed off to Mrs Zambocelli's office without a word until we neared the entrance.

Bella stopped me in my tracks. 'Lucy, thanks for sticking up for me. I suppose it's time we joined forces again. I can't stay angry at you for too long, besides I miss our chats and hanging out.'

'Yeah, me too, and I really am sorry about being so selfish. Hey,' I paused, 'I have to ask you something . . . why are you hanging out with Angie?'

'Well, it's a long story, but a couple of days ago on the way home from school I found her leaning against a tree, crying her eyes out. She's not as bad as you think,' Bella insisted.

'I still need convincing. Anyway I'm so glad we're friends again. I've really missed you. And hey, you are coming to Milan with me . . . aren't you?' I asked with a big smile.

'What? I don't know anything about it! Milan! What!' she answered in confusion.

'You mean to tell me that your mama hasn't told you that you've been invited to come along with us to Milan for the Molto and Favolosa charity fashion parade and Love Lucy film shoot? Or are you messing?' I gave her a quizzical look.

'Oh my god. I honestly didn't know about it. Mum's so busy with her campaign at the moment that we haven't had much time together, but I am definitely coming. Molto and Favolosa? That hip new label?' she screamed.

'Oh thank you, thank you, dreams do come true!' she continued shouting and jumping up and down like a crazed lunatic. Of course she was up on the latest fashion – Molto and Favolosa have just hit the fashion scene. Wait till I told her that Dolce & Gabbana would also be there. She grabbed me and we jumped around together in hysterics.

The moment was priceless. I didn't care about detention or whatever lay ahead. I had my best friend back.

'What's going on out there?' yelled the principal.

# Chapter 24

# Filomena

We immediately stopped dancing around, tidied our hair and uniforms and marched into Mrs Zambocelli's office. 'Lucia Zoffi, was that you making all that racket?' she asked, a serious expression on her face. 'Lucia, Lucia . . . are you all right?'

I felt an elbow in my side and looked at Bella, who was trying to shift my attention to the principal.

'Oh yes, um, Mrs Zambocelli,' I stumbled. 'I'm sorry, I've become so used to being called Lucy that it took me a moment to register.'

To our surprise she replied, 'Oh don't worry, I understand, but Lucia is better than Filomena. I don't know what my parents were thinking. I was named after my Nonna, whom I loved, but I used to get teased about my name. It's very old-fashioned, so I ask all my friends and colleagues to call me Mena. Anyway, what was going on out there?' she persisted.

'Um, I'm sorry we disturbed you Mrs Zambocelli, but we were just celebrating something special and we forgot where we were for a moment,' I said honestly. I didn't want to get into any further trouble and figured it was best to tell the truth.

She surprised us again. 'Well, I wasn't happy about all that screeching outside my office, but I do appreciate your honesty young lady. So girls, we'll forget it this time. I've had an extremely busy day already and I could do with some light relief.'

I'd never seen this side of the principal. She usually comes across as very strict and serious, but with a suave Italian style.

Bella was also astonished, but as usual she was thinking ahead. 'Oh, Mrs Zambocelli, thank you, and if I may say so I love your name. Filomena is Italian for "beloved". I think it's a beautiful name.'

Bella's brain power can come in very handy.

'Well, thank you Bella, and I'm very impressed with your knowledge of Italian. You really are one of our brightest stars. Now, I still don't know why you're both here.' She looked at us inquiringly.

'Miss Hopkins thought we were being disruptive but it had nothing to do with Bella. It was all my fault,' I offered in my best voice.

'Oh no, Mrs Zambocelli. It was me. I dropped my pencil case and –', but Bella was promptly interrupted.

'Obviously you're very close supportive friends but I can't imagine you two causing trouble intentionally. However, I must respect your teacher's instructions, so to keep the peace why don't you stay with me for a while. That way we can keep Miss Hopkins happy and you can help me out by filing these piles and piles of papers,' she said, while trying to straighten them on her desk.

'We'd love to. Thank you Mrs Zambocelli,' I said, knowing that we'd got off very lightly. Bella and I threw each other a grateful look.

'Well, Lucy and Bella, you only have a week left here before you fly off to my hometown, Milano. I'm so envious. I really miss it. I hope you realise how lucky you both are. And it sounds so exciting. Your mama told me all about it. Please make sure that you send me some photos of you modelling in the charity fashion parade and the filming of the Love Lucy commercial. I'll put it in our school newsletter.'

Great, I thought, she may as well pin me up on the wall for a game of darts!

She continued, 'You are very lucky girls. Imagine modelling for a famous Italian label and rubbing shoulders backstage with the likes of Molto and Favolosa. You can't do much better than that. But,' she said warningly, 'I want a detailed journal about your trip, which will make up for missing the last few weeks of school. And it's such a wonderful opportunity for you to practise your Italian, Bella! I know you're becoming quite fluent.'

Bella was bursting with enthusiasm. 'I know we're the luckiest girls on the planet. It's amazing, I'm going to be swanning around backstage at the fashion show while Lucy struts it on the catwalk with cute little Gigi. I'm so excited, I can't wait to get there.'

I just nodded in agreement.

Mrs Zambocelli replied, 'Yes, I would be excited too, but now it's time for your feet to be back on the ground. I want both of you attending the new school football training program. It kicks off this afternoon, straight after school at Rushcutters Bay Park. I'll let our sports master, Mr Williams, know you'll be joining him and the rest of the keen footballers. There'll be a couple of spare school kits for you to wear. He'll be very happy that you can participate, and when you return from Italy maybe you'll both be able to play for the new school team. And don't worry, Lucy, your mama already knows all about it. In fact she was quite supportive of the idea.' That's a surprise, I thought. 'Bella, you can call your mother from here to let her know.'

'Oh, but Mrs Zambocelli, I'm not sporty. I don't know anything about football. Do I really have to?' she pleaded. The principal had her serious hat back on. 'You're a fast learner and I don't think you have much choice.' She looked over the top of her glasses.

'Mrs Zambocelli, we'd love to play. We'll get started with the filing,' I said politely, picking up a few piles of paper and handing some to Bella.

'Come on Bella, let's start working,' I urged. We went into the adjoining back room where the filing cabinets were kept and gently shut the door behind us.

'I can't believe we still waste so much paper. All of this stuff should be kept on the computer and backed up. What happened to saving the trees? Anyway, what are you doing questioning Mrs Zambocelli? We got off lightly: let's keep it that way,' I said.

'How am I going to play football? I don't have a sporting bone in my body. I'd rather be modelling in a beautiful dress in the parade in Milan. Oh, I can only dream of such things,' Bella fantasised, mimicking a model's strut perfectly.

'You'd do a much better job than me in that parade. Now, there's no need to panic about the football session. I'll teach you the basics. But I'm shocked that we're flying to Italy so soon. Mama is determined to keep me away from Max and that's why she's whisking me off to Italy. It's not like she needs to – I don't even know where Max is. He ran off again,' I revealed while trying to file.

'Well, that's Max. No responsibility and totally selfish. Look, you've done enough for that prat. It's up to him to get his life together and he now has the help of his uncle. At least he has a roof over his head and a family member who cares about him. He'll be fine, believe me. It's time for you and I to have some fun together. That's the main reason I'm looking forward to this trip,' Bella said happily.

I laughed, 'So, you're not looking forward to hanging out backstage at a big fashion show and on the set of the commercial? Lights, camera, action!' I teased.

'Mmmmm, well of course I am. I'm ready for my close-up!' She giggled and added, 'Lucy, I have to say that I wouldn't mind being punished with a trip to Milan, parading the catwalk and starring in a commercial that features a label named after me. Most girls can only dream about these things but you're living the dream, so stop with the big whinge! *I'd rather stay here and play football!*' she mimicked. 'Seriously, you've got rocks in your head. There isn't a girl I know who wouldn't jump at this chance. Come on, Lucy, get happy and get excited, we're going to Milan! I mean, we're going to Milano! I'm already thinking Italian. Milano, Milano here we come!' She was dancing with the files in her arms.

'Okay, okay, I get it. We'll have a ball. We'll have the best time, ever!' I promised, trying to get on with the filing. 'Girls, how are you going?' Mrs Zambocelli inquired from her office.

'We're nearly done,' I answered.

'Good, because the bell's about to go. I want you both to get ready to meet Mr Williams and the other students at the oval. Why don't you pop down and collect what you need from your lockers so you're not late? Enjoy the session. I look forward to hearing about it tomorrow,' she said, powdering her nose in front of her compact mirror.

'Thank you Mrs Zambocelli. I'm sure it's going to be a lot of fun,' I said.

'Oh yes, I can't wait,' Bella added with a hint of sarcasm.

And with that, we made a quick exit.

# Chapter 25

# The enemy

'Hi, sir, we were told that we have to join this afternoon's football session,' I reported to Mr Williams.

'Yes, Lucy, Mrs Zambocelli told me to expect you and Bella. Glad you could make it. I think this is a really good way to get fit and eventually I hope that we can form the school's first football team for next season. We already have some good players, including you, and of course Angie, who'll be an asset in the back line. You'll make great team mates and add strength to the squad.'

Oh no, Angie. I hadn't even noticed her, but it made sense that she'd be here. How on earth could we ever be team mates?

'Here are your kits, girls. Go change and meet me back here in five minutes sharp,' said Mr Williams, handing us our outfits. Then he added, 'Bella, it's good to see you take an interest in sport.'

She threw him a forced grin and turned to me and rolled her eyes. I looked back to catch a glimpse of Angie the bully, and spotted her mass of red hair bopping from side to side in ponytails.

Mmmm, we'll see how well those ponytails hold up in the game.

Bella and I headed off to the ladies' room to change. 'Here, you're going to need these,' I offered her my shin pads and football boots. I always carried them in my school bag so I'd be ready for a game whenever the opportunity arose.

She awkwardly held up the shin pads and asked with a panicked voice, 'What do I do with these?

'They are to protect your shins, especially against people who can't play. Otherwise they'll just hack at your legs and you'll go home with lots of bruises and maybe an injury,' I warned as we put on our brown and red school strip.

'Great, that's just what I needed to hear.' Bella squirmed while adjusting her shorts.

'Don't worry, Bella, I'll look after you. All you need to do is stick with me and you'll be fine,' declared a familiar voice from the doorway.

'Oh, hey Angie. Well, maybe this is going to be fun,' Bella declared as we started walking back to join the rest of the girls.

'Yeah, more fun than I expected. I hope you're wearing shin pads Lucy, because you're going to need them,' Angie threatened, striding ahead.

I yelled, 'I don't need them because I have speed – unlike SOME players.'

'Yeah? Well, we'll see what you can come up with this time. I hope it's better than your previous performance. I need a bit of a challenge, otherwise it's soooo boring, don't you think?' Angie sniped back.

'Oh, that cow is really going to get it on the pitch. She's a nasty piece of work. I don't know how you could have hung out with her,' I angrily remarked as we joined the others.

'She's not as bad as you think, Lucy. She puts up a tough front but she's really a big softie. She's had a very difficult time lately – I'll tell you about it another day. Right now I have to focus on staying on my feet and trying to kick a moving ball. I'm not looking forward to it. But please give Angie a chance, she's a good person . . . deep down!' Bella said softly as I helped her to stretch.

'You could have fooled me and I have no interest in getting to know her. She's a cow and a bully and she's going to get another taste of the Zeezou weaponry on the pitch. She won't mess with me again,' I boasted, as we finished our stretches.

'Right girls, I want you in two lines, running in and out of the cones.' Mr Williams blew his whistle and the first girls were off.

'I'll go first and show you how it's done. You'll be fine, just take your time on the first run to get a feel for the ball,' I assured Bella, who was nervously jumping up and down.

I was next up and started running with the ball, weaving in and out of the cones with ease. Suddenly Angie shouted, 'Is that the best you can do, Lucy?' I looked over as she finished ahead of me.

We ran to the back of our lines and I bellowed, 'We'll see who comes up with the goods when it matters.'

She turned her back to me as we watched Bella making her first attempt on the football field.

Angie yelled, 'Come on, Bella, you can do it! That's it, nice and easy.'

Her comments didn't help as Bella looked up in anguish, struggling to weave around the cones. She had no control and moved awkwardly towards us. The other line had finished their run as the next girl and the one after that completed the exercise, while Bella struggled on.

I ran over to assist her, giving her further instructions in how to control the ball. 'I hate this. I feel so stupid,' she cried.

'Bella, you're doing so well for your first time. It just takes practice. We'll get there,' I said, trying to guide her to the last cone.

Thankfully, Mr Williams blew his whistle and put her out of her misery.

'Girls, we're going to play a game. Lucy and Angie, I want you to choose your teams. Angie, you go first.'

I knew she would want to win, so of course she'd pick the best players. I'd noticed during the warm-up that there were quite a few to choose from the thirty or so girls there, but I couldn't believe my ears when she yelled out, 'Bella!' accompanied by a big grin.

Oh, she was really pushing it. She was getting under my skin, but I tried to stay calm and thought I'd sort her out once the whistle blew. I couldn't imagine why Bella thought Angie was so nice. What a load of baloney.

I was eager to get started with my hand-picked team and hoped that we could pull together for our first game and blast our opposition off the pitch. Bella may be my best friend but when I compete there are no friends. In the heat of the battle, I do whatever it takes to score. Today was war and I wanted nothing more than to slaughter our rivals on the pitch.

The whistle blew and once I had the ball I ran down the middle of the park with a determination I hadn't felt since I faced Max at our first meeting. I sailed past one defender and then the next before I came up against Angie. There she was, like a bulldozer attempting to clear everything in sight. She was an intimidating figure but I was dogged. I kicked the ball ahead of her and chased it down with everything I had. She was on my tail but didn't have the pace to keep up. I lunged forward to control the ball but was suddenly forced back. Someone had grabbed my shirt and pulled it with such force that I fell flat on my back and was winded.

I looked up, and of course it was her, with those orange ponytails bouncing with the roll of the ball.

'Sir, sir, you must have seen that! Where's my free kick? Sir, please, she blatantly pulled my shirt,' I yelled with fury from the ground.

But my calls went unanswered and the game continued. Angie was running up the wing without a worry in the world. My defenders seemed afraid of her and she continued until she reached the goal mouth, where Bella was standing around, uncertain of her role.

I raced down to try and stop Angie but I was too late. She'd already managed to flick it to Bella, who was unmarked and had a clear shot.

Angie yelled, 'Bella just kick it straight. Come on, you can do it, Bella! Smack it!' And she then promptly yelled to the keeper, 'Hey, you've got the biggest hole in the back of your pants. Oh my god, it's so embarrassing.'

The keeper fell for it. She turned to check it out while the players fighting for position in the box started laughing. Bella was faced with an open goal. In a moment of perfect timing or simply beginner's luck, Bella struck the ball and BANG, it miraculously rolled into the net for the opening goal.

Angie and her team mates went ballistic while Bella stood still until she comprehended what she had done and jumped up and down in fits of joy.

I yelled out to Mr Williams, 'Oh sir, come on, you can't be serious. Angie cheated. She distracted our keeper. It wasn't very sportsmanlike. Sir, you can't allow that. It wasn't a fair goal.' But he blew his whistle and the goal stood.

And in that instant I felt terrible. How could I try and take away Bella's biggest moment in her very short sporting career?

And my protests didn't go unnoticed. 'You've got to be kidding, Lucy. What is your problem? This isn't the World Cup or the Olympic Games! Whatever! I've just scored my first ever goal in any sport and here you are whining,' Bella scolded, and rightly so. At that moment I was the worst friend in the world. I just wanted to sink into the ground like a worm and disappear. To make matters worse, Bella then shouted, 'Lucy, when are you going to wake up and realise that it isn't all about you?' She stormed off with Angie, who flashed me a self-satisfied smile.

# Chapter 26

# Paparazzi!

Perfect blue skies with a few fluffy clouds paved the way for a smooth flight to Milan. But I was a bit nervous as I was returning home for the first time since the kidnapping. Even though I knew I was safe, I wasn't sure what to expect or how I'd respond to being back in Italy, I just knew that something didn't feel right. I thought that I was over it, but I felt very edgy and didn't know why.

We were halfway through the flight and Bella was napping. I rested on the pillow and closed my eyes, but terrifying images came into my mind. The man's heavy breathing was soaking my neck, and after a brief struggle, I collapsed like a rag doll in his arms as he carried me to their hide-out in the San Siro football stadium.

This had happened when I was there to watch Papa play with AC Milan in the local derby. I'd been snatched away and had struggled with my kidnapper until I fainted. I found myself cowering in a corner in a windowless room. The kidnapper bent down and pulled me towards him, in an attempt to kiss me but I intuitively bit him. Blood poured from his lips, the drops forming a red pool on the ground. His eyes filled with anger as he took a step back and to my horror he pulled out a gun and pointed it in my direction. I screamed, 'No, no, please nooooo!'

'Lucy, Lucy, it's okay. You're dreaming. Lucy, it's me, Mama.'

I awoke feeling a bit delirious to see Bella and my parents looking at me with concerned faces. The flight attendant offered me some water. Sweat was dripping from my forehead and I couldn't calm down. It was as if someone had unleashed a storm above me.

'Please, please hold me,' I cried with fear, as Papa gently hugged me and Mama stroked my head with a soft towel.

I couldn't stop crying. All the horror of the kidnapping was being belatedly released at that moment; it was pouring out of me. Maybe this was good. Maybe it would rid me of these terrifying dreams once and for all.

I was so relieved to be wrapped up in my papa's safe arms, warm in their unconditional love. It was so lucky that he'd been able to come with us. The charge against him had been dropped, which was the best news. Papa didn't deserve to have that case hanging over his head. He's always been such a great role model. I hoped that the Italian media wouldn't focus on it. I hoped they would leave us alone – although I doubted it.

Anyway, the main thing was that I was with my family and my best friend. I knew Bella was still a little cross about my outburst on the football pitch and I really had to make it up to her, but Milan would be the perfect place to do that. I just wished that Max was with us. I wondered how he was going as I stared out the window at the beautiful, familiar view of my hometown.

'Please fasten your seatbelts,' the captain announced. Bella forgot herself as the plane started its descent for landing. 'This is so exciting! My first trip to Italy and in such style. It's so so cool being on a private jet. Lucy, you have it all. You have the best life ever!'

But this was normal to me. I'd known this sort of thing all my life. And even though I was kind of excited about being home again, I dreaded what was ahead of us when we disembarked. I knew they'd be waiting for my family, waiting with their cameras, waiting to shoot.

'Bella, I'm thrilled that you're here and I'm going to make sure that you have the best time,' I said, really meaning it. 'I'm so sorry about my outburst on the pitch. I'm so competitive and I tend to get carried away. I shouldn't have let Angie get under my skin. Your goal was amazing and I'm very proud of you. I stuffed up again, I'm sorry. Please forgive me.'

'I was so angry with you. I couldn't believe that you would dispute *my* goal. Me – the non-sporty girl who wouldn't know one end of the football pitch from the other. I had no idea what I was doing, so my goal was a miracle! But, looking back, I know that it was an awkward situation and that Angie was doing her best to cause trouble. Look, I'm not angry any more. How could I be? Our friendship comes first so let's keep it that way. Just don't ask me to play football ever again.' She laughed and I joined her, relieved.

Now I knew for sure that we were going to have the best time in Milano!

We thanked the captain and crew for a smooth flight and disembarked. We were led out through a back exit in an attempt to avoid the awaiting paparazzi. It was a relief to think that we'd escaped the trigger-happy snappers. But as we stepped out to meet our awaiting car, a blast of light flashed before our eyes. We were greeted by a swarm of Italian media, calling out in Italian and English:

'*Sorride*!'

'How was your flight, Paolo?' 'Ciao, welcome back.'

'Frida, you look beautiful, please look this way.'

Even Mama, dressed as if for the catwalk, refused to share her pout. Were they serious? Did they honestly think that we were happy to see them? They acted as if we were old friends. Papa had got to know a few of the football journalists over his long career, but they were not considered friends. In fact, I regarded them as the enemy. Papa was used to this madness and just took it all in his stride.

I don't know how they find out about our every move.

It's very frustrating having to constantly try and dodge them, but as Papa has told me many times, this is the famous life. We just have to put up with it!

The questions didn't stop, the reporters yelling out: 'Paolo, are you back to see your son?'

'Loretta Sophirelli says she's planning a get together.

Is that true?'

'Frida, are you looking forward to meeting your stepson?'

'Paolo, are you staying with AC Milan?'

'Frida, look this way,' one of the photographers shouted, trying to get a shot.

We remained silent as another invasion attempted to disrupt our privacy and cause further torment and suspicion. Mama's perfect make-up couldn't hide her ashen face while Papa was stoic.

Security guards formed a wall around us and frantically tried to clear a passage through the media throng to our awaiting car. We pushed along as though wading through water and suddenly I panicked. 'Mama, where's Bella?'

She looked around. 'I don't know. I thought that she was with you.' We looked through the sea of people, while trying not to raise the alarm in front of the snap-happy paparazzi.

Then I spotted another group of reporters, who were questioning someone in a red top and jeans. 'Oh my god, Mama . . . look,' I pointed.

The sharks had cornered Bella, probing for information. Mama alerted Papa, who wove his way through the mass of bodies to rescue her. He shouted at the reporters in Italian, grabbed Bella and escorted her towards the car as the cameras flashed in a frenzy.

Great. They'd twist Papa's actions and use them as ammunition for more headline news:

'Zoffi attacks Italian media on home turf.' 'Zoffi's temper flares.'

'Zoffi breaks down.'

We managed to join Papa and Bella a few metres from the car. Bella's face had turned a sickly pale colour as the journalists kept barging towards us. 'Oh Lucy, I can't believe this is happening,' she cried, as I held her tight.

'Don't worry, just stay with me. Everything will be okay, we're nearly there,' I reassured her.

'But they were shouting questions at me and I didn't know what to say. They were asking about you and your parents and Tommaso. I tried not to say too much but I gave them my name and told them a few things. I can't remember. This is madness,' she wailed.

'It's okay. Let's just focus on getting out of here,' I gently insisted.

I held her close to me as we made our way to the car, still surrounded by the photographers in pursuit of the money shot, the photograph that could earn them a fortune, while the journalists fired more and more questions. As soon as we were safely inside the car, the driver put his foot down to take us to safety.

'*Benvenuto a Milano*, as we say in Italian. Welcome to Milan, Bella,' I announced. 'You've just seen the worst of it, but it will die down when they find another story to chase . . . unfortunately at someone else's expense. I'm so sorry. This wasn't the welcome I was planning but I promise it will get better from here on.'

Bella was a bit shell-shocked. 'That was unbelievable. I've had my taste of reporters chasing and questioning my mum – I mean, you can't be the Premier of New South Wales and not be pursued by the media, but this is different. It's so intense! It's madness! And when they cornered me with their cameras and microphones I was in shock. I didn't know what to do. How do you put up with it?'

'Well, I don't find it scary any more because I've grown up with it. I'm used to it but I hate it – it's very invasive and irritating and they never seem to give us a moment's peace. But we have no choice except to put up with it. On the plus side, it's only a small part of our lives, and the rest is a blessing,' I said. I didn't want to upset my parents any further – my true feelings would devastate them. This whole experience really sucked.

Unfortunately the media were still chasing us as if we were criminals. A car was in hot pursuit, as well as a couple of black leather-clad motorcyclists armed with cameras over their shoulders. It reminded me of those wacky racing Xbox games, with us as the target. The driver unleashed a flurry of Italian swear-words as he tried to negotiate a way out of the increasingly dangerous situation. Papa was furious.

Mama had also had enough. 'That's it, I'm calling the police. This time they've gone too far.' She had a line straight to the head of the *carabinieri*, and within minutes we heard the police sirens. They came to our rescue, forcing the paparazzi to pull over.

'Paolo, welcome back,' said one of the policeman, with a wide smile.

'*Grazie*. Please get us home quickly. We've had enough of this madness,' Papa replied.

'We'd be honoured to give you an escort home but before we do, can we please have your autograph?' The policeman handed Papa a piece of paper. The other one had an AC Milan jersey that he wanted him to mark with his famous signature.

'Of course, it's my pleasure. Please just make sure we have no more trouble,' Papa said.

They nodded, happy with their treasured acquisitions and escorted us home. The pesky paparazzi were no longer on our tail.

It was a dramatic start to our trip but it turned out to have one positive effect, when Bella said, 'Wow, Lucy, that's certainly given me an insight into your life here.

It's mad, and now I get why you're a bit nutty *and* selfabsorbed. Now I understand.'

We cracked up. It was so good to have my best friend back.

# Chapter 27

# Green, white and red

The thing I loved about Italy was its obsession with football and our passion for food. Milano was also the hottest fashion spot on the planet – or so everyone here kept telling me. Bella was going to go ballistic when I took her to the famous fashion hot spots.

She was already awestruck on our way home to Brera. 'Oh, look at her gorgeous outfit and those shoes,' she said, as she turned her head to get a better look. 'And check that girl out, she's head to toe in designer. So cool. Oh I think I'm going to really love it here. Look at him, so suave and um, yep, cool. I love it here already.'

We all giggled at Bella's enthusiasm and realised that she wasn't going to have any trouble fitting in. It was a pleasant distraction from the media pursuit at the airport. Mama was quick to add to her favourite topic.

'So Bella, I suppose a shopping trip is the first mission on your list?' Mama smiled.

'Definitely! I can't wait to visit all of the designer stores. The Galleria Vittorio Emanuele, Quadrilatero D'Oro, oh, the list goes on,' she answered with glee.

'Very impressive, Bella. You really are a bright spark and you have a passion for fashion, something we share. We'll get along famously. But I thought that this was your first trip to Milan?' Mama queried, touching up her lipstick.

'Oh, it is, but I did a bit of research before we left Sydney. I quizzed Lucy about her favourite spots but she's not all that interested in shopping, so I checked out Milan's fashion spots on the internet.' Bella was unable to keep the excitement out of her voice.

'Yes, Lucy isn't one for fashion,' she said, peering at me. 'But don't you worry. I'm going to make sure you have the most amazing fashion experience, starting with the M&F charity parade in a couple of days. It's a shame we couldn't bring our little Gigi.'

Poor Gigi. Nanna and Grandpa had decided it was best for her to stay in Sydney to give her more time to heal.

Mama added, 'Also, Bella, I've organised for you to hang out backstage with us, before and after the show. That's, of course, if you'd like to.'

Mama was really earning some brownie points. I was touched that she was making such an effort.

Bella couldn't contain herself. 'Wow, yes please, Frida. Oh, thank you so much. That's a dream come true. I wish I could be a model, but I know that's never going to happen.'

'I don't know about that,' Mama replied with a little smile. I could tell she was up to something but before I could quiz her, Papa interrupted.

'Ladies, we're home at last and thankfully the irritating media are nowhere to be seen.' He helped the driver with our luggage.

We stepped out and then helped carry in all the dutyfree shopping Mama had indulged in. She and Bella chatted about the perfumes, scarves and other fashion items. They were made for each other!

My mind slipped to Max. I really wished that he was here. He'd love it in Milan. We'd go to a big Serie A clash, like Papa's AC Milan versus Inter Milan. And on arrival we'd pop straight over to the park to kick the football.

'Lucy, come on. I want to explore your neighbourhood. I love these cobblestoned streets. They're so quaint,' Bella nudged me.

'Oh, yes, it's very pretty here,' I replied, still wishing that Max was with us.

Mama stepped in. 'Girls, let's get inside, freshen up and relax for a while. Bella, don't worry, we'll have plenty of time for sightseeing and shopping.'

'Okay, cool,' Bella conceded.

I glanced around the street, soaking in the place where I grew up, and took in a deep breath. I think I missed my hometown more than I thought. It was good to be back.

I showed Bella around the house so she could settle in and feel comfortable.

'I've never seen an elevator in anyone's home before.

That's impressive,' she remarked.

'Oh, yes, it's cool, but it's really to give us privacy when my parents' clients meet with them on the top floor. That way they don't come through the living areas.'

I showed Bella all three floors of our house and then we finally chilled out on the lounges. I suddenly felt exhausted from the trip but Bella was still quite chirpy. I think she was running on adrenaline.

'Lucy, this must be the coolest house I've ever seen. I'm so excited, I think I'm going to jump out of my skin. I don't want to waste any time. I want to do all the touristy things and visit all of your favourite places, and all of the fashion stores and see all the sights. And the best thing of all is that I'm going to be backstage at a Molto and Favolosa show. It's a dream come true!'

I couldn't join in her excitement. My eyelids closed, bringing down the curtain for the day.

Over the next few days, Bella dragged me to every shopping strip on the map – and some off it. I discovered spots I never knew existed, thanks to her touristy determination. Sometimes Mama came along, other days she stayed home with Papa to help prepare the commercial shoot, and a bodyguard came with us. It was exhausting! One morning I woke late to the smell of something yummy wafting in from the kitchen. I'd been enjoying waking up in my old bed. It was good to be home surrounded by familiar things.

I got up, opened the shutters to an overcast morning and went to Bella's room, but she wasn't there. I wondered where she was. And where were Papa and Mama? I had to go and find everyone and investigate that yummy smell.

I walked to the kitchen and there she was in unfamiliar territory. Now I knew that something was very wrong. 'Ciao Mama, this is a surprise. Are you okay?'

'Of course I am. There's nothing wrong with your mama cooking in her own kitchen,' she smiled, as I rolled my eyes and grinned, knowing this was a very rare occurrence. 'Sweetheart, you certainly had a good sleep. You must have been having a good dream.' She sat down at the table and patted the seat next to her. I sat down, realising that after all the excitement of the last week or so, I must have been exhausted.

'I think I'm just feeling more settled. Where are Papa and Bella?' I asked.

Mama was quiet. She was looking down at her perfectly manicured fingernails.

'Mama, please, please tell me. What's going on?' I asked.

'It's okay, Lucy, nothing's wrong. They're just upstairs in the office. We were showing Bella the photos from the last Love Lucy shoot and some campaign ideas. I just popped down to organise breakfast. It's been so refreshing spending time at home and keeping a low profile.'

'Oh, okay,' I replied with a smile. 'Bella is so excited about the Molto and Favolosa parade. Thanks, Mama, for organising Bella's backstage pass. She's beside herself and so grateful. And it means a lot to me too, so thank you.'

'It's a pleasure. Anyway, I can relate to Bella's dream. It's nice to know that she appreciates it. Now maybe you have an idea about how lucky you are and I hope that you'll be on your best behaviour during the show. Mario and Franca are very excited that you're appearing in their show – they want to make you their star model. Please perform at your best,' she requested, affectionately squeezing my cheek.

She grinned and added, 'While we're on my favourite subject, we decided to start the shoot later than scheduled by just a few days.'

'No probs, Mama,' I shrugged.

The new Love Lucy commercial was her baby. She was obsessed with making it their best campaign ever, a global success. And the odd thing was that even though I'd rather be playing football, I wasn't all that upset about having to participate in the parade and the commercial, this time around at least. It helped that I could share it with Bella, and it was good to think I could help her live her dream. I was so excited for her. I couldn't wait to see her reaction backstage with the designers. She was going to go crazy.

'Oh, I'm not hearing any protests. Are you feeling all right?' she gasped.

'Yes, I'm fine. I thought you'd be happy that I agreed with you. I can't seem to win either way. I really don't know what you want from me,' I said, a little disappointed.

'I'm sorry, sweetheart. I'm just pleasantly surprised because usually you'd do anything to get out of these fashion events.'

'Well, I don't mind so much this time round, especially since I get to hang out with Bella.'

'I'm thrilled to hear that. I'd also like to add some fresh ideas to the campaign. It's missing something but I'm not exactly sure what it is. Maybe you can help me – well, that's if you're interested. If we come up with something extra special we'll include it in the commercial.'

How could I say no? We don't normally have this sort of time together and I was enjoying the chat, even though it was about fashion. I'd never expressed any interest in Mama's fashion projects before and it was good for our relationship. I just wished Bella could take my place as the face of the Love Lucy label. She'd love it.

Oh, I suddenly had a great idea. Maybe I could wangle a part in the commercial for her! That would make her really happy. My mind went into overdrive and my interest in the Love Lucy commercial rapidly grew. I was determined to find a role for Bella.

'That sounds great, Mama. I'd love to help out,' I replied with excitement. Mama threw me a quizzical look. 'Dreams do come true. I never thought I'd live to see the day when my Lucy would be discussing anything to do with fashion. That's the sort of enthusiasm I've been waiting for! Now let's get started.' A huge smile stretched across her face.

'The television campaign slogan is "Defy gravity in Love Lucy designs". We thought you could use the football as you did in the photo shoot, but instead of playing on the pitch we follow you to picturesque locations – in different outfits of course – and all the time, you're doing that thing you do with the ball. You know, whatever that's called, those tricks you perform.' Mama tried to demonstrate without much success.

'You mean, juggle, Mama . . . like this!' We laughed like mad as I showed her the moves with an orange from the fruit bowl. We hadn't enjoyed time together like this in a long while and we both needed cheering up after the dramas we'd been through over the past month or so. I headed the orange over to her but instead of catching it, she moved out of the way and it flew straight into one of her vases, knocking it to the ground. We watched in horror as it smashed into pieces. I shrugged my shoulders, thinking that our special moment was over, but in another twist of character, she just kept laughing.

'Now that's a goal!' she cackled. I wasn't sure whether to laugh or cry. Mama is very precious about her things. This was most unusual behaviour, but I quickly followed her mood.

We cleaned up the mess, and I put forward my suggestion. 'Mama, I have an idea. Why don't we try, "United in Love Lucy designs", or "Everyone wears Love Lucy", or "No barriers in Love Lucy designs". I could be filmed going through my day catching up with friends who happen to be from different backgrounds, kicking the ball and having fun. So it shows that Love Lucy looks great on everyone; it's inclusive, fun to wear and a global label. For instance, we could choose people like um . . . Bella, who's half-Chinese so she'd be perfect!' I announced with a rush of exhilaration.

I hoped that she liked the idea. Bella would go crazy if this came off. Now, if only I could get Max involved. He'd also be ideal in the commercial, but I didn't even know where he was. Plus, he owed me an explanation. I wished he was here, I missed him. Oh stop it, Lucy, what was I thinking? It wasn't his thing and he was too unreliable. Mama would never agree either. She didn't even like me hanging out with him. And he was thousands of miles away in Sydney.

I waited for a response from Mama, hoping for some positive feedback, but she was looking past me at something. I didn't think that my ideas were that bad. It was very disappointing – one minute she was so keen for my ideas and the next minute, nothing. And then the reason for her blank response suddenly came to light.

'Hey Zeezou. What's up?' A voice that should have been a million miles away was banging in my head. I was wishing too hard. This was ridiculous. It sounded so real, but it couldn't be. Then I turned and locked eyes on him and understood Mama's strange behaviour. Was this for real?

I instinctively grabbed another orange and kicked it straight at him. I'd know he was real if he kicked it back. My jaw dropped as he performed his fancy tricks with the orange, flicking it into the air and straight into the fruit bowl. I screamed!

# Chapter 28

# Wish

Well, my reaction had everyone staring in silence. Papa broke the ice and ran over to give me a big cuddle. 'Princess, I'm glad that you're well rested because you're going to have the time of your life on this trip back home. It's going to be very special.'

Bella followed with a kiss on the cheek. 'Hey Lucy. I think our next shopping trip will have to wait for a bit.' She raised her eyebrows.

I still couldn't speak. Grandpa and Nanna were also there, plastering me with more hugs and kisses. I was overwhelmed but finally came to my senses. 'Grandpa, Nanna, this is the best surprise, ever!' I shrieked with excitement.

'Oh and Lucy, I think you left something behind in Sydney that needs your urgent attention,' Grandpa teased. Then he pulled my little Gigi out from his jacket. Gigi barked with delight and licked me as if I was a delicious gelato. This was amazing! I was in Milan, and the important people in my life were here with me!

'I had no idea you were all coming but I couldn't be happier,' I cried with joy. 'And Max! Wow, this is a very BIG surprise. Oh my gosh, I'm in shock but it's great to see you, um I mean, really good to see you. But who organised your trip here?' I blurted. My cheeks burned with a warm red glow.

Papa jumped in. 'You can blame me. I couldn't let an extremely gifted footballer like Max slip under the radar. After your Centennial Park escapade, I rang Rick to check that Max had gone home. He had and Rick was over the moon. I suggested Max join us here for a little while and Rick thought that this would be a great opportunity for him.'

I was thrilled with his change of heart and that Max had gone home to his uncle's.

He added, 'I also wanted to do this in memory of your Nonno Dino. He would never have turned his back on Max, nor would I. This is what he would have wanted and I know that this is what you want Lucy. It's important to support our friends. And your friends are our friends.' Papa affectionately wrapped his arm around Mama's shoulders, pulling her in tightly in the hope of winning her support.

Mama seemed to be being swayed by Papa's affection and they looked as though they'd patched things up.

'Well said, Paolo. Max is a good kid. He just needs some guidance and a bit of luck. And I can tell you that he's very pleased to be on solid ground. I don't know how we're going to get him back to Oz with that weak stomach,' Grandpa chortled, as he patted Max on the head with blokey affection.

'Yep, my first trip on a plane was unforgettable but for all the wrong reasons. I don't think flying agrees with me. You have a cool house, Mrs Zoffi. Thank you for inviting me stay here, and thank you for not being too angry about my escapade with Lucy last week,' Max said sincerely. His charming approach would serve him well.

'You're welcome, Max. It's my pleasure. Let's forget about what happened in Sydney – as long as it doesn't happen again. And you can call me Frida. Lucy, I think that it would be a good idea to show your friends around while we organise one of the other guest rooms for Max,' she said, with a glint in her eye.

That was an interesting response, especially when she'd ordered me not to hang out with him. But she was really making an effort to make my friends feel welcome. I couldn't fault that. Only time would tell what she really thought of Max, but for now we were on a winning streak. I grabbed Bella, who didn't seem overly happy that Max had joined our party. She whispered, 'What's he doing here? This is our girlie trip.'

I shrugged as I leant over and hooked onto Max. 'Tour of the Zoffi house – follow me this way,' I laughed, hoping that Bella would just accept the situation.

They were on either side of me as we strolled into the hallway and followed me up the stairs to the top floor. I was taking them up to my special spot on the rooftop so we could have a private chat, but before we got there, Max yelped, 'Wow, this is amazing. I'm staying right here.' He'd stopped right in front of Papa's trophy cabinet.

'But we're going up to the roof,' Bella urged, frowning.

The clashes had already started, so I tried to be diplomatic.

'Oh, well, how about we can just hang here for a bit, then explore the rooftop.' I knew how much Papa's trophy cabinet would mean to Max. It's every kid's dream to meet their hero and Max was now surrounded by Papa's trophies from his long and distinguished football career, including FIFA Player of the Year, World Footballer of the Year, World Cup winner.

Unfortunately, Bella didn't get it and crossed her arms in protest. 'Of course, let's do what Max wants.'

Poor Bella. She was peeved but I was so glad Max was here. This trip back home was going to be a little more complicated than I'd first expected, but I knew it was going to be fun!

And it still felt so good to be back in my hometown. Milan was like a box of treasures. It had something special for everyone – the world's best fashions, finest food, and of course football running through its veins. I loved everything about it. Oh, except the paparazzi, who hounded the city's stars like thirsty vampires looking for blood.

Thankfully Bella didn't sulk, and while Max was admiring Papa's awards, she went to check out the internet on the laptop on the desk.

Her next remark echoed my thoughts: 'Lucy, how does your family cope with the constant media invasion? This stuff about your half-brother is everywhere. Dominating the headlines in news and sport!' She mimicked a news reader, while I giggled. 'Zoffi and son united for the *Rossoneri*; Zoffi and Sophirelli a team; football legend and screen siren a big hit!'

'We're used to it,' I answered, serious again, and thinking about my half-brother. 'You'd never believe what they write and I try and ignore it. Most of it is made up. Lies, lies and more lies. Anyway, you kind of know what it's like. Your mother has to put up with this type of gossip, as a politician.'

'Yes, but not on a global scale,' Bella commented. 'I didn't realise that your dad was such a megastar – a worldfamous football legend!' She was still scouring the net for more news and came across ads for Loretta Sophirelli's latest movie. Posters featuring her face were plastered all over the city. Mama's face turned white the first time she saw one.

'Check this out. The life story of Tommaso's mother is being featured. It's a big story,' Bella squealed.

My curiosity got the better of me and I glanced over and read the article.

'Well, that's interesting. She was an AC Milan fan. She must have chased after Papa,' I concluded.

Bella kept scanning the net. 'Oh and here's one about Tommaso. That's an unusual name.' She looked at me inquiringly.

'It's a popular Italian name for boys and the English translation is Tom. Actually, I think it's a nice name,' I responded, surprising even myself with my defensive tone. Max didn't seem at all interested in our chat. He was transfixed – after all, he had entered a new world filled with treasured football trophies, which most fans could only dream of getting close to.

He was so excited. 'This is awesome. He is such a legend!' he said in awe, and then offered, 'Oh and by the way, your half-brother has been dubbed "Tommy the Tiger" because of his knack of scoring incredible goals. He pounces like a tiger – he has incredible agility and explosive power. He's the talk of world football and he's awesome . . . just like his dad.'

That sounded weird. I felt a strange surge of jealousy, and immediately dreaded the thought of sharing Papa with someone else. It was bad enough fighting for his attention with Mama, but a son who was a top footballer could turn out to be my worst nightmare. I suspected Papa would want to introduce Mama and me to Tommy on this trip, but so far Papa hadn't said anything about it.

'Why wouldn't he be the talk of the town, he's drop dead gorgeous! And Lucy, he has your dad's eyes. And check this out – I hate to say this, but

Loretta is stunning too,' Bella offered. She seemed a bit sucked in by the celebrity world.

'Well, it's not all about looks,' I snarled. 'She's probably a nasty cow and he might be one of those cocky guys who thinks he's too good for everyone.'

'But Lucy, you've always wanted a brother. That's what you told me and here he is – a brother who's also a top footballer. That's what you've wished for and the good fairy has delivered. You must meet him soon and when you do, I'm coming with you,' Bella offered, a small smile on her face.

'Look, I can't cope with this right now. Can we just drop it? I'm confused and need time to think about the situation. It's starting to freak me out.' I followed Max's movements as he continued to stare, transfixed, at Papa's awards and trophies.

'Max. Max! You can look at Papa's trophies any time. I'm sure he'd be happy to show you his collection himself and share his stories about each and every one of them,' I said, rolling my eyes. 'But for now, can you please come and hang over here on the lounge for a bit? I'm dying to know how you ended up here.'

'Yeah, yeah, okay I'm coming,' he begrudgingly replied, as he put a glass trophy back in the cabinet. Or so he thought. As he turned to join us we watched in horror as the trophy spun on the edge of the shelf.

'Max, Max, the trophy!' we screamed. He looked over his shoulder and, in an attempt to capture the falling prize, he lunged, heading straight for the polished wooden floor just like a goalkeeper. He twisted in a desperate effort to catch it. He was so close but it was too late, and as though in slow motion it slipped past his hands and crashed to the floor. He'd never make it as a goalie!

Oh no, Papa's trophy! Mama's voice interrupted the commotion, 'Lucy, Lucy is everything all right?'

'Um, yes, Mama, all fine. No need to worry,' I called back, with fake confidence.

'Quick, Bella. She'll be here any minute,' I urged, as we ran to Max's side and sat in front of the smashed trophy. Mama appeared at the door, peering at us and suspiciously scanning the room.

'What are you doing on the floor?' she demanded. 'We were just chatting about Papa's football trophies,' I replied.

Max stood up and addressed Mama. 'Oh Mrs Zoffi, I'm such a big fan of your husband. I was just admiring his achievements but I also noticed a few of your fashion awards. You must be very proud of them.'

'Oh, those little things – they're no big deal,' she said, with a girlie grin on her face.

'But they are, Mrs Zoffi. They're very impressive, especially the one for New Designer of the Year,' Max continued. Wow, he really knew how to play to Mama's ego.

'Oh, well then, thank you for noticing, Max. And remember, you can call me Frida. I'd better go now and check on my parents. We're going out soon, so Lucy, why don't you take Bella and Max to their rooms to freshen up,' she advised, leaving us breathing sighs of relief.

'Bravo Max, very smooth. I didn't know that you could be so charming! And where did you hide the broken glass?' I curiously asked.

'It's in my back pocket. Ouch, it's a little sharp,' he remarked as he tried to remove it. 'Luckily it only smashed into a few big pieces, so we should be able to get it fixed.' He sounded relieved.

'Don't worry, I'll sort it out. I'll ask Grandpa to fix it, he's great at that sort of thing,' I said, as I carefully took the pieces from his hands. All of a sudden my motor mouth raced ahead of me, 'Oh and Max, I am glad that um, you're here with us.' I blushed.

'Oh cool ... yeah ... um, me too,' he responded coyly, leaning against the wall and melting me with his warm eyes.

'Mmmm, well I think it's time to leave you two lovebirds alone,' Bella sneered, turning her back to walk out. I felt myself go beetroot red. She looked over her shoulder to say, 'Well, you got your wish, Lucy.'

'Bella, don't be silly. It's not like that,' I snapped, but Max gently squeezed my hand and threw me a wink!

# Chapter 29

# Butterfly

I was waiting to be given the cue to strut onto the catwalk for Molto and Favolosa. The best thing was that Gigi was appearing with me in her first modelling job.

'Okay, Lucy, get ready. You're up in five!' ordered the lady with a clipboard. She was wired up for sound.

Under normal circumstances, there is no way I'd want to be taking place in a fashion parade, but since this event was raising money for animal shelters I didn't mind. It was a cause close to my heart and of course this was a very special occasion for Bella. She was living her dream, hanging out backstage with the models, make-up artists, and Molto and Favolosa. It was sending her giddy.

It was a crazy scene as all the models had brought in their pets for the show. One girl even had her pet snake hissing around her neck! She sat on her own, as almost everyone else was too scared to go near it. The other models' pets were more of the domestic nature. They included a guinea pig, a bowl of goldfish, a few cats, and even a turtle. It was like being in a pet shop, but with fashion as the backdrop.

Mama was happily chatting with the designers. She had outdone herself this time, and she continued to add to Bella's dream. 'Mario, Franca, of course this is my daughter Lucia, and this is her best friend from Sydney, Bella!'

Mario, dressed in a classic black suit, offered, 'Very nice to meet you and welcome to our show. Lucia, a pleasure to finally meet you.'

Franca nodded, kissed us on both cheeks and said, 'Bella, Frida told us that this is your first trip to *Italia* and that you're a big fan of fashion and our label. We hope that this will make your visit extra special. This is for you!'

She handed Bella a large green leather Molto and Favolosa handbag.

Bella's jaw dropped so much we could have counted all of her teeth and fillings. She couldn't help herself, and started rummaging through the bag only to pull out a new denim dress and a pair of black and silver encrusted M&F sneakers, which even I thought were cool.

Bella went ballistic, jumping up and down like a crazy jack-in-the-box. I grabbed her arm to calm her down.

She rattled, 'Oh, my goodness, this is so unbelievable. I don't know how to thank you. This is the best day of my life.'

Mama replied, 'We're so happy you like your gift, Bella. And that dress is from Mario and Franca's summer range. We thought it would suit you.'

Bella was beside herself. 'It's perfect! I love it, I love it. This is so amazing. It's a dream but even better. Oh my god, I can hardly believe it! You're just the best and oh, this is so beautiful, thank you thank –'

The stage manager ended Bella's rave. 'Lucia Zoffi, you're up. *Andiamo!*'

Mario and Franca seemed to find Bella's approach refreshing. 'You have good taste, Bella. It's so nice to see someone who genuinely enjoys our creations,' Mario declared sincerely. She was a big contrast to many people who would meet Mario and Franca. Most of them try and act cool but Bella certainly showed them some good Aussie spirit.

'Ah, and Lucia, you are perfect for our creations. You are our star! And we are glad that you brought little Gigi along. Go get them!' Mario said, patting Gigi, who was lapping up the attention in her specially designed Molto and Favolosa outfit. She was so well-behaved.

I kissed them on both cheeks, while Gigi licked everyone then I gave Mama an extra hug and whispered, 'You're the coolest. Thanks! Aren't you coming out with me?'

'Not this time. This is your moment. I want to watch my little girl shine on the stage. This is my dream, to watch you flutter like a butterfly, beautiful and free. You look incredible.' She was beaming.

'Oh Mama, thank you, that means a lot to me. I love you!' I answered, cuddling her.

'I love you too. Now go and do your stuff. I've got to race around so that I can capture my girl in her big moment. Enjoy!' she said.

I was stunned! I never thought I'd see the day where Mama would turn down a moment in the spotlight. I guess she really does want the best for me. If this is all I have to do to keep her happy well so be it. I suppose it really isn't that bad after all.

I ran up the stairs and waited for my cue to step out onto the catwalk. And the moment soon came, 'Lucia, ready and go!' ordered the stage manager.

My hair was loosely swept off my face, and I was wearing a short, red, layered sleeveless dress with a black tiger print and a chunky silver necklace and bracelet. The dress was a bit girly for me but at least I was in AC Milan colours, and I felt very comfortable in flat black lace-up ankle boots.

With Gigi tucked under my arm, I walked out into the spotlight and strutted down that catwalk like I owned it – and this time it felt good. I wanted to do my best and make my parents proud of me. The cameras clicked, the onlookers examined every inch of me, but I was at ease. Even though I'd done this many times, it had always been against my will, and I was actually enjoying this parade. Halfway down the catwalk I spotted Papa in the front row, perched high up in his seat with an enormous grin. This was so worth it. I was loving it! He was surrounded by all the beautiful people – actresses, former models and various other fashion types. Mama was on his left side, but sitting on his other side was ... oh no, I didn't know that he was coming.

Max was smartly dressed, and he had a slightly mocking grin on his face. I couldn't take it – our eyes locked, my heartbeat accelerated and before I knew it I'd accidentally bumped into the next model, the one carrying her guinea pig, as she was on her way to finishing her run. I fell and landed with the thump of an elephant – the graceful butterfly had fluttered away.

There was a loud, 'Ohhhh!' from the crowd, followed by silence. Even the Pink song playing was turned down. Luckily, I had Gigi tucked firmly under my right arm and I fell on my left side, so she was okay, while the other model had somehow managed to stay on her feet maintaining her poise. Without hesitation, she simply stepped over us and completed her run.

The photographers went into a frenzy. It was their lucky day. Now they captured my mishap for all the world to see.

I had to redeem myself, and slowly rose to my feet in the bombardment of flashing lights. I straightened myself out, patted my little Gigi, who was amazingly calm, stood tall and continued my walk down the long catwalk with my head held high.

Pink's music filled my head again, the sea of photographers kept clicking and I was back in my stride. As I walked off with Gigi, the stage manager demanded, 'Lucy, wait there.'

Mario and Franca came up the stairs, gushing, 'Lucia, you did it. You even fell with the grace of a butterfly and continued with great bravado! The audience loved it and so did we. And little Gigi, you were magnificent, a natural on the catwalk!' They patted her and added, 'Let's go out together for the finale so that we can show off our new star!'

I was a bit shocked. I thought they'd be upset with me, but as they say in show business, the show must go on!

Backstage after the finale was a flurry of excitement. The models had changed into their party gear and were enjoying glasses of champagne while Bella looked on in awe. She loved hanging out backstage among fashion's elite. She'd already changed into her new Molto and Favolosa dress and sneakers, while I just threw on my jeans and Love Lucy T-shirt.

Bella grabbed me in a tight hug, while Gigi let out a few soft barks. 'Lucy, this is the best time of my life. I can't thank you enough. I never imagined that I'd ever be doing something like this. I'm constantly pinching myself just to check that this really is happening. I'm so excited that I think I'm going to explode. You are my best friend in the whole wide world.' She squeezed me tight and gave Gigi a kiss.

'Bella,' I smiled, 'I'm just happy to have my best friend back, and I'm so glad you're having such a good time. By the way, it was Mama who organised all of this. We need to thank her. But before we do you need to put on something warmer because you're going to freeze out there in that summer dress. Milan is cold at this time of year!' I warned her.

'I don't care. I'm wearing M&F head to toe and no one's going to stop me,' she replied with determination.

Mama came running towards us. 'Lucy, darling. I'm so proud of you. You're a true professional. Everyone's talking about how great you looked and of course how well you handled that situation.'

'It was no big deal. Anyone else would have done the same thing. Oh, and where are Papa and, um, Max?' I casually asked.

'They're on their way over. Sweetheart, you've made me so happy,' Mama couldn't stop enthusing.

Bella was swanning around lapping up the glamorous parade of models and photographers and fashion people, but right now, I just wanted to find Max.

His mop of hair gave him away. I noticed it heading towards me and I didn't know where to look. The next thing I knew, Papa had grabbed me in a tight squeeze and spun me around as if I was a little kid again.

'Princess, you were amazing. My little girl has grown up,' he beamed, as Max just stood there awkwardly, a slightly confused expression on his face as he observed the crazy fashion scene and the jumble of English and Italian words.

I was a bit embarrassed and my voice wouldn't work, and Max didn't say anything either, so we stood there just looking around until Bella thrust herself between us.

'This is the most incredible party. Oh look, there's Stefano and Domenico!' She frantically waved but they were too deep in conversation to notice. 'Oh and there's that's that top model, Cherie Amour! Oh, she's so gorgeous.'

'That's great, Bella. I'm glad you're having such a fab time.' I flashed her a smile. But then she said the unthinkable.

'So Max, what did you think of Lucy's modelling work?'

'Gigi was fantastic, weren't you, girl?' he teased while patting her. 'Oh and Lucy did well. My favourite was the expression on her face when she made her recovery. Now that was cool!' he admitted.

'Yeah, thanks a lot! Come on, let's get out of here,' I suggested, but Bella couldn't get enough.

We were saved by Mama and Papa. 'Time to go, I'm afraid. We have a big day tomorrow,' Mama said.

'Oh but I just want to stay a little longer, a teeny bit, please!' Bella pleaded.

Just then a photographer stepped in. 'Could I get a photo of you together?' he asked.

'Just a minute!' Mama ordered and disappeared for a bit. She returned with a huge surprise. 'Okay, now we're ready!' she said, her arms linked with the designers'. We gathered for a group shot and this time at least it was on our terms. We smiled for the camera. Click, click, click!

Bella was over the moon. She'd had her photo taken with her favourite designers – and us too of course.

'All right, everyone,' Mama said, 'let's go.'

As we reached the door, Bella turned and took in one last glimpse. She said, 'Mrs Zoffi, I can't thank you enough. Life doesn't get any better than this.' One last wave from the fashion icons produced a little Bella shriek.

# Chapter 30

# Lovebirds

On the day of the Love Lucy shoot, the whole house was buzzing with excitement, although Mama was more anxious than ecstatic, and Papa was his usual laid-back self. He's always taken it all in his stride. He exudes that inner confidence that tells you everything will be all right, but poor Mama was running around like a crazy woman, making last-minute arrangements and checking with her assistant that everything was in place for a smooth operation.

There's always something that can go wrong in a big production – a light could break or there could be an electrical fault, or one of the cast or crew could be unwell at the last minute. The list goes on. That's the nature of the business, so Mama, being a perfectionist, always does her utmost to avoid any problems.

I'm not really fussed about all this stuff, but this commercial was different. Mama actually loved my idea and went with the slogan, 'No barriers in Love Lucy designs'. They could be worn by everyone, anywhere, anytime. That was the feel of the commercial and, best of all, Bella *and* Max each had a part to play.

Bella couldn't contain herself. It was like all her birthdays had come at once. She was going crazy making sure that not a hair was out of place before we even left the house. 'Bella, it's the hair and make-up artist's job to ensure that you look fabulous. You don't need to look great on arrival. They'd prefer you turn up with no make-up and clean hair with no product in it. You really need to chill out,' I insisted.

'I want them to think that I'm model material. I'm trying to make an impression,' she blurted, while applying some blush.

'Okay, fine, but you're wasting your time. All that stuff you're applying will be wiped off because the artist has to follow a particular style and colours for the shoot,' I said, watching her apply lip liner.

'Whatever! This makes me feel good so let's drop it, okay,' she begged, finishing off her lips with a dusty pink gloss.

'Okay then, I'll leave you to it, Ms Model. I'm just going to check on Max. I'll be back soon.' I walked out, looking forward to being with him.

'Fine. See you downstairs,' she said, checking herself out in the mirror for about the hundredth time.

It wasn't easy convincing Max to play a part in the commercial. It's not something he's interested in either, but when I told him he'd be kicking the football and he'd only have a couple of lines, he finally agreed.

Max's door was open so I peered in. He was sitting on the edge of the bed staring out of the window that overlooked the quaint cobblestoned streets of Brera.

I gently knocked. 'Max, can I come in?'

I stepped into the room and slowly moved over to him, planting myself alongside him on the bed. He lowered his head, his long unkempt fringe covering his eyes, but I caught a glimpse of tears trickling down his thin cheeks. 'Max, what is it? What's wrong?' I asked, surprised he was in such a down mood.

He shrugged his shoulders.

'Come on Max, please tell me. What's happened? I thought you'd be excited about today's shoot. It'll be fun,' I encouraged, trying to lift his spirits, gently elbowing him in the side.

'It's not that. I suppose I'm not used to being surrounded by all of these nice things and being so comfortable. I don't just mean because of all this luxury. Everyone has made me so welcome, I can't get over it,' he sniffled, trying to hold back further tears.

'But that's a great thing, Max. You can stay here for as long as you like. Don't worry about anything,' I assured him, putting my arm around his shoulders.

'We'll see, Lucy. I'm just not used to this and I know that I can't stay here forever. If I get too attached I'll just get hurt, because in the back of my mind I know that eventually I'll have to leave. I miss my parents, the home we once shared, my family, they're gone! You are so lucky, Lucy. I'm not sure if you realise how lucky you really are and I'm not talking about what you have. I read somewhere that a famous French author said something like, "Without a family, a man alone in this world trembles with the cold".' Max lifted his head and wiped away his tears with his sleeve.

'Wow, Max, that was so beautiful, yet so sad,' I said softly.

'That's my life. I'm not complaining about being here. It's just that seeing you with your parents makes me think of mine. I wonder about what it would be like to have them watching me play football and even kicking the ball with my dad. I just wish they were here with me. I even miss my mum badgering me to study hard. I've promised myself that I'm not going to let them down,' he sniffled.

'Max, they'd be so proud of you. And now you have your Uncle Rick. He really cares about you and wants the best for you. Papa really likes him and told me that he would do anything to ensure your happiness. This trip is an example,' I insisted, looking straight into his sad, chocolate-brown eyes.

'Yeah, you're right. Iam lucky to have Uncle Rick back in my life. He is trying his best to look out for me. Lucy, thanks for listening. I'm fine now,' he insisted. 'I'm ready to tackle anything.' He sat up straight and then tried to tickle me. I laughed and wriggled away.

'Come on, let's get moving,' I said, grabbing his hand. 'We have to leave soon. We can't be late on set, especially on the first day.'

I ran over and opened the wardrobe. I just couldn't wait any longer. This was a good time to spring him with another big surprise. 'Da da da dum . . . well what do you think?' I asked, hoping that this would cheer him up.

At first he stood there in disbelief, but it didn't take long for his face to break into a warm smile.

'Wow, wow, is that . . . my stuff?' he asked, coming over to take a closer look at the perfectly placed new clothes.

'Yep, hope you like them. There's a few Love Lucy things and other cool labels we hope you like. I snuck in the other night to get your sizes. Hope you don't mind.'

'Are you kidding? I really liked the clothes your dad gave me to wear to the fashion show, and I'm happy to have more cool clothes, but I'm paying back every cent. I don't take anything for nothing. Thanks so much Lucy.' His spirits had definitely lifted.

'Well, it was actually Mama's idea. She insisted,' I admitted, a little disappointed not to be able to take the credit.

'Your mum's so cool and your dad, well you know he's my hero. This is so mad! It's a dream to meet him and to stay here in his house. It's incredible! I'm already learning things from him. Hopefully I'll get that football contract, and then my life will be fantastic!' He had so much hope in his eyes that I wanted to throw my arms around him and tell him that everything would be all right. His dreams would come true, he had to believe that, but something was holding him back.

'Max, my papa is great, but you have to chill about the hero thing. Anyway, what contract are you talking about?' I asked.

'Your dad has organised a trial for me with his club and they may even offer me a scholarship with the youth team if I'm good enough. One day I'll play for AC Milan just like him. Lucy, that's the ultimate.'

'Oh, yeah, of course that would be great. Um, I hope you make it. In fact I'm sure you'll get in. No one tackles as well as you and your lightning speed will be a huge plus.' I forced a smile.

What was I thinking? This was Max's dream, a lifechanging experience and all I could do was think about myself. I'd love to play for Papa's team too – but it could never happen. It was strange to think that Max could end up living in my hometown while I was back in Sydney, hopefully playing with the Dolphins, and maybe one day the Matildas.

Now I was getting confused. I think that I want to be with Max. There,

I said to myself. But I wanted to pursue my own football dreams too. I wondered if I'd been selected for the Dolphins. I'd have to check with Papa, since Mama would love nothing more than to steer me back into modelling.

'Lucy, where are you now?' Max interrupted my thoughts, waving his hand in front of my face.

'Sorry, I was just thinking about my football and my life back in Sydney. Let's focus on today and get ready for the shoot. It'll be a good distraction and –'

A barrage of heavy pounding on the door stopped me mid-sentence.

Bella burst into the room with so much excitement etched in her face that she looked like she was about to crack. She was buzzing like a bee. 'Hey lovebirds, let's get going. Oh, Max, you're not ready. What have you two been doing?' she asked suspiciously.

'We've just been chatting, so don't get any stupid ideas,' I said, nervously letting out a laugh. Max just stared.

'Well! Come on. Move it. This is my big chance to become a model or an actress or maybe both. And nothing's going to spoil it. So, move it, move it, move it!' Bella persisted, without even taking a breath. She couldn't stop moving around and checking herself out in the mirror above the dresser. I'd never seen her in such an outgoing mood.

Max gave a wicked grin. 'Wow, Bella, you look like you're going clubbing and we haven't even had breakfast. Or maybe you've just arrived home from a big night out – although I didn't think that you'd be the party type.'

Bella turned from the mirror and threw him a cold glare. 'What would you –'

But before she could really let him have it, I quickly intervened, 'Bella, you look so gorgeous. Like a model. Max is just kidding. He has a very dry sense of humour. Let's get out of here so he can get ready,' I took her by the arm and whisked her out of the room, yelling, 'Max, meet us in the kitchen on the ground floor. Don't be long.'

'What is his problem? And why do you always stick up for him?' she huffed.

'He really didn't mean it. He's having trouble settling in, but you'll soon get to know him and see how sweet he really is. He's really quite sensitive, so just give him some time,' I pleaded.

'I don't want to get to know him. He might be cute but he's a pain in the you-know-what,' Bella countered.

'Please Bella. You're both my best friends and it would make life much easier if you would at least try to get along,' I persisted, hoping she'd be swayed.

'Okay, I'll try, but I'm not promising anything. And I think that he's more than just your friend. It's obvious by the way you look at each other. You're more like a couple of lovebirds,' she teased, and giggled, giving me a gentle knock.

Blood rushed to my face and throbbed through my tomato-coloured cheeks, back for another round of embarrassment. I giggled, 'Mmmm, lovebirds!'

# Chapter 31

# No barriers

The Piazza del Duomo is an amazing place to hang out. The grand, world-famous piazza is basically in the centre of Milan. It's where I'd meet my friends and chill out while enjoying a gelato or a delicious *panzerotti*. Everyone loves these mouth-watering warm, doughy bread creations from Luini's, which is just a short walk from the piazza. You had to get there early or endure very long lines of office workers getting lunch. The ones with melted cheese and ham were my favourite. The only downsides to this piazza were the constant pigeon invasion and the street hawkers trying to sell bird food and tacky bracelets to passersby. They were a menace!

I normally liked to sit at the front stairs, which lead up to the awe-inspiring gothic cathedral, the Duomo; perched on the highest spire is the famous *Madonnina*, the pride and joy of the Milanese and the city's beloved protectress. It made my heart jump every time. It was simply breathtaking!

Locals and tourists alike come here to eat and shop at the Galleria Vittorio Emanuele, which is directly across from the Duomo. Bella already loved coming here. It's a grand shopping arcade, famous for the mosaic bull design laid into the path. Passersby stomp on its delicate area for good luck. I've always had fun digging in my heel but for some it's a bit embarrassing. Of course Bella wouldn't do it, but Max took great pleasure in performing the age-old tradition.

Twilight was my favourite time here. A stunning orange light filtered through the perfect sky, smouldering over the piazza and turning it into a magical place. It was picture-perfect, a haven for photographers and sightseers. It was just the place to film the Love Lucy commercial with Bella, Max and two new cast members, both local young models from mixed backgrounds. One of them was a guy named Julian, who was an exotic blend of Brazilian and Italian. He was a little shorter than me, very fit, with brown wavy hair and dark brown eyes. The other actor was a beautiful Ghanaian/ Italian girl named Sahara. She had long lean limbs, fabulous thick afro hair, pouty lips and high cheekbones.

'Oh, Lucy this is so amazing. I'm having the time of my life. Pinch me, pinch me so that I know it's real,' screeched Bella.

We all laughed, but the huge set that took over most of the Duomo *was* pretty impressive. Max offered his opinion: 'Lucy, I must admit that this is so awesome. I'm not into churches or religious stuff but that cathedral is really cool. It's an amazing building, I've never seen anything like it.'

'Yeah, it's spectacular!' I agreed.

It was only 9 am, but already the piazza was a flurry of activity. The Director of Photography – known in the business as the DOP, the person who films the commercial – and his assistants were tweaking the cameras' positions around the piazza, making last-minute adjustments while dozens of other film people were busy finalising their tasks. The lights had been positioned for optimum effect and lots of other equipment dominated the famous square. The commercial's director insisted on a perfect set-up.

Tourists and locals strained their necks hoping for a glimpse of the stars. I don't think they realised that this was just about a bunch of teenagers featuring in a fashion commercial: they just kept taking photos.

We had no time to comment to our spectators. We were suddenly given our orders. 'Hi, I'm Jasmin, one of the assistant directors. I need all of you in hair and make-up ASAP in that trailer over there with the star on it.' She glanced at Bella and asked, 'Have you already been to hair and make-up?'

'No, I did my own make-up,' Bella proudly announced, flicking her hair.

'Well, you'll still need to be seen by Anastasia, the hair and make-up supervisor.'

I was thrilled to hear that Anastasia was working with us. She wasn't just the best in the business, she was a very dear family friend. She was also Mama's hair and make-up artist and would visit our house in Brera regularly to prepare Mama for big social events. I couldn't wait to catch up with her and find out what she thought of Max.

'And here are the scripts again.' I was relieved that Jasmin and the other models spoke such good English – and that the scripts were in English too. It would make things so much easier for Max, and even Bella had been struggling a little with the rapid-fire Italian spoken in Milan. 'Come and see me if you have any queries. Also, can you all please fill out these forms and make sure you find me at the end of the day's shoot to sign out, except for you Lucy,' Jasmin instructed.

'What are the forms for?' Bella asked, in a businesslike manner.

'They're release forms to give us permission to use your image, and to specify your time on set for your payment – all the admin stuff,' she explained, to Bella's surprise.

'We're getting paid to do this?' Bella looked amazed, and even Max raised his eyebrows.

'Well, of course. This is a job. Were you expecting to work for nothing?' Sahara gave Bella a strange look.

'Well, this whole experience is my dream and I didn't realise that I was also being paid for it. Life just keeps on getting better and better!' Bella gushed, while Sahara and Julian shook their heads in surprise. They were professionals and they knew the deal.

Jasmin then addressed me. 'Lucy, your parents are taking care of your contract, so no need to worry. Max and Bella, the Zoffis will check your forms too, as your guardians on the shoot. Right! Let's go. Please let me know if you need anything, Lucy. Enjoy your first day on the job. Ciao!'

'Oh, thank you so much, Jasmin,' I said, a little embarrassed by the special attention.

Max didn't let it slide. 'Lucy, you're such a star, you mustn't worry. You'll be looked after, princess,' he teased, and the rest of the cast joined in and had a good laugh.

I entered into the spirit of things and attempted my best regal accent. 'I order all of you to enter hair and make-up for a transformation. It's time to strut our stuff in Love Lucy designs.'

We cracked up as they followed me into the trailer, which was set up with chairs facing mirrors that were lined with movie-star light bulbs. Make-up covered the tables and a Love Lucy wardrobe filled the back part of the long room. There was also a bathroom and small kitchen facility with a fridge full of drinks and snacks.

I ran straight into Anastasia's arms. 'Ciao, Anastasia, it's so great you're here. This is going to be the best fun. I want you to meet my friends from Australia, Bella and Max. And this is Sahara and Julian, they're the local models joining us in the commercial.'

They all smiled at her while she checked us all out. 'You're all too gorgeous! It makes our job pretty easy! Nice to meet all of you, and Lucy, I must say you look fabulous and I like this new lively approach. And I think I know why you have so much enthusiasm.' She raised her eyebrow, while obviously checking Max out. My tomato face revealed my embarrassment yet again.

'So, let's get started. Lucy I'll work on you first. Bella, nice job, but we'll need to redo it with special make-up for television. So if you all please, plant your butts on a seat and Sofia, Gia or I will be over to attend to you. Help yourselves to drinks and snacks. We are here to serve and make you look even more *favoloso*!' she said, throwing her hands into the air. She had such an infectious personality.

'This is cool,' squawked Max, looking at all the goodies in the fridge. 'But do I really need to have that make-up stuff on my face? It's poncy for blokes to wear it,' he said in his deepest voice.

'Don't you worry about that, love,' Anastasia assured him. 'You leave all that to me. You must have make-up on to highlight those handsome features and for lighting and so on. Once we've finished with you, our wardrobe miracle worker, Javier, will fit you out in the Love Lucy designs.' She held a cape in her hand, ready to get started.

Max still looked doubtful and lowered his eyes in an attempt to hide behind his fringe. Anastasia quickly stepped into action, 'Max, I think I'll look after you first, actually. Lucy, if you don't mind, I'll do you next.' She winked at me. 'Max, come, sit!'

Without a word he sank into the chair and she went to work. I sat next to him, watching the master at work. She knew how to make people feel comfortable and at ease. After his initial resistance, Max seemed to warm to Anastasia, participating in polite conversation. Meanwhile, Bella was savouring the experience.

'This is heaven,' she sighed.

Well, it wasn't exactly my idea of heaven. My heaven would have a football pitch with games being played 24/7. Football, football and more football! Although I had to admit that I was really excited about this commercial and dressing up for filming, thanks to the football theme and the inclusion of my best friends. And I was thrilled for Bella. I hoped that this experience lived up to her expectations. So far so good – she was still floating from the M&F show.

'Lucy, I know I've already told you this but I can't help it. You are the bestest friend on the planet, thank you! This trip just keeps getting better. It's unbelievable!' she enthused.

We were having so much fun in hair and make-up, with Anastasia's wacky sense of humour and silly jokes that the time passed very quickly. Soon there was a knock on the door. 'Can we please have everyone on set, immediately,' Jasmin ordered, sticking her head in and then checking off her clipboard.

We madly zipped, buckled, touched up lipstick and tied laces. 'Come on! The director's waiting,' she called.

'Okay, we're coming. Quick, I have to take a photo of everyone for continuity. That's it, great, fab, great, great, oh you're all so fabulous! Now everyone out. I'll make final adjustments on set if need be.' Anastasia shooed us out, but she pulled me aside as everyone else rushed out of the make-up trailer.

'Lucy, he's the one, isn't he? I can tell. If you'd really like to know, I think he's very cute and a good boy. He's just right for you,' she said, smiling.

I was a bit embarrassed and whispered, 'But how did you know? I didn't even say anything about him. The weird thing is that I was going to ask you about him, but was waiting for a quiet moment with you.'

'Darling, it's me you're talking to. I know you, and I can see that boy has won your heart! He's a bit rough around the edges but I like that and I can tell that he's right –'

'Lucy! Lucy! You're wanted on set, now!' yelled Jasmin.

'Quick, get out of here before they send the cavalry!

We'll talk later. Go!' Anastasia ordered.

I joined the rest of the cast, still swept up in Anastasia's perceptive comments. Bella shook me out of my daze as she voiced her thoughts, 'We all look like a million dollars. Even you, Max. Not bad for a street kid,' she said, to everyone's horror.

She immediately realised that she'd gone too far and quickly tried to fix things. 'Oh no, I didn't mean it like that. Max, I'm so sorry, please believe me, I didn't mean it the way it sounded,' she said apologetically.

But Max just shrugged his shoulders. 'No big deal, Bella. That's what I am and probably always will be to you, but I know that I'm starting a new life. I'm off the streets and determined to never return to that life. This is just the beginning.'

He opened his arms out to the square, which looked more like a film set than the real Piazza del Duomo. Sahara and Julian didn't seem perturbed about the squabble – they too seemed to be overawed by the mammoth set.

I was very impressed with the way Max handled himself and really disappointed in Bella's comments. I don't think she meant to be nasty. Thank goodness she quickly apologised. I didn't know what to say and decided to stay out of it altogether. They had to deal with it themselves.

Sahara soon moved over to Max and started chatting with him. They seemed to be getting on well. I was surprised with myself – I didn't like the idea of them getting friendly. I couldn't help joining them. 'Hey, what's happening?' I asked, trying to be cool.

Sahara said, 'We were just talking about Uluru. I was there a few months ago on a modelling assignment. It's so beautiful and the Indigenous community there was so friendly. I was about to ask Max what tribe he was from.' 'I'm Wiradjuri!' Max explained. 'So Sahara, tell me about Ghana.'

I felt ill, but before I could do anything about it, Mama and Papa came over with the director. Their timing was perfect. Papa gave me the biggest hug. 'You look so beautiful. I'm very proud of you.'

I decided that today I was going to make him even prouder. I planned to put on my very best performance.

'Lucy, you look so gorgeous,' Mama exclaimed, and quickly added, 'You all look fantastic. Great job, Anastasia.'

'Thanks Frida. I always try my best. It isn't hard to make Lucy look gorgeous, and congratulations on choosing such a great cast. The outfits look divine on them,' Anastasia beamed.

'Lucy, you remember our friend, the director, Marcello Lantini,' she said, and introduced the rest of the cast.

I acknowledged the director while he quickly scanned our attire and told us what he expected. 'I agree with Frida. You all look superb, perfect for this commercial. So remember, I want a sophisticated, yet cool, fun approach. Just be yourselves and focus on your roles. Enjoy it and leave the rest to me and the crew. Oh and Lucy, I love your idea – "No barriers in Love Lucy" is a perfect fit. Everyone wears Love Lucy. And you were right – your friends are ideal for this commercial.'

'Cool, thank you, Marcello. I'm glad you're happy with it,' I responded.

Bella was grinning like crazy with excitement and mouthed 'thank you' to me. Would she ever calm down? 'It's more fun to have you on set. Anyway, you heard the director – you're perfect for the role. Maybe you need to get an agent,' I said when Marcello had finished.

She liked that idea. 'Yeah, an agent! Maybe you're right. I'm going to look into it.'

The director continued, 'This is our stills photographer, Enzo, who is going to take a few shots of everyone on set and will continue to do so throughout the day. Ignore him unless he has a special request.' Marcello grinned while Enzo studied his models.

Enzo came over and greeted me with a kiss on both cheeks. 'Ciao, Lucy. You grow more and more beautiful every time we meet. This is going to be a fantastic commercial and I know that you'll be brilliant – especially with the football,' he winked.

'Thank you, Enzo,' I blushed with embarrassment while the others giggled.

Enzo continued, moving closer to examine the cast. 'Ciao everybody. First I'm going to take photographs of you as a group and then individual ones. So, if you can all stand together, please.' He gestured with his arms like a conductor leading an orchestra. 'That's it, and if you could move in a bit, that's it … just a little tighter. Perfect, don't move. Stay there!' We stood in our pose while he ran back to his set-up and suddenly out of nowhere he threw a football at us. It floated in the air towards the middle of our portrait. We all reacted instantly trying to kick it, except of course for Bella, who moved out of the way, horrified as the rest of us competed for the ball. Max was first to connect, he dived forward, heading the ball straight back at the camera.

There was a click and a scream. 'Nooooo!' And then SMASH!

# Chapter 32

# Tommaso

It wasn't a great way to start the filming of the Love Lucy commercial, but on set anything can happen. We'd certainly kicked off with a blast. 'My camera. Look what you've done to my camera,' Enzo cried, cradling it like a baby.

But before he could confront Max, Papa came to the rescue, 'Enzo, it was an accident, but you must admit it that was a great header. Max is a very gifted footballer, that's why I've brought him here to trial at AC Milan. He is my protégé so let's take it easy. I'm sure you have many more cameras.'

Oh, no. Papa talking protégés reminded me of the dark cloud hanging over the trip. Would I meet Tommaso on this visit? Would Mama? I wasn't sure how she'd cope.

I wondered what Tommaso was like. I wanted to meet him but I was a little hesitant about the whole thing. He'd already caused such trouble between my parents and he wasn't even involved in our lives yet. They'd nearly broken up over the news, and I had been afraid they'd divorce, although now things seemed okay.

There were so many kids at school who'd been devastated by the breakdown of their family. They had to be brave and suffer quietly as they watched their parents fight over custody and a whole lot of other stuff. It was a nightmare and I didn't want to live it. Sure, kids were very good at adjusting and moving on but what other choice did they have? I wanted my mama and papa together forever more than anything else. I loved both my parents so much I couldn't bear to have to choose or to be stuck in the middle of an ugly long-running fight. But then, I did know a couple of kids who were glad their parents had split, because they'd had to put up with regular screaming matches and a horrible home environment. They said that things were better since their parents divorced. But I just couldn't imagine it.

I had realised how important my family was when I was kidnapped. Those people had held me to ransom and I'd really thought they were going to kill me. All I'd wanted was my parents. I understood now that it was the strength they gave me that helped me to escape and act brave in the situation I'd found myself in. All teenagers get antsy about their parents from time to time, and we all fight for our independence. But I also knew now that I was extremely fortunate to have them and I wanted to keep it that way.

But now I had a new challenge! I was faced with a new sibling – this could bring us closer together or pull us apart. I knew one thing for sure . . . I'd always wanted a big brother and I hoped he'd be everything I wished for. And so far it wasn't looking too bad. He was a footballer and a top one at that. I was very curious about what he was like, so I supposed I was looking forward to meeting him.

'Can all the talent please gather round. I want to do a quick run-through of the sequences so you're clear on what I'm looking for. First, as in the script, Lucy will start juggling the ball from right here, near the west end of the piazza, in front of the equestrian statue of King Victor Emanuel II. Max, the camera will zoom out to show you casually leaning against this important monument, nodding and teasing, "Mmmm . . . not bad for a girl!" An enraged Lucy stops the ball, flicks it into her hand and dares, "Catch me if you can!" then runs off with the ball back at her feet. Got all that?' asked Marcello.

'That's called dribbling!' Papa laughed. Marcello was more of an arty person; football wasn't a part of his life as it was for many Italians.

Marcello continued to give us his directions. 'Right, thanks Paolo. So Lucy, you're dribbling along the piazza in and out of the unsuspecting tourists and locals as Max chases you. He then manages to steal the ball from you and the challenge is on for you to win it back.'

Max laughed. 'I'm loving this film business already.

The boys are winners even in fantasy land.'

'We'll see about that. Anyway, I win in the end, so there!' I teased.

'Enough banter. I don't want to waste any time. The chase is on and

Max takes you to the other four locations: first, Max will dribble through the arcade of the Galleria and will lose control after running into a shopper. The ball will end up in the Love Lucy store where Bella is trying on a pair of bright red sequined Love Lucy shoes. Bella will accidently put her foot on the ball as she attempts to check out her new killer shoes.

'We'll do this scene a few times until we get it right. We'll also shoot a few close-ups of Bella trying on the shoes and shots of her with her foot on the ball while she's wearing them.

'To Lucy's horror, Max will then dive into the store and kick the ball from under Bella's heel as she screams and falls back onto the leather lounge. Unfortunately, Max steps on the lounge, leaving a footprint as he collects the ball and dribbles it out of the store. A furious Bella bounces up and instantly starts throwing shoes at him. The store assistant screams as she watches her precious shoes flying through the air! Lucy, who's standing at the door, jumps out of the line of fire while trying to find a way of winning the ball back from Max. Now, does everyone understand?' Marcello looked at us intently.

'Oh, and the dream just gets better and better,' said Bella. 'I have to wear beautiful shoes and I *must* throw them at Max. Well, I was born for this part!' she laughed.

But the director hadn't finished. 'While trying to avoid the shoes travelling through the air, Max continues his run throughout the arcade until he reaches Sahara in the milliners' store, and of course she's trying on hats. Lucy sprints ahead of him, anticipating his next move, but Max cheekily boots the ball past her. It spins around Lucy and shaves over Sahara's fabulous wild afro hair just as she's just about to try on a hat. The ball shoots through her arms, while she's still holding the hat up, and zooms directly into the display window, which shatters into pieces. We'll use special effects for this sequence, so don't worry, there'll be no glass flying around the place. But be careful and watch for the ball, as it may bounce back.'

'Are you sure that the glass won't smash? Someone could get hurt,' said Sahara.

'There's no need to worry. We've already replaced the window with safety glass so it won't break in reality, but in the commercial it will shatter, thanks to the special effects unit,' Marcello patiently answered.

He continued. 'Max then weaves his way around surprised shoppers back into the piazza and kicks the ball high into the air. More special effects – this time the ball lands on the roof of the cathedral, where Julian is posing as a photographer, taking shots of the magnificent marble facade and spires. He's among the tourists photographing the beautiful architecture when suddenly the ball bounces its way into his viewfinder. This sequence will look as if each of his movements is captured in a photograph. Julian scoops the ball up with his foot and starts juggling; he performs a few tricks including taking his shirt off while the ball rolls along his back. That sort of thing.'

'Can't wait to see that!' Sahara cheekily remarked. Mmmm she was very confident. I was definitely going to have to keep an eye on her around Max.

'Yes, now, moving on. In the meantime, I'm getting a few shots of you and Max racing to the roof in search of the ball. It's going to take a while, though, as it's a long climb up the old narrow stone staircase. We'll meet you up there – we're taking the lift.' He laughed. 'Once you reach Julian, who'll be in position on the upper rooftop, you'll both be captivated by his tricks, as I'm sure Sahara will be,' he said, giving her a wry smile. We all laughed now. 'You'll watch him perform a couple more of his impressive football tricks before Max makes his move like a prowling cheetah.' The director imitated the growl of the fearsome, agile creature. We tried not to laugh, but Max was impressed.

'Wow, the whole thing sounds much cooler when you're explaining it. I can't wait to start. Awesome!' Max excitedly remarked.

I thought Max was right. This experience was going to turn his life around. He just needed a bit of luck and this was it. I hoped he'd keep it together and stay interested.

Just as the director was about to explain the final scene, a scramble of paparazzi appeared. Click, click, click, but we couldn't see who they were bothering, as Papa and Mama were standing with us.

Mama, though, had a clearer picture of the celebrities caught up in the mayhem. She started gesticulating, saying, 'Lo . . . re . . . tta Soph . . . irelli! What is she doing here?'

'Frida, sweetheart, no one cares what she's up to, let her be. She means nothing to me. You are the love of my life. Please, let's not make a scene,' Papa quickly pleaded as he desperately tried to prevent an impending clash. He gently kissed her on the cheek and she melted for a moment.

But there was no doubt that the appearance of Loretta Sophirelli was going to cause problems. I positioned myself so that I could check out the source of our troubles, and there before my eyes was the famous actress, heading in our direction. She wore yellow stiletto heels, and a red cape dramatically swaying around a body-hugging, plunging canary-yellow dress, which revealed a petite, shapely figure, all framed by her long, dark, curly hair. The cameras couldn't get enough. She slowed her walk, parading like a proud peacock to allow the media the chance to take a few good shots.

And as if in slow motion, she seemed to call out something that was inaudible to us but amusing to those around her. Suddenly we were back in real time. She quickened her step towards us but it soon became clear that the photographers were also interested in someone else. Emerging from the media throng was a tall, suavelooking guy with shaggy shoulder-length dark brown hair. He was dressed in jeans, a fitted red and black AC Milan T-shirt, a deadly leather jacket and dark sunnies wrapped around his sculpted face. He casually caught up with the actress and they were forced to a halt when the cameras turned on him.

The media circus blocked their path, clicking and urgently yelling, 'Tommy, look this way!' Click click click. 'Tommaso, over here!' Click, click. 'Tommy, Tommy!'

We were all so stunned that no one uttered another sound. Papa was running his fingers through his hair, clearly uncomfortable, while Mama was openly seething as Loretta and Tommy broke from the media scrum and headed our way. The rest of the crew seemed to be enjoying the soap opera, which they knew would end up on the front page of tomorrow's paper and dominate internet gossip and sport news sites.

In an effort to quell the inevitable conflict, the director stopped them just a few metres away from my parents. 'Loretta, this is not the time or place to confront the Zoffis. I have a commercial to shoot and we're losing light, time and money thanks to this interruption. Please, do this in private and out of the media glare.'

Before she could respond, the unbelievable happened. 'No, no it's okay, Marcello, there's no better time than now. Let's get this matter sorted out immediately and that way everyone will know the truth about my son. It will put an end to all this speculation.' Papa was standing tall as the television cameras rolled and the photographers flashed. It was a bizarre situation.

Even though Papa had told me that it was true, I never thought he'd confirm that Tommaso was his son in front of the world media. I was shocked and so was everyone else. Papa was famously private about his family and hated idle gossip. I didn't know what to say or do. Max and Bella stood on either side of me and I could feel Max slowly take my hand and squeeze it. But it lasted just a moment.

As quickly as he'd taken my hand, he was gone. He stepped forward and madly – or bravely – broke the ice. 'Tommy the Tiger, oh man, what an honour. Your last goal was so awesome. You rock!'

Everyone smiled except for Mama, and inside I was bursting with laughter at Max's in-your-face manner and confidence.

'Thanks, man. Are you English?' Tommaso warmly responded, extending his hand. Max vigorously shook his hand for what seemed like an eternity.

'No mate, I'm an Aussie and a huge AC Milan fan,' Max declared, enjoying the media attention.

'It's good to meet an AC Milan fan from Australia. But you don't look like an Aussie,' replied Tommy as they kept snapping.

'Mate, I'm as Australian as they come. I'm Aboriginal!' Max said proudly.

Tommaso's face was a mass of confusion. 'You know, the first Australians. I'm Indigenous Australian!

'Oh, cool, Max. Of course!' Tommaso said warmly. 'Okay, that's enough friendly banter for now, boys.

You two can talk more later,' Papa interrupted. And he pulled Tommaso towards him, hugging him tightly.

The cameras went crazy! The array of flashing lights lit up the square like a bonfire.

Then to everyone's surprise, Papa faced the media with his arm still firmly planted over Tommaso's shoulder and proudly declared, 'This is my son, Tommaso. Tommy the Tiger!'

# Chapter 33

# Fiore giallo

It was bedlam. The media went nuts!

I stepped back to try and take in this wild scene. It was strange to see Papa in a tight embrace with his son, a son we'd only recently learnt existed. I felt forgotten.

I just wanted to run away, but Bella had me in a firm grip while Max kept his eyes planted on his heroes. The cameras never stopped clicking and I knew these images of my papa and his son Tommaso were being sent around the world!

'Lucy, don't worry. It's better that it's all out in the open now, and I wouldn't worry – you're still Daddy's little girl. That will never change,' she said, with her uncanny way of picking up on my thoughts.

Tommaso really *was* my half-brother and now the whole world knew thanks to Papa's bold and spontaneous announcement to the media. The big brother I'd wished for all my life was standing right in front of me and I wasn't sure how to respond. So, I decided to wait for someone else to make the first move. It wasn't long before Papa gently took my hand and included me in the happy family snap, declaring, 'Ladies and gentleman, my family: Lucia, Tommaso, and the love of my life, Frida!'

Papa expected her to join us, but she didn't move. She was standing alongside Marcello near one of the cameras just a few metres away. I thought that she was going to make a very public outburst, but to our relief, she thought better of it.

I didn't know what had come over Papa, but he was taking a huge gamble. It was like a massive weight had lifted from his shoulders but he didn't realise the impact on those around him.

Mama remained still, perfectly aware that all eyes were now on her, but knowingly playing a dangerous game.

Papa softly said to us, 'She wants me to go to her. Let's go and make her happy and show them that we are a family united!'

We nodded, but I was confused by his sudden concern for this sort of publicity. Or perhaps he was just so relieved to finally have all his family together. As we walked towards Mama, a winning smile spread across her face. Papa snugly wrapped his arm around her and squeezed her tight. He whispered in her ear, sharing an intimate moment while the cameras flashed. It was just the sort of thing she would have wanted. She played her part and unleashed a kiss on his cheek and pouted at the cameras. She reminded me of an Olympic champion, standing on the podium with the gold medal proudly hanging from her neck, savouring her moment of glory.

The cameras fired into yet another frenzy, click, click, click, the flashes flickering like fireflies. They now had more headlines to play with:

'The Zoffis home to roost.' 'Zoffi and Sophirelli team up.' 'A family affair at AC Milan.'

Mama's rival, Loretta Sophirelli, was suddenly left to wonder what could have been. The famous actress was, unusually, left in the background, out in the cold with no choice but to watch her son shine in the spotlight with his new family. This was a scene she obviously couldn't bear and she tried to slip away unnoticed.

But she wasn't completely off the radar; some of the media caught sight of as she tried to escape and started to chase her. She was bombarded by journalists and microphones were thrust in front of her face as they fired their questions for all to hear:

'Loretta, when did you break up with Paolo, or are you still seeing him?'

'What are your thoughts on Tommy's new family?' 'What's your relationship like with Frida?'

'What kind of father has Paolo been?

They were so unbelievable – they just couldn't get enough. They weren't interested in a happy family scenario. They only wanted to dig dirt and destroy families and reputations. I started to feel sorry for the actress and noticed Tommy's strained look.

'Tommy, you should go to her. She needs you,' I whispered to my big brother.

He seemed surprised at my advice, 'Of course I'm going to Mama's aid. Thank you, Lucia, you're a good kid.'

Kid? I'm not a kid!

He promptly left my side, but before he reached Loretta Marcello had stepped in to attack the media, 'Okay, that is enough! This is turning into a circus. I am in the middle of filming a commercial. You are costing me valuable time and money. I want you all off my set . . . now! You're all trespassing and I demand you leave now before I call the police.'

He waved his security team over and the media had no choice but to disperse, although they continued to take whatever shots they could while slowly retreating.

Marcello called his assistants, who fell into a huddle with him and within minutes Jasmin emerged, addressing the cast and crew, 'Everyone, we're breaking for a late lunch. Please return to the set promptly, one hour from now.'

With the media off our backs for now, we were all left to ponder an awkward situation.

Papa broke the ice. 'Lunch is a great idea. I'm starving. But let's all go to Cracco, they'll organise a private table for us.'

'Don't worry, Paolo, we already have a table waiting,' Marcello informed him.

'Impressive, let's go!' Papa said, his arm around Mama's waist.

She didn't appear to be too keen, but she went along with him.

Tommy caught up with us again. His handsome face was overpowered by a deep frown but he held his head high and addressed us. 'You must please excuse me, but I must go after Mama. I hope to persuade her to join us. If that is okay with you, Mrs Zoffi?' he bravely asked, looking straight into Mama's eyes.

At that moment I think that Tommy gained everyone's respect.

Mama stared at him and after what seemed like ages, she finally answered. 'Yes, of course it's fine with me. Thank you for asking. You're a good boy. Go to your mama.'

He gave Papa a nod and ran after Loretta.

I was surprised by Mama's response, but hey, it had been a very unusual day. So many surprises!

And perhaps the best thing to have come out of this drama was that it seemed to have brought my parents closer together. I watched them stroll like young lovebirds, Papa's arm affectionately draped over Mama's shoulders and her arm snuggled around his waist as we headed to the restaurant.

Max and Bella kept pace alongside of me. 'I hope Tommy comes back. He is so cute,' Bella burst out.

'Me too, but for different reasons,' agreed Max.

'Yeah, he seems cool. It just feels a bit strange to suddenly meet him. He's real. He's really my big brother. I don't know how it's going to work out and now Papa will have even less time with me,' I fretted.

'Lucy, stop worrying. It will work out just fine,' Bella said, trying to be reassuring. I hoped she was right.

We arrived at Cracco, one of our favourite restaurants. They served delicious modern Italian food and had very cute waiters. Carlo, the owner, gave us his usual very warm welcome and seated us in a special private area.

Max looked around with his eyes popping out of his head. 'Wow, this is a bit uptown.' Bella and I cracked up.

Mama said, 'Max, it's time you became used to places like this. No more eating from those soup kitchens.'

Wow, Mama was really loosening up. I loved this side of her and she was making such a huge effort with my friends. Papa ordered champagne for the adults and limonata and cola for the rest of us.

'Well, that was a very interesting morning,' Mama declared.

Marcello jumped in to change the subject, 'Ah yes, we have a lot of work to do when we are back on set, as we're behind schedule. Kids, you must be sharp and on the ball so to speak when we resume filming. We can't lose any more time.'

'After that drama, the rest of the day will probably be smooth sailing. Although I've gotta say that it was so cool to meet Tommy. He's a great footballer. You must be very proud of him, Paolo,' Max said.

'Well, yes I am. He is very talented, but more importantly, today he demonstrated that he's a very considerate young man. It's going to be great to have him involved in our lives,' Papa announced.

Well, that was all I needed. How on earth was I going to compete with my new brother, a top footballer playing at the same club as my papa?

'Princess, are you okay?' Papa asked. Bella gave me a quick nudge.

'Whoops, um, oh I'm fine, Papa,' I blurted.

Mama interjected, 'How about I order for everyone – unless you'd rather choose your own dishes?'

'No, no – you choose,' Papa replied and we all agreed. At that moment, I didn't think I could eat anything – my stomach was full of scattering butterflies as I thought of my new family situation.

Mama asked, 'Is anyone allergic to anything?' 'No!' they all answered in unison.

She loved taking the leading role and went about her duty with precision and little fuss. In the meantime we chatted about our scenes in the commercial. Bella was still beaming as she talked about her role, when suddenly her eyes locked onto the restaurant's entrance. Max and I followed her gaze.

Tommy had arrived, and as he strode up to our table, I could see the effect he was having on everyone. He even walked like Papa. He smiled at us all. 'Ciao! Apologies for my late arrival. Unfortunately my mama won't be joining us, but would love to meet you all soon. She has pressing engagements to attend to in the lead-up to the opening of her latest movie, *Fiore Giallo!*' He greeted Mama and Papa with kisses on both cheeks.

'Mrs Zoffi, I want to thank you for your understanding. Papa was right, you truly are a wonderful woman. He has told me so many great things about you.' He smiled charmingly at Mama. The arrow was released and . . . bullseye. He'd won her over already. Her perfect red lips stretched cheek to cheek in a delighted grin.

'Well, they're all true,' she giggled. 'And I've heard lots of about you, too. But please call me Frida.'

Papa interrupted, 'I had originally planned to organise a special dinner to introduce Tommy to the family, but his unexpected arrival with his mother on set seemed the perfect opportunity to tell the world about my son. I apologise if the situation made anyone feel uncomfortable, but it had to be done and I wanted to confirm the news myself. Hopefully those gossipmongers will now leave us alone – at least for a while.' He patted Tommy on the back.

'Papa, I think that you handled it beautifully. I'm very touched that you made such a personal announcement to the media. That was the proudest and most exciting moment of my life!' Tommy declared.

'What? Even better than scoring that incredible goal against Inter?' Max interjected, as we all laughed.

'That's a tough one, but yes, nothing beats being acknowledged by the Papa you've dreamed of all of your life. Nothing!' Tommy answered with complete honesty and conviction.

It was so weird to hear him refer to my papa as his. Mama also looked taken aback, but swallowed her emotions. It was going to take some time for Mama and I to get used to having Tommy around as a family member. It was going to change our lives forever – hopefully for the better.

Bella interrupted my thoughts. 'Oh my god, he is so cute. You've got to introduce me properly.'

'Okay Bella, but there's no rush. I've only just met him myself, remember? And don't start getting hung up on him, that would be too weird. Let's take this slowly,' I suggested, surprising myself. The last thing I needed was for

Bella to have a crush on him.

Instead of taking his seat next to Papa and Mama, Tommy darted towards me. He leaned over and said, 'Lucia, I'm so pleased to finally meet you too. I hope that we can become good friends. Papa told me that you're a very talented footballer. I noticed earlier that you even walk like one, you have a striker's gait. Let's play when you can fit it around your filming schedule.'

The tide had rapidly turned. He'd also won me over. My new brother actually got me after just a brief meeting. He wanted to play football . . . with me. This was amazing!

Beside me, Bella was almost drooling over him, and she joined our conversation. 'Oh, that's a great idea. I also love, um, football but I can't play, so I'll come and watch instead. Is that okay?' She fluttered her eyelashes.

I kicked her under the table to stop her making an even bigger fool of herself. What, now she's suddenly a football fan?

But she wasn't alone. Max couldn't wait to join her. 'Yeah, do you mind if I come too? I'd love to show you some of my tricks,' he said, while tucking into some garlic bread. 'Of course. I was going to ask you all to come, anyway.

It's settled then,' Tommy confirmed.

'That's a great idea. I will also join you. We'll go to Milanello. Bella, that's AC Milan's training facility and while we are there I will introduce Max to our team mates. I'm also looking forward to catching up with them and getting back into training, so it will be great for all of us,' Papa added.

'*Fantastico*!' Tommy exclaimed, slapping Max on the back.

Max's expression was priceless. I wish I could have taken a photo of that moment to show him.

My brother was proving very popular. I hoped that Mama maintained her friendly approach. So far it was all working well: fingers crossed it stayed that way.

A huge selection of food arrived at the table and it didn't take long for us to devour the delicious dishes.

Everything was going well until Mama abruptly enquired, 'So, Tommy, when did you find out that Paolo was your papa?'

We were stunned into silence at her query, but Tommy kept his cool and was about to answer when Papa jumped in. 'Leave it Frida, please!' he insisted, touching her hand.

Mama, to my surprise, zipped it and instead kept sipping her champagne.

'Papa, please, I'd like to answer,' Tommy said quietly.

Papa looked at his son with great pride. 'Of course, if that's what you wish.'

'Frida, I just found out a couple of years ago. I've grown up playing and loving football and the funny thing is that Mama was always trying to deter me from the game. She was really against it. But I was relentless and pursued my passion. Funnily enough, I'd always supported AC Milan. Last year when I made it into the AC Milan youth squad, people kept saying that I had an uncanny resemblance to Paolo Zoffi. Mama then felt compelled to tell me before the gossiping escalated any further.'

Papa stepped in. 'At least now it's all out in the open. We all have a lot to talk about, but for now, let's discuss the commercial. Marcello, I'd like you to include Tommy in the commercial, maybe in the closing scene. After Lucy finally wins the ball back from Max she could run with it and find Tommy walking by the equestrian statue in the Piazza del Duomo. She calls out his name and he looks up to see the ball in the air heading towards him. He takes one step back and leaps into the air with a perfectly timed scissor kick, which propels the ball straight into the barrel of the camera. What do you think?'

'That sounds awesome!' yelled Max.

Papa threw Max a wink and Marcello added with excitement, '*Smash*, the lens shatters, then we cut to Tommy and Lucy celebrating as though they are team mates. And the rest of the cast runs to them to shake hands. Enzo steps in with his camera, directing them to pose together for a team shot, flicking from one glamour shot to the other. We zoom into a close-up of Lucy and Tommy. He looks straight down the barrel of the camera and says, "No barriers in Love Lucy designs". I love it!'

'Yes, I do too, but that's only as long as Tommy is interested in appearing.

Well, Tommy?' Papa asked, with a very warm smile.

'I would be very honoured to play a part in the commercial. Thank you, Papa!' he declared. 'Frida, what do you think?'

She raised her champagne glass. 'I'm on the team.

Great idea!'

The surprises kept coming.

'You're the boss, Paolo, and I think it's a brilliant idea. It will work beautifully and give us much more publicity and marketing potential, thanks to Tommy's high profile. But Tommy, don't you have to check with your agent and AC Milan? Will we be able to work around your training sessions?' Marcello inquired, while we all digested the latest exciting twist to our first commercial together.

'I'm all yours. I'm sure the club will be supportive of the idea. And in regards to my manager, there'll be no issue there. I'm doing this for my family and nothing or no one is going to stop me. Lucia and I will have a ball. After all, I am a Zoffi,' Tommy said eagerly.

Papa held his head high and responded, 'Yes, son. You are a Zoffi!'

Mama kept sipping her champagne.

And then it struck me . . . Tommy was the son Papa had always wanted. Where did that leave me?

# Chapter 34

# Take two

Back at the Duomo, Chinese whispers were infiltrating the set. The crew was screening the piazza with greater intensity, keen to pick up more gossip. The paparazzi drama from earlier that day, and of course Papa's major announcement, which was by then all over the internet, were the only subjects of discussion.

'A boy for Zoffi. He's seventeen!' 'Another Zoffi at AC Milan.'

'Will Tommy live up to the Zoffi legend?'

It's fascinating how people don't seem to have anything better to do than to read about other people's lives!

Jasmin, the assistant director, addressed the cast. 'After a quick check with hair, make-up and wardrobe, I want everyone on set in fifteen minutes ready to shoot scene two, where Bella is trying on the red shoes in the Love Lucy store.'

Anastasia and her assistants checked us carefully from head to toe. 'Thank goodness no one spilt anything on those outfits. Next time you leave the set, please change first! Luckily you all still look fabulous. A little touch up here and there and you'll be ready to go.'

After a dab more lipstick and blush and some extra spray in our hair, Anastasia gave us the go-ahead. 'Right, you can all go, except for Lucy. I just need to make a few more adjustments and she'll join you in a moment.'

She took me aside. 'Sweetie, I really felt for you earlier. That was a very confronting situation you had to face, especially in front of the scumbag media – you handled it very well. I just want to make sure that you're okay. You can talk to me about anything, any time.'

'Thanks, Anastasia. I was a little bit shocked at the time, but I'm okay. Tommy's really nice. I like him. It's just going to take a little time to get used to having him around. In fact I think it'll make me happier having a big brother to hang with on and off the pitch. I guess I am a bit scared about sharing Papa with him,' I divulged. It was good to get that off my chest and I knew that I could trust Anastasia.

She hugged me and whispered, 'I know that your papa loves you very much and would never leave out his princess. It won't take you that long to get used to Tommy, especially since you both love football. Anyway, he won't be around that much – as you know, he'll be spending most of his time with AC Milan and travelling the world playing football.'

'You're right, there's nothing to worry about. I feel so much better talking to you about it. I'd better get out there before they send a search party. You're the best,' I said. It was at that moment that I realised what had been niggling at me.

Tommy was living my dream and more – he's going to be playing alongside Papa every week. They would be together all the time, training, travelling, playing football all over the country and around the globe while I was stuck at school and back in Sydney.

I ran across the piazza to the Love Lucy store and found Bella in her element: it was actually a Prada store, which we rented and rebranded for the shoot. She was admiring the merchandise while getting final touch-ups. Marcello called me over for my final instructions. 'Lucy, you'll be chasing Max along the Galleria. Once I call action, I want you both to keep going until you hear "cut". We'll probably have to do this sequence a couple of times until I think we have what I want.'

And there was Tommy standing alongside Papa and Mama near the director's monitor. His arm was around Papa and they laughed together as if no one else existed. I knew it was probably silly, but I felt as if I'd been punched in the stomach. Something rotten was swirling and I felt ill. I was in a fit of jealousy. I knew I had nothing to be jealous *of*, but I couldn't control my raw emotions.

I suddenly felt saliva filling my mouth. My gut heaved and before I knew it, I was vomiting. It was vile and humiliating but it was too late – the damage was done.

Everyone ran to me as I crouched to the floor. An unfortunate crew member had to clean up the horrible mess, while I tried to hide my face. I was dying of embarrassment.

Mama sped to me and put her arm over my shoulder. 'Lucy, come with me. You need to sit down and rest. Someone get her some water. Now!'

She took me back to the make-up trailer, where Marcello, Papa and Tommy joined us. 'My little princess, are you all right? Maybe we should call it a day,' Papa suggested, his face creased with concern.

'No, I'm fine, Papa. It must have been something I ate. I just need a short rest and I'll get back on the set. I'm sorry,' I blurted, still embarrassed.

'Lucy, are you sure you're feeling up to it? We can shoot Bella's close-ups now and do your main scenes tomorrow,' Marcello reassured me.

'No, really. I feel much better now. I just need a few minutes and I'll be ready for action,' I declared, trying to sound upbeat.

Marcello spoke to his assistant, who in turn yelled out to the crew, 'Let's get the close-ups of Bella while Lucy takes a short break.'

Tommy sat next to me. 'Wow, Lucia, you're a tough kid. I like that. I'm glad you're feeling better. I think that we're going to have lots of fun doing this commercial together.'

Feeling like a fool, I gave him a forced smile. How could I not like him? He said everything I wanted to hear, he was so considerate and more importantly, he was trying! He also knew how to grab my attention.

'Lucia, perhaps our game after today's shoot should be changed to something a little gentler? If you're feeling up to it, how about we just go shopping, grab a gelato or whatever tickles your fancy. Of course, as long as that's okay with Papa and Frida.'

Wow, a guy who liked shopping. He was most girls' dream. And even though shopping wasn't my favourite pastime, I knew I'd enjoy finding out more about him over a gelato.

Papa immediately nodded with approval while Mama followed with a forced smile, 'That's a lovely idea, but why don't you do it another day? I think Lucy needs to rest.'

'Oh Mama, I'm fine. I'd love to hang out with Tommy,' I insisted.

'Okay, it's fine with me then, as long as you're up to it,' she reluctantly agreed.

'Lucy, how are you feeling?' Anastasia asked while touching up my make-up.

'Great, I'm ready to go,' I replied with renewed vigour. More ready than I'd ever been. I couldn't wait to show Tommy – I mean my big brother – my football skills.

'Positions, everyone!' yelled Jasmin.

'Max, you've just come from the piazza where you won the ball from Lucy. She's giving chase and mustn't win the ball back. It's the battle of the sexes and for now it's the boys who reign supreme. Keep going until you reach the store. Then we'll work out a move to get the ball to Bella's feet.'

He nodded, grinning.

'Cool, but I don't like to lose. Max, you'd better be at your best,' I cockily challenged.

'I'm ready for anything, Lucy. Bring it on!' he countered.

'Yeah, like she's going to beat a boy,' I heard a crew member say sarcastically.

I'll show him, I'll show them all!

'Quiet please and ACTION!' called the director.

Max took off through the Galleria as I gave chase like my life depended on it. The cameras were invisible to me, I just focused on the ball, trying to win it back. Max was weaving in and out of the extras and really showing his talent. The only way I thought I could secure the ball was through the element of surprise, and without a second thought I leapt into the air and caught the ball on my way down, my legs unfolding into the splits.

'Oh my god!' I heard someone shout.

I swung my outside leg around and moved up to my feet, flicking the ball up to my chest to keep control while Max stared in shock.

'Game on!' I snarled back.

That's all he needed to chase after me. We bolted along the Galleria, constantly dodging extras playing locals and tourists. But Max was one of the best defenders I'd ever come across and it didn't take long for him to steal the ball from under me. He flicked it up into the air and volleyed it. The ball spiralled away from us with a lot of power and flew into the Prada store. Bella was ready, but instead of moving or trying to head the ball, she froze. The cameras kept rolling as the ball hit her in the face. The force pushed her back onto the sofa and she delivered her first – unscripted – word. 'Arghh!'

'Cut, cut! Oh dear, Bella. How's your face?' asked Marcello.

We all ran to her side, except for you-know-who. 'It'll be fine when I throw the ball straight back at that big goose. Max, where are you?' she yelled, a hand pressed over one eye. A crew member attended to her with an ice pack while Max wisely kept out of her sight.

'Thank goodness you're fine. Max and Lucy, great action back there. Where's Max?' called the director, while the crew gave us a round of applause. Max stuck his head out from the store next door and awkwardly waved. Marcello called him over, 'Come on Max, it was an accident.'

Max cautiously walked out, anticipating Bella's fury. But he soon forgot his troubles when showered with praise.

'Lucy and Max, that was something else, except of course when the ball hit Bella. You should both be playing for AC Milan,' boasted Papa.

I wish! Maybe I should have been a boy. Then again, I could just keep chasing my dream of being a Matilda!

'Max, you idiot! What were you thinking? How could you aim the ball at my face? Now I have a black eye at the worst time possible. I was about to live my dream and now it's shattered because of you. You've ruined everything. I hate you. I hate you!' Bella cried, holding an icepack over her left eye.

'Bella, I'm so sorry. I really didn't mean it. I didn't aim the ball at you. It was an accident,' Max pleaded.

'Bella, you poor thing. But it won't take long to heal.

Max really didn't mean it,' I said sheepishly.

'He was supposed to kick it to my foot so that I could try and stop it. You're the footballers, not me! I was in shock. He's an idiot. He did it on purpose. And you're always defending him. Why can't you for once be on my side?' she snarled, tears rolling down her face.

'Can we chill out, please? Now is not the time or place to talk about this,' I said through clenched teeth, trying to calm her down.

Marcello stepped in. 'Bella, let me take a look at your eye. Oh, that's a bruiser all right, but don't worry, it will heal sooner than you think. We got the ice on quickly and we've already shot your close-ups, so you'll have fun throwing Love Lucy shoes at Max, which we'll film tomorrow. Anastasia will work her magic around your eye and you won't even notice any bruising. It'll be fine. Just remember that when the time comes I want lots of aggression when we film you throwing the shoes at him.' The director knew how to get the best out of his cast. 'You're on! There won't be any problems coming up with that emotion. I can't wait,' Bella said with a satisfied grin.

Marcello didn't stop there: 'Oh and Bella, you're a natural. I think that you have the potential to be an actress or model. You shine on camera, you have that star quality and it's not something you can teach.'

Bella fluttered her eyelashes – then fainted like a true actress!

# Chapter 35

# Princess Lucia

This was the most fun I'd ever had on a shoot. I wished it could always be like this. And of course you couldn't beat the football aspect.

'Marcello wants us to set up for scene three with Sahara in the milliners' store,' Jasmin instructed the crew, while Enzo captured each moment, clicking his camera at every opportunity.

'Wait, I've just been told that Tommy's ready for the last scene. Quickly set up back in the centre of the piazza, now! I'll need all the talent, including Bella, standing by,' ordered Marcello.

The crew frantically began setting up for the final scene, giving us time for a quick drink. I grabbed a limonata and tried to stay out of sight behind one of the stores to get some time to myself. It had been a big day and I was reflecting on the unexpected events that had caught all of us off-guard when I heard a familiar voice.

'Princess, I've been looking all over for you,' Papa said.

'What is it, Papa?' I asked.

'I just wanted to let you know that I'm very proud of the way you've been conducting yourself. I'm blessed to have such a beautiful and intelligent daughter. I love you so much and I want you to know that no one will ever come between us. There can only ever be one princess, my Princess Lucia!' Papa said, giving me a hug.

I suddenly found myself crying. I had so desperately needed to hear that.

He held me close to his chest and added, 'I didn't mean to announce this important news in front of a media circus like that. I hope you'll forgive me.' I nodded, as I couldn't be angry with him. I knew that he loved me but it felt even better when he told me. 'I'm touched by the way you have accepted Tommy and how you are making an effort to spend time with him. I want nothing more than the two of you getting along. It means a lot to me. I'm lucky to be blessed with such great kids. You're my best girl and he's my best boy!'

I wiped my tears and mumbled, 'Papa, I'm very happy to have a big brother like Tommy, but why didn't you tell us about him sooner?'

'Lucy, it was all too complicated at the time, and I felt it was best to keep him a secret, especially in my position. I agreed to help Loretta financially. Even though she now earns big money as a movie star, the minute I discovered I had a son, I wanted to contribute to his upbringing. I couldn't turn my back on them. I want you to know that I knew Loretta before your mama. Frida is the love of my life and Loretta is the mother of my son, so I have to be courteous with her. We are only in contact because of Tommy. As you know, our lives are blown out of proportion in the media and at the time they could have destroyed me. We all have our secrets, some bigger than others, but I promise no more like this. Anyway, I'm glad it's out in the open, but let's talk about it in more detail another time. It looks as though they're ready to resume filming,' Papa said.

'Okay, and Papa, I love you with all my heart.' I blew him a kiss, while I thought about the secrets I'd kept.

I was relieved. I knew Papa loved me and that we'd be happy as a family once again, but all this had happened so fast and I guess it was going to take time to come to terms with everything.

Right on cue, Tommy appeared from the dressing room, wearing Love Lucy designs – a white fitted T-shirt with a big red heart, a black jacket covered with zips, and dark denim slimline jeans and black D&G gymboot-type sneakers.

'What a honey,' someone whispered in my ear.

'Oh, Bella, settle down, that's my brother you're talking about,' I laughed, worried that her crush was growing.

'Man, I've got to get myself an outfit like that,' Max remarked, checking out his other idol.

'Der, Max, you're wearing the same label but different colours. Anyway, it doesn't matter, there's no way that you could look as good as him. Dream on!' Bella stirred.

Bella was hooked and she was right. Tommy was perfect for the commercial. The label looked great on him – mind you he'd look great in anything – and more importantly his endorsement would attract football fans to the Love Lucy label.

'All the talent are wanted on set, now!' yelled Jasmin. Anastasia and her assistants made some more lastminute adjustments and touch ups and we ventured back on set. We gathered around the director and he didn't waste any time.

'Tommy, it's great you're playing a part in this commercial. In the final scene, young Julian here will head the ball from the top of the cathedral. Again, we'll use special effects here. We'll shoot the close-ups of Julian's scene tomorrow. As the ball comes spiralling from the sky, Max and Lucy will be racing down the steps of the cathedral to reach it first as it drops onto the piazza. It's a fight, a tussle, a challenge to win it and it's Lucy who gets to the ball. Max is forced to defend and desperately tries to steal it from her.'

Max interrupted, 'I don't think this is fair. I don't want to look like a sissy,' he complained.

'Max, you must follow what's in the script and my directions. Lucy's the face of the label, so she must win at the end,' Marcello asserted. For a director he was being extremely patient with us.

'Max, what's with the attitude? I thought we were past that boys-are-better-than-girls thing. I can kick your butt any day. And you know it!' I teased, while the crew bellowed, 'oooohhh!' in unison.

Max's mood changed immediately. His face heated up with determination, like a boxer trying to intimidate his opponent.

Marcello was frothing at the sight of his actors preparing for a heated battle, and he gave us the final direction for the scene.

'Perfect!' Marcello said. 'This is just what I'm looking for. Final places everyone. Now Lucy, when you win the ball, Max will chase you and then you'll spot Tommy walking near the equestrian statue. Call out his name and kick a floating ball or cross, or whatever you call it, towards him so that he can scissor kick it straight at the camera lens. Now, instead of the illusion of it shattering, we've decided that we're going to make it look as though Tommy has scored a goal, but then the ball ends up hitting the crossbar. It bounces back out and Lucy, you pounce and clean up for the winner. Just do whatever you would normally do when you have a chance to seize the moment and score. And with another slight change in the script, I'd like you to look down the barrel of the camera and with your arms punching the air, say, with attitude, "There are NO barriers in Love Lucy". Got it?'

'But where's the goal?' I asked, confused.

'It's at the San Siro stadium. That's where the ball ends up. It's all an illusion and at the end the viewers will be celebrating Lucy's winning goal against AC Milan.'

Everyone laughed. 'Wow, you mean we beat AC Milan? That's amazing,' I exclaimed.

'Yes, well you'll beat their first team keeper. Paolo managed to convince the club to be a part of the campaign. It's very exciting. And you have to love technology, it can take you anywhere! Let's shoot while we have the right mood. Everyone in positions . . . and action!' Marcello ordered, endeavouring to capture the competitive tension.

As the ball fell from the sky among the swarm of frenzied pigeons flapping to get out of the way, Max didn't stick to the director's instructions, but emerged ahead of me from the imposing cathedral and onto the piazza, which was a hive of activity. There were people shopping, tourists checking out the historic area and taking photos, the Milanese chilling out, a few cyclists – they were all actors playing their part to make the piazza look realistic. They were also trying to avoid the flock of pigeons, but that didn't stop Max from breaking ahead. He bolted out with the determination of a hungry lion chasing its prey while I followed on his trail, like a hunter trying to capture the majestic beast.

And it was the king of the jungle who conquered, as the hunter weaved and taunted its target to no avail. His stride was longer and faster and with the ball at his feet he was nearly unstoppable.

Max savoured his brief moment of victory, but the smile on his face soon faded as I came up with the unexpected. I drew on a ballet move to take him by surprise once again. I leapt into the air, aiming for the grace of a gazelle, propelled myself forward and landed perfectly in front of him.

He froze on the spot with the ball parked under his left boot. 'Unbelievable!' he squealed.

I threw him a quick grin. 'Who's better now?' I boasted, as I swiftly swept the ball from under him and dribbled along the piazza, looking up to kick a floating ball to Tommy. But he wasn't on his mark. I frantically searched for him as Max caught up with a vengeance. I managed to keep the ball but there was no sign of Tommy. I breathed a sigh of relief when the director finally yelled, 'Cut!'

# Chapter 36

# The key

Elite footballers like my papa were revered across the globe. This was especially true in football-mad Italy. They were treated like gods, sent expensive designer gifts, inundated with invitations to exclusive parties and functions, wined and dined by film stars, high-profile business people, and politicians, and adored by anyone and everyone with a passion for football, sport or celebrity.

But you couldn't always know who your friends were. Who did you trust? That was something I'd learnt as the daughter of a famous footballer. Lots of people just wanted to hang around you and be seen in your company because it might help them become famous. They saw it as a springboard to success, or perhaps they enjoyed the taste of fame of being photographed with famous people. It was funny to watch them in action. Because of this, Papa was very wary of who he allowed into our inner circle, which was mostly made up of childhood friends and his close team mates. It was very hard for an outsider to find a key into the group. There was always the question of what they wanted from us and whether they could be trusted.

I was lucky to have Bella and Max. I trusted them completely, and now Tommy had come into my life, my new brother in my inner circle. And maybe he'd be my new confidante. He could certainly trust me with anything.

But because he was in the public eye as a new star striker for AC Milan, and most importantly as the son of Paolo Zoffi, he had to tread carefully. There'd be high expectations and comparisons to the Zoffi legend, even though they played in different positions. Everyone was going to want a piece of him for various reasons and women would desperately try to grab his attention in the hope of winning his heart and leading a glamorous highsociety life.

I couldn't think of anything worse than having to be so careful, but I was a little envious in one respect. Tommy was fortunate because he held the key to the door of the football world, the world I wanted. He was living my dream as an AC Milan elite footballer, running out of the San Siro tunnel to the roar of the devoted *rossoneri*, the AC Milan fans, and – if Papa stayed in Milan at the end of the shoot – alongside Papa. It was something I could never achieve, being female. But it wasn't going to stop me from following my dream to go to the top of world football. Even though the women's game didn't receive the high profile and respect that the men's game did, I knew that one day it would. Passion was every- thing, and along with hard work it would lead me to my ultimate destination – playing in the Women's Football World Cup.

In the men's event, the best national teams in the world battle it out for the game's most treasured prize, the ultimate trophy on the planet. And Tommy had a chance to be part of it, with a high possibility of being selected for Italy's World Cup squad. He had already made everyone take notice of his goalscoring ability. There was already talk in the media that he'd be an integral part of the striking force in the Italian national team, the *Azzurri*. It was just a matter of time before the national manager gave him the call-up. He had it all! My dream life was being played out right in front of me.

But right now a hunt was on for Tommy and it had turned the Piazza del Duomo into a madhouse. Papa tried to reach him on his mobile, but it just kept ringing out.

The security guards indicated that they hadn't spotted anything unusual but then again, they hadn't even noticed whether he'd made it onto the set. He was hard to miss and I could have guaranteed if they were female guards they wouldn't have taken their eyes off him.

We were becoming extremely concerned and Papa was starting to get agitated. 'This isn't like him. He wouldn't just leave without notifying us, and I know that he had cancelled all his other plans so he could work on the shoot with us this afternoon. It's very strange. He wouldn't just run out on us . . . unless something was very wrong.'

We were standing in front of the monitor, searching through the footage we'd just filmed in case there was a shot of him in the background that might give us a clue. And then Anastasia came running towards us from the make-up van.

'Marcello, I'm sorry, I didn't realise there was such a panic about Tommy. I tried to warn you earlier but you'd started filming so I had to wait till you were finished,' she said, breathlessly.

'Warn me about what?' Marcello impatiently asked.

'That Tommy received a phone call just as he was about to come out onto the set to take his position. He was listening intently to the person on the other end and then became distressed and started shouting, "What? How did this happen?". His face turned a sickly white and he ran out of the van yelling, but I couldn't catch what he was saying as I was steaming an outfit. I'm sorry,' Anastasia apologised.

'It's all right. We'll get to the bottom of this. I think we're going to have to call it a day and resume filming early tomorrow morning,' Marcello informed us. He called over his assistant and instructed her to dismiss the talent and crew after giving them the call sheets for tomorrow.

And at that moment Papa's phone rang and he answered. After listening in silence for a few seconds, he exclaimed, 'What, no! No, it can't be. But how did it happen? I'm on my way.'

Papa looked at us with a very grim face, 'I must go to the hospital now.'

'What's happened?' Mama asked, but he didn't answer.

We stared at Papa and I was sure we were all thinking the same thing.

I built up the courage and asked, 'Is it Tommy?' I could feel my head swirling, hoping that it wasn't him, that he wasn't hurt.

But Papa was already sprinting ahead to our car and before we could catch up he was gone.

Marcello yelled after us, 'Frida, Frida, wait, I'm coming with you. I've seen the news headlines on my phone – it says "Sophirelli seriously injured", but it doesn't give any more details. It must be Loretta.'

# Chapter 37

# The star

Loretta Sophirelli was Italy's leading actress, a screen siren and megastar whose performances on film and on stage received great acclaim. She was a brilliant actress – she not only made the screen sizzle, but was renowned for delving into her characters so deeply that she'd often need some time off after each film to recuperate. Women wanted to be just like her and men viewed her as the ideal woman. She was often compared to Italian film legend Sophia Loren, but Loretta was her own woman – feisty, intelligent, uncompromising, and a natural dark beauty. She had the curves in all the right places, an hourglass figure, yet petite. Although quite short, she was larger than life. She was considered one of Italy's most beautiful women, the best actress of her time and an ambassador for the nation. She represented the modern-day Italian woman and was a role model for single-parent families.

She had come from very humble beginnings. Her parents used to run a small bakery in the northeast of Milan, which struggled to survive. Loretta had to be up every morning by 4 am to help bake the bread. Once she had finished helping her parents she'd have to make breakfast for herself and her brother Franco before they headed off for school. She and Franco grew up to become fanatical AC Milan supporters, just like their father. But she also dreamt of girlie things, and escaped from her everyday life by going to the local movie theatre. That's where she wanted to be, she had decided from an early age – on the big screen, unreachable, and leading a life of luxury.

She was also captivated by the theatre and in the little spare time she had, she volunteered to work on local productions, working backstage, making props and helping the actors with their costumes. She used to memorise the lines of all the characters as she sat backstage, dreaming of the day when she would get her chance to act on the big stage.

And one day that opportunity arrived. It was during a season of Shakespeare's *Romeo and Juliet*. On the fourth night the lead actress was off sick with flu. Halfway through the play, the understudy who'd stepped in to play Juliet went over on her ankle and had to limp for the rest of the performance. When she came offstage, she fell in agony, her ankle swollen and blue.

The cast and crew were devastated and thought that the play's run would have to be cancelled, but the stage manager alerted them to Loretta's talent. 'But we don't need to close the show – Loretta knows Juliet's lines. In fact she knows each character's lines and actions by heart.'

The director had approached her and said, 'Loretta, is this true?'

Dressed in her overalls, dirty from her work backstage, and with her hair in ponytails, the then fifteen-year-old replied, 'Yes, I can recite the whole play word for word.'

No one had ever really looked closely at Loretta before. She had assisted the stage manager, made coffee for the actors and helped with their costumes, make-up and anything else they needed. But now she had captured everyone's attention and the director noticed her gorgeous big brown eyes for the first time. He realised that tied up in those ponytails, she had luscious curly hair. His eyes lit up when she recited a few of Juliet's lines from the play, and the rest of the cast was immediately convinced. The director was thrilled. 'Perfecto! We have our Juliet.'

That was the start of Loretta's career and she never looked back.

It was a strange feeling having a big brother and driving off to the hospital because his mama had been hurt. I wondered what had happened to Loretta. Mama kept trying to reach Papa on the mobile. 'What's going on? I can't get through,' she moaned. 'This is so frustrating. I hope Tommy's all right.'

'I pray for that more than anything,' I surprised myself by saying. I hadn't realised until now how much he really meant to me. Mama seemed to relate to this. She put her arms around me and as if reading my mind, said, 'Don't worry, I'm sure he's fine.'

The taxi pulled up and we all sprinted into the hospital. Mama asked the receptionist about Loretta and was directed to the emergency department.

I whimpered to Max and Bella, 'This can't be good.' 'Quick!' Mama yelled and stormed ahead with such an urgency in her step, it must have worn down her heels.

We trotted to the waiting room to find Papa pacing up and down the room. I ran to him crying, 'Papa, Papa, is Tommy all right? Please tell me he's okay, please. What's going on?'

'Lucy, Lucy, he's okay. At first, I also thought something had happened to Tommy, but –'

Before Papa could finish, Tommy appeared from behind the white swinging doors. He was pale and a bit unkempt, but he was okay! Everyone was so relieved. Tommy was wiping away a few tears, and we were all wondering what had happened. In such a short time Tommy had already made a huge impact on my life and had also impressed everyone else. I was so glad to have a big brother!

Tommy leant over to Papa, 'She's going to be fine. The knock on the head left her unconscious for a while, but thank god it isn't serious. She just needs to stay here overnight for observation.'

Mama stepped in. 'Tommy, we're so relieved that you are okay, but we don't really know what's going on. What happened?' she asked.

'It's Mama. She was hurt during a press conference while promoting her latest film. The media were hounding her about Papa and me, instead of asking questions about her film, so she stormed out. They chased her down the street, bombarding her with more questions, and she tripped over and hit her head on the pavement. It instantly knocked her out, but thankfully she's going to be all right.'

I was so relieved for Tommy but I knew he was hurting and had been shocked to find his mama unconscious. I leant over and wrapped my arms around him.

'Thank you, Lucia, you really are a good girl. I'm lucky to have you as a sister,' he smiled. Papa also unfolded a smile of satisfaction. But then he became serious.

'Those paparazzi are devils! They never know when to stop,' he said. 'Come on, let's go. There's nothing more we can do here. The good news is that Loretta is going to be fine and she'll be well looked after. We have the best doctor taking care of her and the staff will ensure that she is comfortable, so Tommy, there's no need to worry. It's been a very big day for all of us. It's time we went home and rested. We'll come back and visit her in the morning.'

'You're right, Papa. I just want to go in and see her once more before we leave. Will you come with me?' Tommy gently asked.

Papa hesitated. This was a bit awkward, but Mama just looked at him and nodded her head.

'Of course, I'll come with you, Tommy,' he replied.

I suddenly blurted, 'Can I come too?' I don't know what I was thinking, it just came out. I guess my curiosity got the better of me. I think I wanted to share this moment with them.

Tommy briefly looked at me and answered, 'Okay, Lucia, let's go.'

Mama didn't seem to mind and took a seat next to Bella and Max to wait for us.

We stepped into the white clinical room, eerily silent except for the sound of a beeping machine monitoring Loretta's heartbeat. The leading light had faded to a falling star. Yet although she lay in a hospital bed far from the spotlight, she still looked beautiful. She was perfectly still, angelic in her sleep.

Tommy tenderly lifted his mama's limp hand and kissed it. He whispered, 'I love you Mama. I'll be back soon. Ciao!'

And we walked out after him. Papa put his arm around Tommy in support. Mama looked up. 'How is she?' she asked.

'Sleeping peacefully. Hopefully, she'll be up and out of here tomorrow,' replied Tommy.

I rejoined Max and Bella, who'd been waiting on the seat but Max's patience had run out. 'I've got to get out of here. I can't take this much longer. I hate hospitals. I haven't been in one since I lost my parents. See ya!' he cried as he stood up to leave.

I wasn't sure whether to go with him or not. Bella made the decision for me. 'We must stay here for Tommy. Anyway, Lucy, your parents won't like you running off. Max, let's just stay put and be cool.'

'Sorry Bella, you don't understand. I can't be here any longer' he stressed, shaking his head.

'But Max, where are you going?' I asked, worried he'd disappear again.

'I just want to go for a walk. I need fresh air. I can't breathe in here. I'll meet you back at the house later,' he said breathlessly.

'I'm coming with you,' I insisted, standing up.

Papa stepped in. 'Max, perhaps we should all go. The hospital will call when your mama wakes up, Tommy – and I'll bring you back myself.'

Tommy nodded grimly. 'I guess you're right.'

We huddled together solemnly and headed for the hospital's exit. As soon as we were out the doors we hit a wall of nosy reporters and television cameras, fighting for prime position on the hospital's front steps.

Tommy threw his hoodie over his head, trying to hide his tortured face as they rapidly fired questions.

'Tommy, what's your mama's condition?' 'How are you coping?' 'Do you think it was an accident?'

Tommy unexpectedly yelled, 'If you hadn't chased her, she'd be fine. Now leave me alone or you'll end up in there where you all belong! Scum, you're all scum!'

His outburst didn't stop them. In fact, the media was pushing for blood. It was a frenzied attack as they jostled with one another, took photos and threw more questions into the air, and I lost sight first of Max and then of Tommy. They had both escaped, running for different reasons, although they shared a strange bond. Their manoeuvring skills on the pitch served them well, as they must have weaved out of the media's glare with relative ease – out of sight like sly old foxes.

Tommy would have to get used to the media circus, because they'd never leave him alone. But for now he had escaped the pack to find solace somewhere – and so had the other fox!

# Chapter 38

# Amore

In one of those ironic twists of fate, the drama surrounding Loretta's accident brought my parents closer together. They were hanging out more on set, laughing, embracing each other like new lovebirds. I was so happy that they seemed to have sorted out their problems.

They signalled me over as I waited for my turn in make-up. They were in each other's arms and Mama brought me into the huddle. 'Lucy, I'm sorry if we caused you any concern, but from now on we're a family again and a very happy one. It's important that you know that I've accepted Tommy as a member of our family and we will do everything we can to make him feel comfortable. As for Loretta, we will help her as much as possible to ensure that she's back to full health soon. I'm very proud of you and I must say that your friends have also impressed me on this trip. Max especially. He may be a little rough around the edges, but he has shown me that he's a well-rounded young boy with hopes and dreams just like you.'

Max and Tommy had turned up at the house late last night. They'd apparently hung out for a while together and then crashed on the lounges in the main living room. And there was no missing them at breakfast, as they ate nearly everything in sight. I was so relieved that they were home and safe, and I think Papa felt exactly the same, because he fussed over them as if they were toddlers. 'Can I get you something else to eat? Would you like some hot chocolate?' But there was no answer because they were too busy munching.

Mama took my hand. 'Lucy, I meant to tell you before, but with all the drama, it slipped my mind. I thought you'd like to know that we've had a call from Sydney. You have been accepted into the Sydney Dolphins team. Congratulations, I'm so proud of you, sweetheart.'

'Oh Mama, thank you. That's so cool. I'm a Dolphin! It makes up for missing out on the Beckham Academy scholarship,' I said cheekily.

Mama coughed, clearing her throat. 'I'm so sorry about that, but I just want what's best for you.'

'I know, Mama,' I said. 'I understand now. I have everything I want, anyway. Maybe one day Papa could organise a kick-around for me with his friend, David. That would make up for it!' We all laughed, a happy family together at last. 'I love you both so much. Where is Tommy?'

'We trained earlier this morning, which was a great distraction, because he also went to see his mama beforehand. The doctor wants Loretta to stay in hospital for more tests, although they're confident that she's fine. Then hopefully she can go home. But Tommy is understandably concerned, so I hope training – and the commercial – will help him forget his troubles,' Papa said. 'He's just in the park now, and is due back on set very soon.'

Mama stepped in. 'And guess what? Tommy has already spent some time with Grandpa and Nanna – they like him a lot – and of course Gigi. In fact, he's quite smitten with Gigi. They're strolling in Parco Sempione at the moment. Your grandparents are happy enjoying the sights. They'll meet us at home later tonight, perhaps. I think that they're having a romantic holiday.'

We all giggled at the thought. At last we were getting back to normal as a family. I just hoped that it stayed that way. 'It's a shame Gigi can't be here on the set,' I said, missing my munchkin doggie.

'Well, she'd be too much of a distraction. She'd try to chase the football and get in the way of the filming, and Marcello wouldn't be happy about that! Anyway, Gigi's having far too much fun with your grandparents,' Papa stated.

'Lucy, they're ready for you in make-up,' called Jasmin.

I stepped into the trailer and there he was. My big brother in a make-up chair, with Anastasia taking care of him. I sat in the make-up chair beside him as Gia started on my face.

'Ciao Tommy, how's your mama?' I asked, surprised he was already on set.

'She's much better thanks, Lucia. She'll be out this afternoon,' he smiled.

'That's great news. Hey, can you do me a favour? Can you please call me Lucy?' I asked.

'Okay,' he agreed.

I was watching the fuss Anastasia was making over him.

'You have a fabulous mop of hair, but it needs a good treatment, or maybe a meeting with my scissors.' Before Tommy could say anything, she snipped her weapon in the air. His locks started to fall rapidly to the ground. Gia was finishing up my make-up as I giggled at Anastasia's boldness.

Anastasia called out to Sofia, 'Sweetie, please let Marcello know that Tommy will be ready in two and Lucy won't be far behind.' She knew the drill and she also knew how to make people feel at ease. I don't know what we would have done without her during filming. She was really amazing!

'Okay, Tommy, you are ready, and I must say that you could be on the cover of a fashion magazine with a face like that. Do you really need to play football?'

Tommy flashed a grin and replied, 'Football is my passion. Modelling isn't for me. But I'm happy doing this for my family and, besides, it's giving me the chance to hang out with my little sister, Lucia ... I mean Lucy.'

I gave him an affectionate knock on the shoulder. 'Music to my ears! I'd also rather have a football at my feet but this isn't so bad. In fact I'm enjoying it – especially knowing that I get to score the winner and beat the AC Milan keeper. That's priceless.'

'You're both mad. I'd rather be pampered and have everyone fussing over me as I pose for a photographer than run around after a football getting sweaty. But each to their own. Now, you crazy thing, fly out of here and knock them dead,' Anastasia encouraged. 'You guys make the Love Lucy label look like the *IT* label. Every cool young person will want to look just like you. *Bellissimo*!' Anastasia said proudly.

Then she called out, 'Strut it, Lucy! Strut it, girl!' I just laughed.

Soon after, the rest of the gang joined me on set, ready to plunge into the scene.

The director's assistant, Jasmin, instructed, 'We're shooting the final scene with Tommy. Marcello is just checking a few things with his DOP and will be over shortly to give you further directions.'

Bella, Max, Sahara, Julian and I stood around chatting. But Tommy was standing alone. His face lit up as he peered at a building close by. I moved next to him and followed his eyeline – an enormous billboard for Loretta's latest movie, *Fiore Giallo*, was plastered high above the street. Her smiling face dominated the heavens and I couldn't help staring. She was so beautiful.

'Tommy, she's so stunning,' I remarked.

He murmured, 'Yes, she is beautiful. She's the most beautiful woman in the world. I'm so lucky that she's my mama. Even when I was little, she took me everywhere with her. I remember my first red-carpet event with her. We stepped out of the limousine into a swarm of photographers who captured her every move. She was so confident and graceful in her sweeping red long gown with her curly hair falling down to her hips. Her big dark eyes mesmerised the fans as she waved and blew kisses. She was a film star promoting her movie, surrounded by adoring fans screaming for autographs and photos, but to me she was also just Mama, and she's always made sure that I came first. The media always badgered her to reveal my father's identity, but she insisted that it was none of their business. I'm so lucky to have her and I'm even luckier now.'

'I can relate to that, Tommy. I know just how you feel,' I said.

Then we heard Papa's voice. 'Tommaso! I thought you didn't have to be on set until much later than this.'

'I wanted to get here early and catch up with Lucy. We're just talking about Mama. Do you have any stories about her you'd like to share?' Tommy teased, patting Papa on the back.

'Well, yes, why not? I remember when I first met her. She was a vision in a long flowing gown, the new up-andcoming actress surrounded by admirers and the life of the party. I couldn't believe it when she came up to talk to me. I thought she was moving to the next guy, but she stopped at me and started asking me some questions in her confident, almost intimidating, way. I was so stunned that I couldn't speak, but when I eventually found the courage it came out all wrong. But eventually she was charmed and we ended up dating for a little while. We had a great time together, but we were so young – still teenagers really – and both of us were just starting to make names for ourselves so we decided to take it slowly.'

Tommy was captivated. He looked so pleased to have heard Papa's version of events. 'And then what happened?' he enquired.

'Well, the club wanted me focusing on my football, which they thought was negatively affected by the romance. The pressure was too much. It made us fight constantly, and in the end we decided it was best to break up. I didn't know back then that she'd fallen pregnant with you, Tommy. At the time the media reported she'd gone to film a movie in the US, but really she wanted to stay out of the limelight until you were born. She told me much later that she wanted to keep it quiet to protect me and my career. I wish I'd known about you earlier, but we're together now and that's all that counts. We were young and foolish and did what we thought was best at the time.' Papa added, 'Tommaso, I would never have abandoned you if I'd known. I'm so, so sorry.'

He grabbed Tommy and they embraced so tightly it seemed that all those years apart were wrapped into this one hug.

I realised that I didn't feel jealous. Instead, my heart went out to Tommy, who had never experienced growing up with Papa. I was the lucky one!

Life may not be fair at times, but you can make the most of it and be whatever you want to be. Tommy achieved his dream, he found his papa, and I was so happy for him. And for me.

Jasmin put an end to our family moment. 'I want all the main cast standing by in their positions. Marcello is on his way to start shooting.'

We raced to our spots and it wasn't long before we heard the magic word, 'Action!'

# Chapter 39

# Milanello

A few days later, Papa took us to visit his home away from home. AC Milan's training facility was a world-class sports centre equipped with the latest technology and the best trainers to nurture the most talented footballers on the planet. Milanello, as it was known, was also a special place for me – I had spent a lot of my childhood visiting it. When I was a kid I had thought we were in a different country because Milanello is perched at the top of a hill, like a castle – remote yet magical. Well, to me, anyway. It seemed so far from Milan. Of course, I later found out that in fact it was only fifty kilometres from the city centre.

It had everything the players and coaching staff could need, even a track through the pine forest especially designed for physical training and recovery sessions. But for me it was a place to play and get lost in my thoughts. My favourite part, though, was the 'cage': a small outdoor pitch which was enclosed by fencing from top to bottom. The aim was to keep the ball in motion and make sure that play never stopped. This helped to improve the players' speed of execution and it was so much fun to watch – maybe not so much for the players during a tough training session. I had played there with Papa in the good old days. Maybe now he'd prefer to play with Tommy.

Papa had trained at Milanello throughout his career with AC Milan, which spanned almost twenty years. After this long family break to recover from my kidnapping ordeal, he'd just been told that he still had the captaincy and could even be called up to the national team – although this could possibly be his last season on the pitch. His experience in the back line was still needed, because the World Cup squad was depleted due to injuries.

Papa said that Tommy also looked set for a call-up. The AC Milan coaching staff were positive he would get a run, as long as he kept up his good form.

He was itching for a chance to play the world's biggest sporting event, and we were itching to get on the pitch too. Well, except for Bella, of course. She was still making eyes at my new brother.

'Oh, he is a yummy honey!' she said. It wasn't the first time.

'Look, Bella, you've got to stop carrying on about Tommy. It's so weird. Just be cool about it, especially here. He'll get paid out so badly,' I warned her.

'I can't help it. He really is so gorgeous and sensitive and considerate and too cute,' she sighed.

'Right, that's enough. I've heard it all. Please take it one step at a time. Remember, he's my brother! And we've only just met.'

'Okay girlies, enough gossing. Lucy, let's play football. I'm desperate to get onto one of these perfectly groomed pitches. But you know, whatever pitch we're on doesn't matter, because I'm going to kick your butts,' Max announced, a cheeky grin across his face.

'You're in trouble now, Max,' I bit back.

Tommy jogged up to us. 'Game on!' he said with excitement.

'Lucy, you still don't get it. You must know now that the male of the species is superior to the female. Do I really have to keep proving it to you?' Max taunted.

'Well, Max, I would have hoped that by now you'd have realised that no girl in her right mind would believe such an ignorant comment,' I snapped.

'I'm with you, Lucy!' yelled Bella.

'So get ready to be wiped off the pitch!' I barked at Max.

Tommy found our banter amusing. He fit right in, just like we were old friends.

Bella couldn't help herself. 'Oh hey Tommy, I bet you can sort them out,' she purred, giving him her best girlie look.

Oh, how embarrassing. I'd never seen her carry on like that, she looked ridiculous. I'd certainly have words with her later.

'Thanks Bella. I'm just going to check with Papa which pitch we can play on,' he replied as he ran off to the players' lounge.

'There are six regular pitches to choose from and the two synthetic ones. Why don't we just go on this one?' I pointed to the nearest one, but he was already too far off to hear me.

'Lucy, this is amazing. I never would have thought in my wildest dreams that I'd have a chance to trial for AC Milan. Me! And here we are at my dream club with my heroes. This is incredible. I can't thank you enough. Maybe, you're not so bad for a girl after all,' Max joshed.

'And you're not bad for a boy,' I smiled, nudging him gently.

'Okay, you two little lovebirds, that's enough. Why don't you just kiss and get it over with?' Bella teased.

That kept our lips tightly sealed. Both Max and I turned a deep shade of red. I even moved away from him in case he did try anything, although I doubted he'd want to kiss me, especially in public. Although he *had* given me that gorgeous bracelet on that wild day in Centennial Park, so maybe, just maybe … Oh, why was I even thinking about it? I could have killed Bella. How could she embarrass me like that?

I was relieved when Tommy came out dribbling the ball. It was a welcome distraction. He hollered, 'Okay, let's go. We can use that one over there,' he said, pointing. 'Papa is going to come out with some of the boys soon and they may even join in.'

'Wow! That would be cool,' I gushed.

'Yep, it doesn't get much better than this. Something's going right in my life at last,' Max agreed. He was still in a state of disbelief.

'I'll just hang on the sideline and admire the view,' Bella said.

Yeah sure, I thought. The view she was admiring was Tommy!

We did a quick warm-up.

'Good ball control, Lucy,' Tommy yelled encouragingly. And then he gave us the drill. 'Max, I heard that you're a hot defender and you look like quite a handy player. How about you try and stop me getting one past Lucy?'

'Yep, no problem,' he replied.

'Cool, so Lucy, you're in goal until you make a save, and then we'll swap,' he instructed.

'I'm up to the challenge. Let's see you try and sneak one past me,' I teased, even though I'd never played in goal before.

Tommy started playing from a few yards outside the box as Max did his best to stop him. It was a very tough contest, probably tougher than Tommy expected. He tried to get past Max with a few fancy tricks but was marked like a hawk.

I spotted Papa joining Bella on the sidelines with a few of his team mates. They all seemed very interested in the competition unfolding before them.

'Come on Tommy, show him what you've got,' called Papa, nudging one of his team mates, who included the likes of Nesta, Pirlo, Gattusso, Dida, Pato, Ronaldinho and David Beckham.

But Max was incredibly focused and he hadn't even noticed the star-studded line-up watching him.

The first team coach had also joined them, inspecting the talent on display.

Tommy pulled out a move which took Max completely by surprise. He found enough space to get a good strike on goal. I lunged desperately to the right, stretching out to stop the shot. But I had no hope – the ball screamed past me into the top right-hand corner.

'Gooooaaaaaaal!' shouted Tommy and he lifted his shirt to reveal his very fit physique. I thought Bella's eyes were going to pop out of her head. She drooled at him as though nothing else existed. This was getting really awkward.

Everyone on the sidelines clapped, except for Bella, who looked like she was in a trance. She was probably still thinking about Tommy's six-pack. What else could I do but laugh?

Tommy and Max shook hands. 'Yep and that's why you're playing for AC Milan and I'm not. Well done! Great goal but watch out next time!' Max warned, as it was his turn to attack.

Max was very explosive off the mark and extremely competent. With the ball at his feet, Tommy was finding out what he was up against as he struggled to mark him. Tackling wasn't Tommy's strength and it didn't take long for Max to pull the trigger. I tried to reach the ball, throwing my body into the line of fire, but it ripped past me for another goal.

Well, I'd never make it as a goalie, but I was happy for Max. He kept his cool in front of the mounting throng of onlookers and thrust a jubilant fist into the air.

Tommy picked up the ball and handed it to me. 'Here, Lucy, you have a go. Let's see what you're made of. He's a very tough competitor. Fifty euro if you beat him and another fifty if you beat me.'

'You're on. Get ready to lose your money,' I teased, eager to have a chance to prove myself in front of Papa and his team mates.

'Max, this is your moment, but I'm not going to make it easy. You have to earn it. The AC Milan coach and most of the squad are watching so don't stuff up,' I warned him. I knew that Max performed even better under pressure. I wanted him to impress them more than anything, but a little part of me would have been relieved if he messed up. At least then he would be coming back to Sydney.

'Bring it on, Zeezou!' he screeched, staying focused.

Wow, I hadn't heard that for a while, and it made my blood rush with excitement. It was so good to be on the pitch again, doing what I loved more than anything. Max was in for it now. He was going to have to be at his best to stop me.

I took him on with the ball at my feet and tried every trick in the book to show that I was confident and unafraid of facing him. As I approached the 18-yard box, my plan was to dummy to the left and make a break on the right, but Max didn't fall for it. He was on his game and wasn't going to let me get by. I took a risk and kicked the ball ahead as we both chased it. At one stage we were level, pushing and shoving, and as we caught up with the ball I stretched forward to connect. But, incredibly, Max swept the ball from under me. I lost my balance and fell in the box.

'Penalty!' I yelled. 'That's a penalty.'

But instead of appeals or support for the decision to go my way, all I could hear was laughing. I couldn't work out what all the fuss was about until Max pointed at my bottom. Somehow in the clash, my shorts had been pulled down below my waist and exposed my undies, which – of all colours – were red.

Tommy came over to help me up. He extended his hand, but I was too embarrassed to take it. 'He must have handled me, otherwise how did my shorts come down?

It was clearly a penalty. I was on my way to scoring,' I argued from the ground.

Papa came running out onto the pitch. 'Come on, let me help you up.'

'It's okay. I'm fine. I'll pop up in a sec, just let me try and work out how my shorts fell on their own,' I retorted.

'Oh princess, up you get, it's just a casual kick and I hate to tell you, but it was a fair tackle and one of great quality. He won the ball fair and square. Max plays like an Italian. Are you sure he isn't?'

'Ha, ha, Papa. Now you're all against me, three to one. How can I win?' I asked, feeling especially cross that he'd openly supported Max over his own daughter.

Bella ran on to join us, although I just think she wanted to get closer to Tommy rather than side with me. Anyway, she has no idea about the rules.

But Papa insisted, 'I'm just being fair. Anyway, gather round, I have great news to share.' He patted Max on the back. 'Great work Max. You've really impressed me and the boys, but more importantly, you've impressed our manager. He wants to offer you a full-time scholarship with the youth team. You don't need to trial next week. This was your trial. You're in – but only if that's what you really want and naturally, we'll have to discuss the move with your Uncle Rick. If all goes to plan you'll be living here and playing for AC Milan. And don't think you'll be getting out of school – getting an education is a part of the scholarship. School in the morning and football training in the afternoons.'

Max was stuck to the spot, speechless. He looked at me and Tommy and then at Papa and gazed at the football stars watching from the sidelines. His jaw dropped as though he'd witnessed someone walk on water.

'Well, Max, what do you think?' Papa pressed with a grin while fluffing Max's hair. 'You'll certainly fit in with that mop, so you're halfway there already. Are you sure you're not Italian?'

We all laughed, and that was all Max needed to ease his nerves and comprehend the offer of a lifetime.

He looked at Papa and with trembling lips uttered the words I both wanted to hear and hated hearing, 'I want this more than anything. *Grazie!*'

# Chapter 40

# Glamour game

While we were in Milan World Cup fever hit the planet well and truly. It's the most revered competition on the football calendar and it's bigger than the Olympics. Over the last few years around two hundred national teams had battled it out in qualifying rounds to fight for just thirtyone spots. The host country was lucky because it enjoyed automatic qualification, making up the 32-team draw. Mama would have mixed feelings, as Australia had also qualified for this World Cup – which was going to make it even more interesting for our family.

But the huge news was that Italy, the defending champions, were going to include Papa and Tommy in the national team. Italy's coach had made sure they were fit and available before he named his full squad. Papa had played in the campaign four years ago, beating France in the final, and he treasured his precious World Cup medal and hoped for another. It was the special memories of winning the most prestigious prize in his sport that kept him hungry to continue before he could finally call it quits. This would be his last World Cup and I was sure it would be the most special, since he would be able to enjoy this experience on the pitch with his son.

I couldn't help feeling a little jealous, as I wished it was me sharing the pitch on the world's biggest sporting stage with Papa. But I just had to be realistic and get over it. As for Max, he was about to start a new life, living his dream at AC Milan's youth academy in Milanello. He was Papa's protégé, and would play in the same position – left-back. In such a short time he'd also become very close to Tommy.

It was ironic that he was getting to play for my dream team's youth squad, and I was going back to pursue my football in Sydney with the Dolphins rep team.

Sometimes life wasn't fair, but I'd finally grown up to understand that I had to stop living in fantasy land and face reality. And to be honest – I didn't think I minded the glamorous life after all. Whoops, I guess Bella's influence was rubbing off on me! The glamorous life could be fun, but football would always be my passion. My next goal was to make it into the Matildas squad – that would be so cool. I knew I could play for Australia in the Women's World Cup one day, but right now all I wanted was to hang out here with the boys and Bella.

We were having so much fun in Milan and this was our last day on the set. They had to shoot the cathedral sequences with Julian on the roof and get some close-ups of the final scene with Tommy. But Bella was driving me crazy with her obsession with him.

'Bella, this is becoming ridiculous. Tommy probably has loads of girlfriends, so just chill out,' I told her, wishing she'd find some other interest.

'Can't you just ask him if he has a girlfriend? Please!' she persisted, her face all squashed up as she pleaded with me.

'No way, that's embarrassing!' I remarked. I was desperate to change the subject.

I called Mama who was milling around chatting to Anastasia in the make-up trailer. 'Mama, when are we flying back to Sydney?'

'Our plans have changed, sweetie. The whole family is staying in Milan for Christmas. I hope you don't mind. We've cleared it with your school – there will be some assignments, but nothing too big. Max's uncle is flying over in a few days and so is Bella's mum.' She smiled cheekily.

I screamed with excitement and danced around like a crazy ballerina; the rest of the gang went wild.

Jasmin came running in and shouted, 'Can you all please calm down! We're supposed to be working. I need everyone on set, now!'

Nothing could quell my excitement. I was having the time of my life and everything seemed to be falling into place. Dressed head to toe in our Love Lucy gear, we followed Jasmin until we reached the director in the middle of the piazza.

Marcello gave out his instructions. 'Tommy, we're going to film you connecting with the ball and volleying it towards the camera, and then we'll get a shot of Lucy kicking the rebound for the winner.'

As he was directing us I noticed Sahara chatting to Max and it made my stomach curdle. I didn't know what to do, but as it happened, I had the ball in my hand and the director conveniently yelled, 'Action!'

I was supposed to kick the ball to Tommy but the devil in me couldn't be suppressed. Instead I blasted it towards Max. Sahara ducked out of the way as Max instinctively stepped forward and collected the ball on his chest. He controlled it with precision, juggling it onto his left boot and striking it back to me.

He came after it with the determination of a possessed bull chasing the matador with the menacing red cape. I got a foot to the ball and started dribbling along the piazza as Max charged in my direction, trying to win it back, but I felt as though I had already won. My family was back together, my football was on track and Max was chasing me. What more could a girl want but to play a role in the glamour game?

Life was great after all!

Suddenly Max caught me and the ball, keeping it held firmly under his boot. He stood before me . . . we were frozen in time, just the two of us. His big brown eyes stared deeply into mine, sending my head spinning. I was suddenly breathless, but not from the chase, consumed with a feeling that made me feel weightless, my heart accelerating. Is this love?

I think that life just got better. *Amore*!

# ACKNOWLEDGEMENTS

I'm grateful to my publisher at Popcorn/Fair Play Publishing, Bonita Mersiades, who's also a passionate football fan, for her vision and support in reigniting *Lucy Zeezou's Glamour Game* to give football fans a chance to get to know her as we kick off the 2023 FIFA Women's World Cup in Australia and New Zealand.

I would like to thank my dear friend, former Matilda Heather Garriock, a role model and leader on and off the pitch for paving the way for others to succeed and always supporting me.

To my friend Craig Foster, former Socceroo, and human rights advocate - thank you for believing in me.

Warm thanks to Tim Bauer for his magical photography and Brenda Dwyer for her friendship and expertise.

I'm so proud of our national women's football team, the Matildas, for their inspiring leadership, advocacy, passion, and fight for equity. From the days (two decades ago) when I was the only television journalist covering their games to the Matildas becoming the most popular sporting team in the country and recognised as one of the best teams in the world, it's rewarding to see the massive growth of women's football in Australia.

I'm eternally grateful to the former Matildas for their invaluable insights into the game and paving the way for future generations. I am grateful for the support of former Matildas captain and trail blazer, Melissa Barbieri, as well as the engaging and talented Clare Hunt who is living her dream as a Matilda playing for Australia in the 2023 Women's World Cup. Big thanks to my friend and former Matildas Coach, Tom Sermanni, for connecting us.

ACKNOWLEDGEMENTS

I'm also thankful to the following incredible people for helping keep my Lucy Zeezou dream alive especially during this exciting time in women's football: my friend and literary agent, Jeanne Ryckmans who has been instrumental in my game changing career moments; Amanda L. Tyler, Charlotte Perry, David Basheer, Helen Deep, Tracey Deep, Marcella Kaspar, Alex White, Ray Gatt, Pablo Bateson and George Donikian for their invaluable support; my colleague at the ANU Andrea Morris for being unstoppable; Mena Labbozzetta's unique Italian stories and delicious cuisine at *Figo* restaurant.

My family and friends without whom none of this would be possible, especially my hubby Derek, who came up with the title; son Dylan, (a Manchester United fan) for keeping the teen language real on and off the pitch and my daughter, Izabella who worked with me on the Lucy manuscript at bedtime and after much convincing agreed to be on the cover.

My gorgeous nieces and nephews who keep wanting to hear more Lucy tales: Conor, Lee, Brandan, Jared, Jasmin, Cocoa, Sahara, Daley, Zakk, Khobi, Chase, Zali, Asha, Jackson, and Riley.

My extraordinary late Mum and Dad, Jeanette, and David Deep Snr, who opened my world to endless possibilities and instilled my belief that anything is possible!

Diehard AC Milan fan and Milan Academy Australia President, Anton Tagliaferro and former AC Milan player, Andrea Icardi for connecting me with football legends Paolo Maldini and Gennaro Gattuso.

And to my wonderful Lucy Zeezou fans for their continuing support and inspiring me to write the next Lucy adventure. It's a privilege to be able to share my crazy imagination with you. Never give up on your dreams because they do come true!

# ABOUT THE AUTHOR

Liz Deep-Jones is a published author, journalist, producer, presenter, film maker, curator and the inaugural Freilich Arts/Media and Activism Fellow at the Australian National University in Canberra. Her best-selling young adult novels, *Lucy Zeezou's Goal* and *Lucy Zeezou's Glamour Game* have been re-released for the upcoming 2023 FIFA Women's World Cup in Australia and New Zealand. Liz is passionate about football as it breaks societal and race barriers and is a champion for human rights, inspiring young people to take action through her mentoring role at the ANU in media and arts activism. The proud Sydney-sider is travelling her *We Bleed The Same* anti-racism exhibition and documentary across Australia. She's also writing her third novel, hoping to inspire young readers to never give up on their dreams.

# MORE REALLY GOOD FOOTBALL FICTION FROM POPCORN PRESS

Jarrod Black
Chasing Pack

Anna Black
This girl can play

The End of the Game

The Gaffer

Game

The Yawning Giant

POPCORN
PRESS

www.ingramcontent.com/pod-product-compliance
Lightning Source LLC
Chambersburg PA
CBHW070633170726
48291CB00003B/995